AF655806

# Half a Face

Published by
NIYOGI
BOOKS
D-78, Okhla Industrial Area, Phase-I
New Delhi-110 020, INDIA
Tel: 91-11-26816301, 26813350, 51, 52
Fax: 91-11-26810483, 26813830
email: niyogibooks@gmail.com
website: www.niyogibooks.com

Text © Nonda Chatterjee

Cover Design: Kartick Paul
Editor: Madhuparna Banerjee/Niyogi Books

ISBN: 978-81-89738-56-3

Publication: 2010

This is a work of fiction. The names, characters and incidents portrayed in it are the work of author's imagination. Any resemblance to actual persons, living or dead, events or localities, is entirely coincidental.

All translations are author's.

All rights are reserved. No part of this publication may be reproduced or transmitted in any form or by any means, electronic or mechanical, including photocopying, recording or by any information storage and retrieval system without prior written permission and consent of the publisher.

Printed at: Niyogi Offset Pvt. Ltd., New Delhi, India

# Half a Face

Nonda Chatterjee

NIYOGI
BOOKS

*For Rupa, my first-born,*
*who inspired me to write this story.*

With thanks to:

Dr Choi Chatterjee, Professor of History at California State University, Los Angeles, USA, for her valuable ideas and input.
My editor, Ms Madhuparna Banerjee for all her help.

# FOREWORD

In this novel, Nonda Chatterjee uses the recent history of India as a canvas to explore the contemporary themes of feminism, subjectivity, and the complicated path to self-realisation. Priti, the young protagonist in the novel, is a serious journalist, and an independent professional. With her strong sense of self and consummate professionalism, Priti represents the new generation of emancipated women in modern India. But modernity comes in many guises, and in India it sometimes takes unrecognisable forms. Despite Priti's attempts to lead a life of independence, to choose her own partner, to come and go as she pleases, she is still bound by tradition. She is beset by the emotional demands laid on her by the loving members of her joint family. While Priti is trying to negotiate terms of independence within her family, she realises that she is perhaps not the first woman in her family to attempt to live life on her own terms. In this riveting murder mystery about Priti's formidable great grandmother, Gauri Debi, Chatterjee takes the reader on an exciting journey from pre-Partition rural Bengal, through the Partition, and into contemporary times. As the novel unfolds, Gauri Debi becomes part of the horrendous exodus of a traumatised population that pours into Calcutta in the second half of the twentieth century. Their unintended travels set into motion by the manufactured demands of religious frenzy, ethnic politics, class struggle, and the ruthless accumulation of the burgeoning capitalist order.

While the tale is ostensibly about Gauri and her adventures in the world of *jatra* and the provincial politics of Bengal, Priti, however, through her investigations into the life of her great grandmother, begins to realise that her own feminist independence is based on family stability, solid education, and the economic freedom that only inherited property can confer. Her great grandmother, on the other hand, had grown up in conditions of abject poverty in rural Bengal, and had created for herself an important presence in the artistic community of Calcutta. While Gauri Debi found fame and fortune in the unconventional world of theatre, she also pursued abstract notions of justice and truth in her own inimitable fashion. Chatterjee's characters refuse to be cowed by their circumstances and move towards their goals with tenacity and purpose. But life and history intervenes in mysterious ways and forces both the heroines to question their own dreams and aspirations. In this novel about generational conflict, Chatterjee deftly displays the inter-connected nature of selfhood. She shows that self-realisation can only come through an empathetic understanding of other people's lives, and that the modern feminist stands on the shoulders of countless, unsung heroines. According to Chatterjee, history is not just a story of the past, but a mirror beset with restless spirits. It contains many illusions and disturbing images. If you stare in that mirror long enough you will discover uncomfortable truths about yourself, and about the adulterated nature of your own perceptions. But as Chatterjee would say, perhaps truth is the greatest illusion of all!

Chatterjee writes with a keen ear for the nuances of both languages—Bengali and English, and recreates evocative details of daily life from this period in fine detail. She weaves in snatches of folklore, bits of poetry and song culled from the popular heritage of Bengal into her novel. Chatterjee also includes her own translations from various literary and dramatic texts, and her obvious mastery of the history of Bengali theatre, both popular and literary, helps in the creation of this multi-layered literary narrative. She recreates forgotten worlds for younger audiences, and reprises nostalgic memories of pre-Partition Bengal for the more mature reader. But caveat emptor, the novel progresses at a murderous pace and the reader is swept along through gothic twists and turns, beguiled by the fluid prose, and mesmerised by a cast of unforgettable characters. The denouement is as unexpected as the mysterious beginning—an unfulfilled death wish, a series of unanswered letters, and an unread diary of a woman whose very name is forbidden!

Choi Chatterjee

# I

My great grandmother's name had always been taboo in our family. This was particularly strange in view of the fact that as a family, we clung fiercely to tradition and our past. Uprooted from our ancestral home in East Pakistan by the partition of the Indian subcontinent in 1947, my grandparents had been compelled to join the stream of anonymous humanity who came to be known in Calcutta as 'the refugees', and the only way to maintain their identity was to link what 'had been' with what 'was' and 'is'.

To this end, the walls of our large house in Ballygunge were crowded with memorabilia—photographs, paintings, framed *kantha*s depicting traditional icons, images of gods, goddesses, gurus—all jostling for space on their whitewashed surfaces. Particularly striking were the scarlet imprints of two pairs of feet on faded white cloth, framed and hung over the main entrance to the house. These had been taken from the dead bodies of my great grandfather and uncle as they lay on the funeral pyre, prior to cremation, as was customary. For as long as I remember, the imprints had been suspended there and had forced themselves on the attention of every household member, relation and guest attempting to leave the house. My childish imaginations had woven wild fantasies around them, and the images that emerged in my consciousness were always malevolent. Most often, I saw them as baleful eyes that had the power to look into the innermost recesses of my heart and divine my most secret thoughts; I ran past them, with my eyes lowered, whenever I had something to hide.

As I grew older, other thoughts bothered me, particularly the absence of female feet. Why this emphasis on patriarchal feet only? Why had the imprints of my great grandmother's feet not been framed and displayed? My parents parried my questions with great dexterity; my grandmother openly declared that women did not deserve such honour and hinted broadly that there was a touch of blasphemy in the thought. Only my grandfather's voice softened when I asked about his mother, but that too only momentarily. Very soon the inscrutable mask would be back in place and he would advise me mildly not to venture where my elders feared to tread. This of course, whetted my curiosity further, and the desire to investigate this mystery began to take on the proportions of a secret mission.

Time flows swiftly and I am past childhood, past school, past adolescence and in my second year at Jadavpur University, reading comparative literature. Contact with new ideas and varied experiences have weakened my links with the past and rendered them tenuous. Born and bred in this city, I am a Calcuttan first and last and am breaking out of the mould that has been created for me. I see sweeping changes in the homes of my friends in terms of décor, modern conveniences, lifestyles, and a steady trend of drifting towards a nuclear family structure. These changes only have a fleeting and peripheral influence in our home which has remained uncompromisingly archaic and 'East Bengali' in every aspect. My grandmother and father have always stifled any attempt at change suggested by my mother. It is only due to my grandfather's gentle insistence that I am 'allowed' a book shelf in my room, a few secular paintings on the walls, and several tapes of devotional songs of Tagore and other composers. My friends have been allowed entry to my room, where they are permitted to converse, provided they keep their voices low. My grandmother does not approve, particularly of my friends of the opposite sex, and loses no opportunity to voice her disapprobation. At times I am hurt and rebellious; in rare moments of clearer vision, I realise that she is fighting a rearguard action against time and change, determined to prevent encroachment on her territory.

Soon, I graduate with First Class Honours and enrol myself in the Master's programme. My professors tell me that I have a flair for writing, and the occasional acceptance by respectable magazines and newspapers of my literary essays, poems and short stories strengthen this conviction. The question of a future career looms large on the horizon, and fending my grandmother's attempts to marry me off, I decide to try my hand at journalism.

A year later, armed with appropriate diplomas, I apply for the post of a junior reporter at an esteemed news bureau, and to my utter astonishment, am accepted. Six months of hard work as a probationer earns me my rewards: I am confirmed in my position.

I cannot quite believe my good fortune or my dramatically altered status within the family. From a lowly student dependent on pocket money and occasional income from tuitions, I have finally risen to the ranks of the 'honourably employed' with 'real' money in my pocket. The 'paper' gives me a mobile phone for 'immediate access', a computer in my home, and puts at my disposal a car and a photographer for 'late-night' and 'distant' assignments. I don't hurry home 'before the lights go on in the streets'—a cardinal rule for women, particularly the young and unattached, in our family—but march in at 11.30 p.m., my head held high, for I have been out on an 'urgent assignment'. At times, this is true; at times it is just an evening with my friends. The reactions of my family members to my new lifestyle are mixed and interesting—my grandfather and mother see in my career a vindication of their own desires and are frankly delighted; my grandmother and various visiting aunts make dire predictions about my future as well as the unlikelihood of procuring a 'decent' boy for a 'fast' girl like me; my father, caught between the two camps, is elated and depressed by turns!

A couple of years slip by. I am presently a career woman of undisputed status and am emotionally involved with a colleague who shares my passion for 'getting at the truth'. 'Investigative journalism' is the latest buzzword, and we increasingly veer in this direction. I foresee a storm ahead of me when I will be compelled to announce my commitment to Ranjit, for in respect of caste and religion, he is in no way compatible, and I keep delaying the evil hour. I have given some hints to my grandfather, but even he quails at the prospect of facing his wife and son with this revelation!

2 July 1996, and the bottom gets knocked out of my world! My grandfather, the most disciplined, abstemious and controlled human being that I know of, has a massive heart attack. The doctors are at a loss to account for this mishap and advise transfer to an intensive-care unit at the hospital. I inform my office that I am unavailable, and that Ranjit will handle my assignments. I cling to my grandfather in fear, apprehensive of incertitude. All my life, I have taken his support, understanding, affection and comforting presence for granted. How will I ever survive without him?

He is scheduled to move to the nursing home on the morning of 4 July. The excruciating pain has eased slightly and he is sleeping at uneasy intervals. Conversation is strictly forbidden. We sit around him in the agony of suspense and cope with an endless stream of concerned well-wishers. We realise anew that his charming presence is of paramount importance not only to his immediate and extended family, but also to his erstwhile colleagues, friends and the community at large.

On the night of the 3rd, at about 10 p.m., he opens his eyes and a faint smile touches his lips. It is evident that he wishes to say a few words. The nurse, rather reluctantly, relents and leaves the room. Very clearly, his words drop like pebbles in the pool of silence in the room, and send out concentric waves of meaning to each one of us.

He begins speaking gently: 'My papers are in order. You are all aware of the will I have made. I leave most of my property and money to my wife and son jointly. There is a special bequest to my dear daughter-in-law who has been my good friend all along. There are certain donations to charities, which I know my son will take care of. There are legacies for both my daughters and their families, mentioned in the will. My books, I leave them to my granddaughter, Priti, for I know she loves them as much as I do.'

We think that he is tired, and my grandmother is about to call back the nurse, when he opens his eyes again, and his voice takes on a new strength and urgency. He continues, 'There is another matter of which I have never spoken before, and it is of this that I wish to inform you tonight. There is, on the bottom shelf of my cupboard, a locked suitcase. I leave this suitcase and its contents with my granddaughter, Priti, who will know what to do with the material, and in doing the needful, she will fulfil the greatest wish of my life. Here in the presence of my entire family, I give the key into her hands with complete faith in her sense of responsibility.' He slips his hand underneath his pillow, takes out the key, and presses it into my hands.

As I stare at the key on my palm, his hands close over mine, and I feel their reassuring warmth which I know so well. Our eyes meet for a moment, and the appeal in those grey clear orbs is unmistakable. I lean over him and whisper into his ear my acquiescence and reassurance. At these words, a calm look erases the anxiety from his face, and he closes his eyes indicating that the communication is over.

The tension in the room is electric and the questions in the minds of the people present, almost tangible in their insistence. So I take the key, thread the gold chain I wear around my neck through it and put the chain back on. The key nestles close to my heart and I have a fleeting vision of my grandfather, smiling and young, merging into my being, my consciousness, my very soul. I am sure now that he will never desert me, not till it is time for me too, to pass into the realms where he has headed with such faith and calm assurance.

He never did get to the nursing home; he slipped away in the night as peacefully as he had lived, wearing the usual, faint smile on his lips. A true *karma-yogi,* he had lived and died effortlessly as his beloved text, the Bhagavad Gita, had instructed him:

*From untruth into truth,*
*From darkness into light,*
*From death to immortality*

I had always shared my grandfather's study with him, and we had worked here in perfect harmony since my schooldays. My scholastic success was mainly due to his unfailing interest and support, and it is a shock to realise that I will not be able to turn to him in moments of intellectual, emotional and spiritual need. However, when I am in this room, I actually feel his presence, and gradually, it becomes my retreat and refuge. My family appreciates this need, and allows me to take over the room as my own.

The suitcase has been the source of constant conjecture ever since the funeral rites have been completed, and subtle pressures have been brought to bear to share the contents, at least with my grandmother, but I have been obdurate, reckoning that if my grandfather had wanted his wife in the picture, he would have said so. I have brought the 'case' to my study and put it behind some books on the shelf, where it is temporarily out of sight. I hope that if it stays that way for some time, its existence will gradually fade out from the minds of the people in the family. I have discussed this stratagem with Ranjit. He too feels that I need to put time between my grandfather's death and the revelation, so as to get a clear perspective. Ranjit is sure that this is a sacred trust, a serious mission, and that I will need all my intelligence and strength to bring it to fruition.

I have brought my computer into the study and when I work late, I just curl up on the divan in the corner, instead of going back to my bedroom. On 2 September 1996, I work on an important 'story' till the big clock in the next room chimes twelve times. Realising that I have to leave the house at 8 a.m. on the morrow, I shut down the machine, switch off the light, lie down on the cot and pull a light cover over myself. It is a moonlit night and through the window I can see the branches of a neem tree with its delicate foliage stirring in the breeze. A night bird calls lazily; another replies; a third, more raucous, objects; a dog barks in the distance at a passing car; I gradually drift off, my mind deliciously empty of thought. But this does not last very long. Slowly, a clear and most unexpected image fills my vacant subconscious mind.

There is a large hall with pillars; the floor is of pristine white marble with black inlay; the chandeliers are half-lit, casting more shadow than light. There are priceless carpets on the floor; at one end, sits a woman with a *tanpura* and her accompanist with a pair of *tabla*s before him. She is not wearing the garb of a professional singer, but is dressed in a white silk sari with a red border, the kind one would associate with the matriarch of a family or a simple housewife. Her slim fingers touch the wires, drawing melodious harmony, but when her voice joins the strains of the *tanpura,* the melody produced is so exquisite that it takes my breath away – such passion, poignancy, infinite anguish! The lyrics are in Bengali and unmistakably those of Tagore:

*When my life is lost in aridity,*
*Come to me as a stream of compassion,*
*When all sweetness is lost*
*Come as an ethereal flow of music...*
*When work and duty take on power*
*And their urgency obfuscates vision,*
*Enter the portals of my consciousness*
*On gentle feet, my Lord.*

*When my life is wasted and barren,*
*Find your way in a compassionate*
*stream, my Lord.*

*When my mind is without liberality,*
*When I seek to conceal my meanness,*
*Open the door wide my Lord*
*And enter in glory like a king.*
*When all sweetness is lost, Lord,*
*Soothe me with your music…*

The strains of the song die out, but the echoes continue to reverberate long after. She then stares with intense longing at someone to her left—a small boy, about a year and a half or two, is trying to make his way to her, but is held back by an invisible force. She holds out her arms with anguished desire, but the boy cannot move. Slowly, the boy turns back and disappears from sight. She throws herself on the *tanpura* in a paroxysm of grief and her long, dark, lustrous hair blots out her face; only the fragrance of the jasmine strands woven into her hair lingers in the air.

When I wake up, it is almost six. I am rushing to complete my morning routine, when I realise that the fragrance of the jasmine flowers still persists in the room. I seem to carry it away with me when I leave for work.

I tell Ranjit about my dream. To my surprise, he does not laugh it away. On the contrary, he says that my conscience is sending me subliminal messages to get on with the job that has been entrusted to me.

'This Saturday,' he says, 'hopefully you can sleep late the next morning. Why don't you open the box and take a look?' Suddenly his expression changes, he turns to me urgently and asks, 'Do you realise, yesterday was the 2nd and today, we are exactly two months away from his death? I don't think you should waste any more time.'

I tell him he is becoming superstitious, but his words have an uncomfortable ring of truth that I cannot gainsay. Also, my curiosity is getting the better of me, and my desire to 'know' more importunate. So I take his advice, have dinner with my family where conversation turns inevitably to our recent loss, and try to appear as normal as possible before turning in, so that no one has an inkling that anything unusual is about to take place. However, I lock my door firmly, for tonight of all nights, I want no interference. Inevitably, there are knocks on the door: first my grandmother brings me my flask of coffee which I had forgotten; next my father enters looking for a book. Finally, at about 11.30 p.m., all seems quiet. I take out the suitcase, place it on the cot, draw up my chair and remove the key from the chain. I am surprised to find that my fingers are trembling and that I am perspiring profusely in spite of the whirring fan. I have absolutely no idea what to expect when the key turns smoothly in the lock.

When I eventually muster courage to lift the lid, I almost scream—I do not know if in terror or in surprise. For, whatever images my mind had conjured up have nothing to do with what stare me in the face. On a piece of paper yellowed with age, I find the song I had heard in my dream; the handwriting is bold and formed and has faded and turned to sepia, but the words are quite unmistakable. I pick it up gingerly and the brittle paper rustles in my hand threatening to disintegrate. With infinite care, I place it on the writing table, mop my forehead, sit back in my chair and close my eyes. This song had been a favourite of my grandfather's and he had taught me the words and tune with great care. He would ask me to sing it to him in rare quiet moments, and sometimes his eyes would be moist during the recital. 'Why? Whose handwriting is this? What is the connection?' I wonder.

I go back to the suitcase and examine the rest of the contents. There are several bundles of what appear to be old letters held together with faded blue ribbons; a large envelope of newspaper cuttings; a couple of old diaries; and finally, right at the bottom, a slim, white envelope with my name on it in my grandfather's firm, neat handwriting. My eyes blur with sudden tears, and I pick up the envelope and lean my cheek against it. When I open it, a time-bound cheque flutters out carrying indeed a very large sum. There is also a letter which reads as follows:

*My little Priti,*

*First things first: the money enclosed herewith is yours. Pay it into your account tomorrow. If the family makes a fuss when you tell them about Ranjit, this money will come in useful and will enable you to set up home. Don't worry, I have saved it for this contingency and have not deprived anyone else to give it to you. If the family behaves sensibly, it will be my little gift to you. Please use it for things that will bring joy to both of you.*

*You must be wondering at this cloak and dagger affair of the suitcase and why I made such a fuss about it. But if this venture has to succeed, it will only do so when handled with caution and circumspection. If the entire family gets involved, you will be defeated even before you begin. So, little Priti, the contents of this suitcase are meant for your and Ranjit's eyes only, and 'mum' is the word.*

I had absolutely no idea that my grandfather had formed such a favourable impression of Ranjit on the basis of a few hurried meetings, but then, he was a man who kept his own counsel at all times. I now realise with a pang that had he been around when I revealed my intentions to the family, he would have stood beside me like a rock and helped me to face the storm of opposition. I go back to the letter again.

*Priti, what I am about to tell you is something that lies at the very centre of my being, more precious to me than anything else till you came into my life; a trust which I have been unable to fulfil, a burden that I carry with me even in death. You have often asked me about my mother and I always encountered these questions with irreverence, even though my heart broke in the process. You must have also noticed the frosty attitude of the rest of the family members concerning her. Well, this is because she left home in dubious circumstances, when I was about two years old and turned up years later as the owner and chief protagonist of a* jatra *company. This company went all over North India and not only achieved some fame, but also a great deal of notoriety. Very often, performances were stopped midway due to the intervention of the police or district authorities. I have assiduously collected all the newspaper cuttings that I could find about her shows and put them in bundles chronologically. Hope they will be of use to you in your investigation.*

*Yes, investigation is what you will have to undertake if you are to make sense of this strange woman's life! No one has ever had a good word to say of her except for drama critics, who not only commented on her extraordinary good looks and talents as a musician, singer, dancer, actress, but also spoke of her caustic tongue, bursts of temper, love of liquor and general unpredictability. She did make one or two attempts to establish contact, but of course the family and particularly your father, spurned her advances with righteous indignation.*

*Then came the dramatic finale. She was found in her room in a state of dishabille, with a bullet wound on her right temple. There was no suicide note, so, 'wilful homicide' by person/persons 'unknown' was the verdict returned. However, the whole affair was kept under wraps and ultimately hushed up. Why? Was her death the inevitable outcome of the life she led, or was there somebody who needed to silence her permanently?*

*Priti, do you think because I lost her at the age of two, I am unduly sentimental? Do you also think so at this moment? Or, do you think that she was an enigma and that the world never got to know the real woman behind the façade she had deliberately created? Was it that she could not bear to be 'understood' and therefore became an adept at misguiding people?*

*You are wondering, I am sure, why I think this way, and will feel I am unduly romantic if I say that the first picture does not match the image I have of her in my mind's eye. The memories of a two-year-old are not to be trusted, surely! But believe me Priti, I am not mistaken; she was a good and honest woman, who tried to do her best for everybody, including my sick and ill-tempered father. But because she left home and he died soon thereafter, presumably of a broken heart, he has been turned into an icon and my mother's name has been blackened beyond redemption. But the truth has never come to light, and I, her only child, who owed her rehabilitation, have failed her. Perhaps I was too emotionally involved to do perfect justice? Perhaps I was looking for 'my truth' rather than 'the truth'. But you will not make that mistake. You are trained to sift the lies and arrive at the truth, however unpalatable it might be, right? And that is what you will do for me, and once and for all, the mystery will be cleared: if she was who I think she was, my soul shall rest in peace. If not, so be it; I shall still be at peace.*

*You are thinking perhaps that I am fanciful in imagining that all this will matter to me beyond the funeral pyre, but because I have felt my mother's presence so acutely after she died, I know that I will not be too far away from you, at least till you have carried out my behest.*

*So, best of luck, little Priti, I do hope your first 'real' enterprise in 'investigative journalism' will be as rewarding to you as I believe it will be for me.*

*Love and blessings always,*

*Your Dadubhai.*

*PS. I received a parcel by post, three days after I wrote this letter. I never found out who the sender was, even though I made extensive but discreet enquiries. The parcel contained the two diaries I have placed in the suitcase. They are obviously my mother's, but how they found their way to me, I do not know. I have read them carefully, but have not been able to relate to the true character of the writer – far too complex. Also perhaps, it takes a woman to understand another woman? I hope they will be of help rather than place obstacles in your way!*

I read the missive several times before the letters stop dancing before my eyes and I can make sense of the words. But I don't even contemplate the option of not taking up the challenge. Apart from the fact that this is the first time in my life that my grandfather has made a serious request of me, the project itself is too fascinating to ignore.

Who had my great grandmother been – the proverbial bad woman, or the misunderstood and maligned good woman, or the ambitious woman who had given up home and child for a career? Did she really want to 'live' life? Did she find the confines of a traditional home too suffocating? Was she a woman who did not want any blank page in her life? Was she one of these, some of these, none of these or all of these? I will have to find out. I decide to go no further till I have discussed with Ranjit the strategies to be followed thereafter, but cannot resist a peek at the cuttings. One look at the faded photographs convinces me that the woman who is portrayed in the newspapers and the one I had encountered in my dream are one and the same; only, in the photographs she somehow looks coarser and harsher. Is it the younger woman, the one whom I saw in my dream, who is craving for understanding rather than the older one? I wonder in amazement. As I fall asleep, the fragrance of jasmine fills the room, and I am not sure if all of it is coming in from my neighbours' balcony where a creeper has recently come into full bloom.

When I speak to Ranjit the next day and show him the letter and the cheque, he is as astonished as I had been. He is also greatly moved, and for the first time since we became friends, I see tears in his eyes.

Being a reticent sort of chap he brushes them away but cannot quite keep the emotion out of his voice when he speaks, 'Priti, you know, when I met your grandfather, I think I fell in love with him as much as I did with you, and I think he also approved of me. But somehow, I had not been prepared for such generosity and this degree of trust. I do hope I will prove worthy and not disappoint him.'

However, when it comes to the investigation, Ranjit seems strangely loath to participate. He is prepared to help me with the external arrangements—travelling, meeting people, extricating information—but feels that *I* must make sense of the material given to me as best as I can.

He says, 'Priti, I will not intrude where your grandfather had been wary of venturing. This is the story of a very unusual woman and you have been *chosen* for a very special reason. I think that you must try to see things as she did, feel as she did, interpret situations as she had done and understand why she responded to them as she did. Don't you see Priti, at some point you will empathise so completely with her that you will begin to think and feel as she did? And, when that happens, her story will become your story!'

It had seemed a rather tall order at that moment, but when I start reading and appraising the material, the persona of the dead woman slowly begins to emerge, and soon, I feel that I am not dealing with a stranger, but someone I have known at another time, another place, that I am renewing an acquaintance, re-establishing contact, revisiting partially known, familiar territories. Ranjit is proven right, as usual.

The newspaper cuttings are mostly about her shows and some about her mysterious end. The letters are the ones written to the family begging for a meeting so that things could be discussed, pleading for a glimpse of her son; and some are copies of the replies that had been sent to her. However, the writers on both sides had been lawyers who had smothered the emotions of the parties in jargon and caution. There is one short, direct, passionate appeal from her to my grandfather, to which presumably, no reply had been sent:

*Dear Mr Roy,*

*I dare not address you by any other name as I have forfeited the right. A mother who deserts her son at the age of two can have no claim on his affection or respect, as no doubt you have been told many times. In any case, why would you want to re-establish a relationship with a person of my notoriety? It is entirely at variance with the sober, disciplined ambience in which you have been nurtured. Also, I am a very different person from your aunt, Mala, who raised you and gave you all the love that I denied you.*

*But no one has ever heard, or wanted to hear my side of the story—why I left home, how I survived, and why I am what I am today. No one ever looked into my heart and noticed how bloody it was, how torn and lacerated! No one ever guessed the anguish that lay behind the hard yet glittering façade. No one looked beyond the labels at the merchandise within. As Tagore says,*

I am eager to express the pain in my heart,
But no one asks or listens.

*Will you give me only one chance to talk to you, to explain, to unburden my overcharged soul? My explanations may not be good enough to convince you, but at least I would like to make an attempt. I feel as though I were walking around bound by heavy chains of guilt, self-recrimination and hopelessness; they clank and grow heavier as days pass by; and I move closer to the confrontation with my Maker. Will you, 'son', help me to unfasten these chains, make their load a little lighter, give me the right, if only for one brief moment, to call you my only link to immortality?*

The signature at the end of the letter is so garbled that it can be hardly distinguished, whereas the rest of the letter is written in the firm, bold hand I know from the song. Had she too been overcome by emotion to write clearly? But on closer inspection I understand the reason behind the garbled signature: her present name was not what it had been before, and she had not wanted her son to scrutinise it too closely. Whatever be the case, he had not replied and no contact had been made. Who had been responsible? Was it my tight-lipped grandmother, or my parents and aunts, or my grandfather's reluctance to confront the past?

Yet it had mattered to him greatly, so much so that he had begged his granddaughter to respond to the dead woman's appeal, so that not only her burden but his own could also be lightened.

The diaries, therefore, are my best hope. A chronological narrative would provide the surest clues to this enigmatic woman's life and enable me to find a logical interpretation, assign cause to effect, and build up a defence that would stand up to close scrutiny. But, when I begin to read the diaries, I realise immediately the problems that my grandfather had faced as there are neither dates, nor a connected chain of events; these are mere jottings that had been made at different moments. Besides, the constant movement between the past and present is totally bewildering. Very often, lines of a song or poem, odd references had been used to replace statements and facts. Her memory is the obvious link between these entries, but how was I, seventy odd years distant in time from the birth of her son, and eons apart in terms of experience, to make sequential sense of this? For instance:

*My mother says there is very little rice in the house today, so the women will have to go without a meal; I am five years old, do I count as a woman? I do, and am staring at a boiled yam—my midday meal; a teardrop or two falls on the yam. When my father puts a handful of rice from his own banana leaf onto mine, my great grandmother is not pleased and her raucous voice fills the air.*

The whole household is asleep; the street dogs have put their heads between their paws; and the night guard has completed his rounds. I am sitting at my writing table and the diaries lie open before me; the only source of light in the room is a table lamp near the open diaries before me. I lean back and close my eyes.

Gradually, an image of the house of the 'five-year-old' forms in my consciousness—a small cottage, mud and thatch, the floor smooth with its daily layer of liquid mud and cow dung dried to a plaster; a niche in the wall for the household gods where ironically, Lakshmi and Ganesha, icons of wealth and success, predominate. In one corner is a *chowki* under which the few meagre possessions of the family are stored, and on it is seated the matriarch of the family, half blind, toothless, semi-paralysed, but rapacious for her share of life, pitting her needs in shrill, garbled words against those of a five-year-old child. What did the child do? Did she put the rice into her own mouth before it could be taken away or did she obediently give a share to the old woman?

I resume reading and another entry catches my eye:

*My mother gave my sister and me a bottle to collect snails from the banks of the pond that is close to our cottage. The snails are clever and hide under the leaves of plants that grow on the edge. The best time to catch them is at dawn when they come out for a touch of the sun. When cooked with a lot of chillies, they taste very good. We left long before dawn, but a drunkard came in our way and we had to hide. By the time we got to the pond, the best snails had been taken by other people; we decided not to be late on any account next time and then, after the harvest, I would help my mother to crack the snails against a stone and take out their soft flesh, juicy and delicious!*

A chill runs up my spine as a possible image of the real person is conjured up in my mind. Here was a fighter who would stop at nothing to survive, kill before she would starve, claw her way up a slippery precipice to get to the top, and never count the cost. Was this iron-willed woman now impelling me to delve into her past and get at the truth—*her* truth?

I put away the diaries, switch off the lamp and try to get some sleep, but try as I might, one persistent image fills my consciousness—a little girl of seven, pretty as a picture, with her hair tied in a tight braid and a torn sari wrapped around her frail body, is sitting by a large stone cracking snails on it with single-minded deliberation, lifting out the writhing creatures from their fractured shells with deft fingers and depositing them in a glass bottle; her chiselled features appear sharper with concentration merely in anticipation of a square meal, or perhaps something else? The snails do their best to climb out but the slippery glass defeats them, and she watches their helplessness with malicious glee! I am surprised at how such a disturbing image is created in my mind, but why, I have no clue!

I examine my own feelings the next morning. In the sanity of daylight, I realise that this personality is getting a hold on me, that I want her to be vindicated and find valid reasons for her actions. The question here is whether she is naturally cruel or whether this is merely an exercise in survival. I find that I am loath to accept the former and would rather prefer to find evidence to support the latter view.

I turn the pages of the diaries frantically for corroboration. Finally, tucked away in the pages, I find a few lines of doggerel verse on a slip of paper:

*A bird sits on a tree*
*A worm in its beak,*
*The hawk kills the bird*
*With a sharp tweak.*
*The man shoots the hawk,*
*It falls on the ground,*
*The ants fill its body*

*And the ground around.*
*Who will kill the man?*
*Who will eat his flesh?*
*The worms will have a feast*
*And the bird will find them fresh!*

I wonder where she had found this, or had she written it herself? At what age had this vision of life come to her? I find another entry on a different note:

*Krishna and I lean down and look at our reflections in the pond. The water is as clear as a mirror and you can see the mud and the plants at the bottom. The fish flit by in twos and threes.*

*Krishna's face is as perfect as mine, but she is dark. My mother says, 'How will I get rid of this baggage? Who will marry her? How much will it cost?' Perhaps she does'nt notice, but Krishna flinches at these words as though someone has struck her physically and she desperately tries to wipe away the tears that well up in those limpid, beautiful eyes. Is it the same in rich homes? Or is it a crime to be dark only if you are poor? I feel ashamed of my own fair skin and guilty too when I look at Krishna's sad face.*

It is the age-old problem of the dark and fair; nothing at all seems to have changed in half a century. I wonder what these girls were looking for in the water on a lazy afternoon? Was it a premonition of their future that lay beyond their reflections? Did they think that colour would decide their destinies? Who was Krishna? Was she a sister or a cousin? Was Krishna the dark beauty as described by the classic poet Kalidasa or like Jagyaseni Draupadi, the heroine of the famous epic Mahabharata—slim, tall, dark, with lips like ripe fruit and a smile like lightning? Would no one look at Krishna with desire because she was not a king's daughter?

I imagine the reflections of the two damsels dancing in the water—sometimes their eyes appear elongated, sometimes their noses disappear, teeth and lips goes through kaleidoscopic motions and trigger forth ripples of laughter. At that point, the female gender, the vagaries of colour, the problems of marriage must have receded into nothingness and their own images must have held them spellbound. Did they fall into the water like Narcissus and emerge as blue and white flowers? Or did they masquerade as girls in daytime only and retain their identities as flowers at night? Did their fractured identity explain the duality of my great grandmother's later life?

I find out on reading further that Krishna was Gauri's (as was my great grandmother's name) twin sister and that they had been inseparable. People inevitably must have remarked on their similarity of figures and features and difference of colour. In this context, my eyes fall on a particular entry.

*Our aunt (father's sister) came on a visit to us after many years. In our village, they say, two rivers meet often than two sisters after marriage. How will Krishna and I survive if this happens to us? Our aunt had seen us only as babies and was delighted to find us grown. She placed us both on her lap and put a gold ring on each of our ring fingers. They were not heavy but very shiny, and we were overjoyed! She scrutinised our faces very carefully and said to our mother, 'Sister-in-law, you have produced two goddesses—one made of gold and the other of black marble, and I think the black one is the handsomer of the two!' Hugging us close she continued, 'We have to find two princes for the two of you—then they will put you on their horses and carry you away to their kingdoms where you will live happily ever after.' Her voice trailed off leaving us dreaming.*

I try to speculate over what they had dreamt of, as their own reality could conjure up no images of splendour or luxury, for there were no points of reference. So their dreams must have been culled from the fairy tales they had heard—of golden palaces, flower-bedecked beds, gold jewellery, pearls as large as pigeon's eggs, saris as blue as the sea, as fine as the sky, as light as air. There were ogres and monsters lurking everywhere, but the princes would make short work of these with their swords. There was the 'good queen' and the 'bad queen'; which one would be their mother-in-law? Their aunt must have told them to build Shiva *linga*s with mud, place them near the *tulsi manch,* and worship them with garlands made with their own hands every morning. On special days of worship, they must starve without water till evening, complete their prayers and then break their fast with the holy *panchamrit* that they would receive from their priest, for, all this would get them husbands like Shiva. I wonder what had they thought or made of this concept?

To me Shiva is a terrifying figure—clad in tiger skin, with a snake draped around his neck and a throat blue with poison which he can neither swallow nor regurgitate. He rides a bull, lives on Mount Kailash and frequents charnel houses and burning grounds. What kind of a husband would someone like him be and how would the sisters receive him? In the end, did they prefer their own mundane world to the uncertainties of the imagination? Deprivation is after all a relative term, and those who know no better are not unduly saddened by the rigors of a sparse existence. This idea seems to be corroborated by a later entry:

*Today is Saraswati Puja. A lot of people will come to our house because my father is a Brahmin and therefore, entitled to worship. After he completes the* puja *in the house, he will go to other houses and they will give him many things—money, fruits, sweets. Today we can eat as much as we want, no one will stop us. My mother soaked armloads of* shefali *in water. The flowers have turned the water into bright saffron. Then she dyed two red-bordered white saris for us in this water and now they are sunshine yellow with red borders. Krishna and I will look beautiful!*

Saraswati Puja has always been an important event in our family and it is comforting somehow to find that the roots reached so far back. I wonder how much the two little girls understood of the event's significance—the worship of learning? The fact that they had been literate is obvious, but what access did they have to books in an age where society believed that an educated woman would be widowed early? By linking education negatively with their only hope of security, men and women had succeeded in holding back women effectively from formal education and books. Krishna and Gauri's father must have been ahead of his times to introduce his twin girls to the alphabets and primers, but how useful was this learning to them? Had they been admired or derided for it?

My eyes catch a fragment of another verse:

*The wind blows, the leaves fall,*
*The grass sways strong and tall,*
*The water ripples, the fish swim,*
*The bird sips water at the brim,*
*The sunlight fades across the field,*
*What will our futures yield?*
*Fine hot rice or hunger cold,*
*Dull black mud or shiny gold?*
*What will happen to Krishna and me?*
*When the clock points to half-past-three?*

I think and think about the last line and its possible meaning, but can come to no satisfactory conclusion. In this case, there is no doubt about the identity of the author, and I marvel at the simplicity, profundity and sheer beauty of the lines and the philosophy they reflect. At what age had this realisation come to her? How had she viewed her uncertain future, with calm fatalism or trepidation? Or, had the mature woman written these lines thinking back on the past? If so, she had certainly not lost the immediacy of the moment.

My eyes are tired and I lay my head down on my arms folded on the table. I must have dozed off for a while and wake up only to find the clock chiming thrice sonorously, and then the decisive half-hour! The last line of the verse comes back to me immediately, and in a sudden flash of recognition, the meaning becomes as clear as daylight. She had compared life to the dial of the clock and the four quarters to the stages of life—childhood, youth, middle age and old age, a familiar concept in Hindu folklore. Half-past-three indicates stepping over from the first quarter to the second—puberty—after which no sensible parent in those times would leave a daughter unmarried, as it would be too dangerous. In any case, rural society would not have permitted it, would have declared the girl *arakshaniya* and ostracised the entire household for failing in their duties.

The coincidence of waking up at the designated hour does not escape me, and again I have this strange feeling that a greater force than my own curiosity is impelling me to move on. That I am correct in my conjecture becomes apparent several pages later, when an older Gauri, as I interpret, looks back and tries to recapture a terrifying experience of youth:

*What is this dark, clotted stuff that flows out between my legs? When it happened for the first time I was so afraid that I hid in some bushes for hours, trying to hold back the flow by contracting my muscles. But it made no difference and my sari got more and more soiled. Finally, when evening fell, I could hear my mother calling for me, a touch of anxiety in her voice, so I covered myself as best as I could and slunk home.*

*My mother looked at me and laughed, but then perhaps she saw my frightened expression and said gently, 'This is a curse that every woman must bear; it comes to plague us once a month and only stops when you carry a child in your belly. Gauri, you are a big girl now and must be careful that no man touches you in the wrong place.'*

*My mother only succeeded in worsening my terror and filling me with vague and nameless fears—curse, child, men, wrong place! What did these things have to do with me? And how would I protect myself from them?*

*My mother showed me how to fold a piece of old cloth, place it in position and secure it with a strip around my waist. I can still feel the discomfort of this device and the horror I felt every time I took it off and saw the fresh blood on it. I also had to wash the cloth myself, dry and reuse it, for cloth, old or new, was a precious commodity for us. When I watched the water redden, I felt as though my very life's blood was flowing away under my hands. How would the blood I was losing be replaced? Would I ultimately die of this loss of blood? Krishna was in the same plight and we clung to each other for reassurance wordlessly. But as the months passed and we lost no weight but gained some, we were less afraid and one day I said to Krishna, 'If our mother, grandmother and other females have not died in all these years, why should we? I am sure Goddess Kali fills fresh blood in our veins when she is no longer thirsty and we are asleep. However, we have to be careful of men so that they never touch us in the place where blood comes from, otherwise the blood might come out of our mouths and kill us!'*

The diaries lie open before me; the leaves stir in the breeze. I close my eyes and will myself to go back through the years till I stand beside the two young girls who can only advise each other. I listen as they talk and I am amazed at the mixture of myth, ingenuity and robust realism that comprise their thought processes. They are submerged in matters they do not understand, trying to make sense of them with their limited knowledge and experience of life, but with total conviction. They sit under a silk cotton tree flaming with blood red blossoms, where the mauve periwinkle flowers in profusion, the jasmine emits its fragrance with passionate abandon to the breeze that wafts it far and near while the cuckoo sings its heart out reaching a crescendo of ecstasy. I wonder what they are thinking of. The two sisters, Gauri and Krishna, are so similar yet so different! What do they see of their later lives as they stare into the horizon? Do they have any premonition of what the future holds for them? Or do they say 'sufficient unto the day', and take the morrow as it comes? Have they realised that events have their own volition and that nothing can change? Have they discovered at this 'half-past-three'-stage a truth that so-called 'educated' persons chase for a lifetime, and do not see even at the end of the road? I remember my own pampered childhood and youth and feel very small in comparison to these two girls. I also realise that by being chosen by her grandfather to carry out his behest, I have been privileged beyond measure.

Ranjit is completely fascinated by my findings and suggests that we make a visit to Bangladesh, to the village where Gauri came from. Perhaps there will be someone who can recall what others have said? He is convinced that such an interesting and intense personality like Gauri would not have been forgotten.

In the unending struggle for power and 'one-up-man-ship' that we call daily life, the forces are so delicately balanced and camouflaged that very often they go unrecognised and masquerade as 'love', 'idealism', 'principles', 'philosophy', 'tradition', 'concern'; the list is endless. I had suspected this for some time but the change in attitude of my family after my 'legacy' came to light, has convinced me. Overnight, certain icons were replaced with others and the power ratio was reversed. By empowering me, thus, my grandfather has set me free and it is nothing short of a miracle he has wrought for me. Ranjit now comes more often and freely to the house and is welcomed much more cordially, even by my grandmother.

I overhear her telling my parents one day, 'The winds of change will blow; time will evolve; this is *yugantar*. We must bow to the inevitable and make the best of what comes our way; after all, none of us wants a rift with Priti!'

I wonder if anyone had done as much for Gauri and Krishna, would they not have been also empowered? If so, how? I cannot wait to find out.

In the following week, I become busy at office with several assignments that take me to various suburbs of Calcutta and to some villages beyond Uluberia, a provincial town about thirty miles from Calcutta. I am particularly attracted to a village by the name of Banibon where the Brahmo Samaj runs an orphanage and a big school. The village is scrupulously clean, and small tiled cottages nestle amongst large clumps of bamboo. The roads are undulating and full of surprises—the picturesque landscape is dotted with ponds, clumps of trees, little streams and meadows that follow in quick succession. Apart from farming, the villagers occupy themselves with various crafts to bring in extra income, the most prominent being *zardozi* and *shola* artefacts.

A homemade embroidery frame on which yards of material are spread tight, and which is clamped firmly down at floor level particularly intrigues me, for it enables the worker to approach it from all directions. The array of bright materials, twinkling *zari* and sparkling sequins in all colours, fill the dim rooms with a warm radiance.

The orphanage is a miracle of dedication, ingenuity and good management. The premises are sparse but spotlessly clean. The boys are not only given academic instruction, but are also trained in useful trades like poultry farming and carpentry. They want to start a farm and a dairy but are held up by the shortage of money. I make a mental note to address this problem on my return to Calcutta. The boys are lean but stand straight and tall and their shining faces belie their neatly darned clothes. On a green field against a backdrop of green bamboo and flaming yellow laburnum they sing for me:

*You live in the abode of joy,*
*In the realm of peace,*
*Truth and beauty personified...*

And again,

*Forgive me my fatigue my Lord...*
*If on the path of life I fall back or falter,*
*Or in the scorching heat of the sun*
*The flowers on my salver wither,*
*This weakness overlook in me*
*My Lord...*

It was a picture that would haunt me for ever. I remember a line by Thomas Hardy: 'So little cause for caroling', yet so much faith in life!

I am so fascinated by the place that I stay on even though my assignment is completed. The caretaker of the guesthouse where I am staying, advises me to spend the night for the show to be staged in the evening. I have seen the posters all over the village and found out that the show is sold out.

*Jatra* or folk theatre has a long tradition in Bengal. Till the time video became popular, it was the main form of entertainment in rural Bengal. Originally, themes were mythological or historic with a simple plot pivoting around the conflict between good and evil. During the nationalist movement, *jatra* played a key role in awakening the spirit of nationalism and desire for freedom from foreign rule. Though with time and political influences, it started to focus on more complex issues and social questions with more sophisticated overtones, in essence, *jatra* has remained strident and didactic.

This evening's show is called *Shakuntala* and is an adaptation of Kalidasa's famous play set in modern times. Each ticket costs ten rupees. The caretaker assures me that if I pay twenty rupees, he will find me a seat in the 'VIP enclosure'. I silently hand him three ten-rupee notes, the extra one for his services, and the die is cast.

The caretaker and I turn up exactly fifteen minutes before the scheduled time of the show. He too has a ticket, as do other members of his family. He wills to sit with them but reassures me that he shall accompany me back to the guesthouse at the end of the show.

The VIP enclosure proves to be a makeshift affair wrought with gunny cloth and bamboo poles. The chairs are placed about five feet away from the stage which is made of several planks of wood lashed together to create a platform. There are jute mats laid on the platform to facilitate movement. There is no front curtain, but the area on the two sides is curtained off to provide 'wings'. The backdrop is a crude but colourful depiction of a forest fading into a cityscape. The people with ten-rupee tickets sit on the ground on canvas sheets to keep the damp out. The play is staged in the open air and there is no protection from the natural elements even in the VIP enclosure! I find that several local dignitaries including the village *sarpanch*, the headmaster of the school, the doctor, the block development officer and their wives are seated in the VIP stall. There are two or three teachers from the school as well, and one of them, well advanced in age, is seated next to me.

A new face, an unusual persona naturally excites curiosity and I find myself at the receiving end of a barrage of questions! I parry them as best as I can, and soon the conversation becomes general. On finding me truly impressed with their village, the elders become doubly gracious and even the ladies venture a comment or two. We are in the middle of a spirited 'city versus village' debate when the bell is sounded, and a hush settles on the restive crowd.

*Shakuntala,* the play, is based on the timeless themes of love and betrayal; a story of love between a simple forest maiden and a king, an outsider to the forest, and the plot interweaves divine displeasure, curses, loss of memory, reversal and the failure of recognition. Owing to the universality of its theme, the play can be easily adapted to any age, milieu or culture. In this case, the emphasis is definitely feminist, and the current production has turned Shakuntala into a strong woman, fighting tooth and nail for her son's rights. In the end, it is only *her* determination and not divine intervention that compels the city slicker's reluctant acquiescence. The final scene is set in court where Shakuntala pushes her counsel aside and conducts her own case.

I am truly impressed by the force and conviction of the actress's portrayal and remark on it to my neighbour Mr Sen, the schoolmaster who teaches history at the local school. He smiles and says, 'It's obvious that you're not very familiar with *jatra*s or you would have known that this is a gem from the Gauri Sikdar repertoire.'

My senses reel and then for a moment, all appears dark before my eyes. I finally get a grip on myself to find the elderly gentleman peering into my face and enquiring anxiously, 'Are you all right?'

I explain that the heat had overpowered me for a moment, but I am fine now and urge him to tell me something more about Gauri Sikdar. I come to know that she had written and directed several such adaptations and played the lead role in many of them. Mr Sen actually remembers seeing her as Shakuntala thirty years ago, and he remarks excitedly, 'What fire, what emotion, and what consummate theatre presence she had! What you saw today was not even a shadow of the original!'

When I enquired whether copies of her plays were extant, Mr Sen laughs and says, 'I doubt if they were ever printed. She always managed with handwritten scripts. As for the idea of copyright, she had probably never heard of it. This is why other theatre companies, who got hold of these handwritten scripts somehow, are using them so shamelessly without even acknowledging her contribution. When people like me die, Gauri Sikdar will also be forgotten.'

I try to convince him that I am genuinely interested in these plays, that I will try to get them published and so give back posthumously to Gauri some of the credit that is due to her. He looks sceptically at me, mistaking my enthusiasm for a passing fancy, but in the end I think he recognises the sincerity in my voice and promises to respond to my letters. He also says that he will speak to the proprietors of this particular company and try to get me a photocopy of the script. I insist on leaving a thousand rupees with him for incidental expenses although he is most reluctant to accept the money. He would have been shocked if I had said that I was prepared to pay five times that amount as a bribe for the script, so I refrain. I do not want to lose his trust which is tenuous enough in any case.

I leave a note with the caretaker for him before I leave for Calcutta, early next morning. In it I explain that I am a journalist, am interested in doing a 'story' about Gauri Sikdar, am completely serious about publishing her plays, and that I would be eternally grateful for his support in this worthy cause. I also add that if some monetary investment is required, I am prepared to bear the expenses.

Ranjit is wildly excited when he hears about this episode and feels that I have been incredibly fortunate. He is also convinced that from now on the investigation will be plain sailing.

This state of euphoria lasts exactly one week, when a letter and a cheque of thousand rupees arrive from Mr Sen. The proprietors had refused to give him a copy of the play and had even denied that it was written by Sikdar. They mentioned that their own man, who was planning to get a copyright for it, had written the play, and till that happened, they would not let the script out of their custody. Mr Sen is predictably outraged and promises to continue his efforts. He also urges me not to give up and to maintain contact with him. But I am bitterly disappointed and feel as though a barely opened door, through which exciting vistas had beckoned, has been closed firmly on my face.

For two days thereafter, I am too depressed to do anything; even the diaries lie untouched and my dwindling confidence makes me wonder whether I will ever be able to carry out my grandfather's request. Am I not too small and inadequate for such a grave responsibility?

Ranjit finally talks me out of my despondence when he comes up with a plan that seems workable. Accordingly, he makes a trip to Banibon and meets Mr Sen. They spend two days discussing matters during which time Ranjit takes him into confidence and tells him much of the truth including my relationship with Gauri and my grandfather's request. Ranjit also convinces him that we have the capacity to undertake a moderate financial outlay. Finally, Mr Sen agrees to become one of a team of three and to carry out investigations on our behalf. Since he has no outward connection with us, he feels that people will take his queries as part of an independent research project. He proposes to begin by placing advertisements in provincial newspapers in the vernacular that will offer rewards for valid, documented information about Gauri Sikdar. Once responses start coming in, he will contact us and we will then devise the next stage of our strategy. Ranjit leaves behind a very excited Mr Sen before returning to Calcutta; elderly and on the verge of retirement, Mr Sen has found the perfect antidote to ennui and obsolescence.

I go back to the diaries after a lapse of more than two weeks and find that I now have a fresh insight. My brush with the mature and creative Gauri, albeit only through her play and Mr Sen's words, has convinced me of her strength, determination and above all, creative prowess.

Seen in the light of this newfound vision, the entries come to life as the utterances of a 'real' person rather than a shadowy, almost mystical presence. I find that 'half-past-three' had indeed been a watershed in her life and that the quality of her entries in the subsequent period is not only more mature, but also anxious and poignant:

*What is to become of Krishna? She has been 'inspected' by so many parties, but been rejected by all prospective grooms and their families on the ground of colour alone. Can no one see her wonderful face and body? Can no one see the wealth of love in her heart? Can they not see that she is like an urn of honey with the capacity to slake all thirst? That anyone who accepts her with love will have a lifetime of sweetness to enjoy? Some of the young men who came to 'see' her were so plain and ordinary in every way; what makes them so desirable and so arrogant?*

*My mother says that men are like gold ornaments; crooked or misshaped, they never lose their intrinsic value. What is this value—the capacity to earn a few rupees and impregnate women? Given a chance, Krishna and I could beat most men at most of their own games, but...*

Her voice trails off, helpless in the grip of a social system that had not changed despite the efforts of noted social reformers of this country like Ram Mohan Roy and Ishwar Chandra. I think it became increasingly clear to Gauri and Krishna that no one was going to 'help' them, that if they wanted something out of life, they would have to fight alone and unaided.

Another entry:

*I have told my father not to think of my marriage till he has made some arrangement for Krishna. They will probably marry her off to someone who is lame or disfigured or mad. Such is the burden of a dark, marriageable girl to a poor family! My father does not want to do this, but will he be able to stand up to the pressure my grandmother and mother will put on him? Why are women so cruel to their own kind?*

I realise with a shock that there is a similarity between Gauri's predicament and mine, and that only formal education and economic independence have saved me from others taking charge of my life and running it as they thought fit. It is a male however, that has come to my rescue, much to the chagrin of the women folk in the family!

Has nothing changed then except for the façade? Is the much celebrated, post-Independence woman power not a social, but a purely personal phenomenon, at least in India? To go back to the diaries:

*Krishna has been different lately—a little absent-minded, making mistakes with the simplest household chores. Today, she put salt twice in the daal and my mother was livid. There is more to it than meets the eye. I must get her to confide in me.*

A little later, on the same page, another entry:

*...It is not easy to get Krishna to talk. The slightest hint of a breach of privacy, and she stares at you blankly, total incomprehension on her face as though blinding rain had smudged out the landscape. She has no worries, no fears, she is sure her parents will do what is best for her. She laughs off her absent-mindedness, but the laughter rings hollow. I know Krishna too well to mistake the signs. She only behaves in this fashion when her total concentration is focussed elsewhere. I will have to find a way.*

After this, the entries are abrupt and cryptic. For instance:

*I saw her when I was returning with my urn of water from the pond. She was standing in the shadows talking to him.*

Or,

*She trusts him but I don't, I am afraid.*

Again,

*He is well built with rippling muscles, very manly but very crafty. In any case, his caste is all wrong. But how will she convince the family?*

Further,

*That he has courage, I know. I have seen him kill poisonous snakes with ease. Once he caught a cobra by the neck, twirled it around and beat its life out by repeatedly flailing its body against some rocks. When he put down the creature, it was twitching in its last agony and his palm had turned blue; the whole village marvelled at this feat.*

I can only presume that *she* is Krishna, but nowhere is she mentioned by name. Who the *he* is, I have not the faintest notion, even though I have a startlingly clear mental image of him—dark, stocky and powerful, with muscles as of a leopard move under his shiny skin; a face with strong features and piercing eyes, not handsome but compelling; the whole persona replete with a sheer animal magnetism that would be quite irresistible, especially to a girl who has known nothing but rejection.

I turn the pages of one of the diaries with frenetic eagerness, but there is not a single entry that pertains to Krishna after this. She fades out as though she had never been, never existed, not been an alter ego to Gauri for so many years. Why had Gauri so firmly shut her out? What had Krishna done, or what had been done to her? My mind ranges over a vast spectrum of possibilities, each more fantastic than the other, but a sense of tragedy seems to predominate, mainly due to Gauri's silence. Would Gauri not have made a jubilant entry had there been a happy ending to her twin's story? Or had uncertainty about her life caused Gauri to turn her face away? Was her silence merely a façade for the gnawing anxiety that had desperately sought solace in forgetfulness?

Try as I might, words such as 'rape', 'murder', 'suicide', 'betrayal', melodramatic but likely, bombard my consciousness with the insistence of a swarm of torpedoes till I seek refuge in sleeping pills.

However, the next morning, I try to rationalise. Perhaps Gauri had known something that she did not wish to commit on paper for fear of it being found or her being caught out? She must have been questioned mercilessly whichever way Krishna had decided, for their closeness was well recognised by the family. She must have feigned complete ignorance both in self-defence and to protect her sister, which came through clearly in the diaries. This hypothesis however does not satisfy me completely, and my thoughts chase each other endlessly like two bits of driftwood caught in an eddy of water till I am again compelled to acknowledge defeat.

At lunch, I convey my perplexity to Ranjit and look at him hopefully for ideas.

He takes my hand in his and says affectionately, 'You look like a little girl waiting for the magician to pull the proverbial rabbit out of the hat! I agree that this silence seems inexplicable, that you have examined all possibilities and none of them is satisfactory, but there must be a clue or hint that you have missed, for such a cataclysmic event in her life cannot go unrecorded.'

We both sit in dejected silence for a while when a colleague of ours joins us at the table. He works in another department, the literary to be precise, but forms part of the 'young gang' that we moved around with. The common factor that unites us is our dislike of the upper echelons—their stodginess, conservatism and caution. He has a slim volume in his hands and on enquiry says, 'This is a fantastic collection of conundrums that a little known author has put together. They are very clever and reveal amazing political insight. I would like to review the book in the literary section, but do you think my boss will allow it? No! He's the kind that would ask Naipaul to present his credentials if he turned up on his doorstep!'

I ask for the book and on perusal, the verses do indeed prove witty and interesting. One item especially catches my attention:

*Black is white and white is black,*
*Is common knowledge to the political Jack!*
*Only methods vary from Jack to Jim*
*How they, the murky waters, swim;*
*The ruling party provides the bait,*
*The opposition seals its fate,*
*The fish they catch is solid grey,*
*The Truth is safely hidden away!*

We both promise to praise the book to all and sundry, so that the 'buzz' may ultimately reach his boss, and he goes away less angry than he had been on arrival. We too prepare to get back to work when Ranjit clutches my arm so hard that it hurts!

'That's it!' he exclaims, 'white and black – of course! Gauri was too clever to put anything directly on paper. It is a wonder that she managed to save her diaries from being confiscated. She must have required a deal of craftiness and ingenuity. She must have written these happenings in riddle or allegorical form so that even if the diaries fell into wrong hands they would not betray Krishna or her secrets. It's up to you, Priti, to unravel this mystery and put it in a coherent form! Let's see whether you are half as clever as your great grandmother!'

So that night I settle down with a whole flask of coffee determined to work through the night if need be, to get to the bottom of this question. As mentioned before, Gauri had often written down verses and prose passages on issues that had caught her attention at different times. I glance through them and it is evident that her choice indicates an unexpected sophistication.

I had assumed that they would provide valuable clues to her personality and also thought that when I got a clearer picture of her life, I would attempt to place these entries in context. But compelled to change my mind, I decide to make these entries the focus of my research tonight and begin to go through each of them meticulously.

It is obvious that Gauri had some access to books that children read at that time. Perhaps these had been acquired for her brothers and she had managed to get hold of them. There are references to popular fairy tales, poems, verses that are called *chhara*s which are very popular in Bengal and similar to 'nursery rhymes', and like them, record important events in village life, and even happenings of historical importance. A typical one reads:

*The boy is asleep,*
*The locality is at peace,*
*The Borgis have arrived in the country,*
*The bulbul bird*
*Has consumed the harvest,*
*How will I pay my dues?*
*The paddy is finished,*
*The betel leaf exhausted.*
*How will I pay?*
*Wait a few days*
*And I will pay,*
*For I have sown the field with garlic.*

One book that seems to have caught her fancy particularly is a children's classic, all but forgotten today, by the name of *Lal Kalo* (Red and Black), an inspiring tale about two camps of ants, red and black, by Girindra Shekhar Basu. I have read the book, thanks to my grandfather, and find it fascinating; so I can understand Gauri's preoccupation with it, but am surprised to find excerpts from it occurring with increasing regularity and in narrative progression. This is unusual, and I decide to go through these entries before perusing the others. The opening lines, I know, is the inimitable *chhara* that introduces the book:

*Beyond the seven seas, thirteen rivers and the island*
*of Sri Lanka*
*The dark night descends on a faraway field;*
*In the centre of this field grows the silk-cotton tree,*
*And on its tip sits the 'Kankurshinge' fish, and*
*In the belly of the fish is a jewel glowing like*
*a thousand lamps.*

*The field is drowned in dark, deep blackness;*
*You cannot see the leaves of the trees; you cannot*
*see the ground,*
*And by the water the bullfrog hops gently around;*
*Suddenly the bullfrog looks up in awe and fear,*
*The owl has swooped down and caught him in the rear!*
*The python climbs the silk-cotton, into the cleft of the tree,*
*The Kankurshinge wakes up and feels he needs to flee.*
*One jump and the Kankurshinge fish is off the tree,*
*The python slithers and falls off the smooth bark, free;*
*The tip of the silk-cotton crashes and tumbles down,*
*The broken python falls and the crane on him swoops down.*

*Happy and at peace the Kankurshinge swims in the sea,*
*The baby wakes up and smiles, says, 'Look at me!'*
*The brightness of the early dawn touches the tip of the tree,*
*The little boy and girl will read 'Red and Black' with glee.*

The story itself is a complicated one where the red and black ants clash and go to war because a red youngster insults a young black wife who is very beautiful and a favourite with the queen. This conflict grows and draws in the entire insect population, the birds, the chameleon, the frogs and the snakes. While the moves and countermoves are strictly in keeping with animal behaviour, the text itself is a biting political fable that parodies the Indian national struggle for Independence. 'Red and Black' represent the 'British' and 'Indian' respectively, yet the author had not permitted the animal characters to lose their specific identities. And this brilliant and amusing book is barely known beyond the confines of Bengal.

It is obvious that Gauri had been fascinated by the book and transcribed large chunks of it; but on reading, I begin to find small but subtle differences. For instance, the first two lines of the song of the Red youth are:

*Dusky wife for my sake*
*Beware the waves in the lake*

Gauri had replaced the word 'wife' with 'girl' or 'maiden'. In the book, the king and queen are sympathetic to the victim and are determined to avenge the insult, but in Gauri's retelling of the tale, they harshly instruct the dark girl not to transgress the limits of modesty. In the original story, the chameleon wishes to fight the Reds because they have bitten him; in Gauri's version, the chameleon takes the dark maiden under his protection because he is attracted to her. The fable takes on the features of an epic with the conflict developing into full-scale war and the various heroes, the frog, the snake, the birds are ranged on opposite sides. Gauri's interpretation is less spectacular, subtler; craft and guile have to be used to save the girl. The snake strangely is on the chameleon's side and helps him to escape with her. When D day dawns and both sides are drawn up in the battle array, the snake comes and informs both camps that the *casus belli* is not to be found, neither is the chameleon! The birds and flying ants take on the role of spies and look for them high and low, but so adept is the chameleon at camouflage that he cannot be spotted, and the black maiden too has donned disguise. She looks more like a cricket than an ant in the costume that the chameleon has given her. There is a memorable bit in the book where the author says:

*The king came and the queen came,*
*They put the sweet corn in the fire,*
*They cooked spinach, baked bread and ate,*
*And all were awed at the sight*
*Of his great beard!*
*Then they conferred among themselves, making plans...*

Gauri had added:

*The chameleon clings to a twig*
*Just above their head,*
*Another stiff, brown twig*
*Which could not be read.*
*To hear better he slid down*
*A leaf among the leaves,*
*Green and slim he swung*
*Almost to their sleeves!*

On another occasion, in the original narrative, the bullfrog guards the mouth of a hole in the bole of a tree to prevent the chameleon from escaping, not realising however, that the snake is his friend.

*The snake slid up to the hole*
*The bullfrog leapt up high,*
*The chameleon, ant in mouth,*
*Climbed the tree to the sky!*
*Under leaves he crept,*
*The hawk circled above,*
*Yellow, blue and purple*
*Such is the power of love!*

But what is significantly missing, I observe, is the banquet at the end, when the triumphant blacks celebrate; instead, the ants, birds, frog and others sit in a circle and solemnly curse the pair.

*May they know no happiness*
*Only sorrow and pain,*
*May there be only loss*
*No blessing and no gain.*
*To flout friends and family*
*To think a stranger near,*
*Can only bring tears and shame,*
*Agony, toil and fear.*
*We reject them both,*
*To us they are dead,*
*May twenty million curses*
*Fall on their head!*

Where was Gauri when her beloved sister was condemned in the name of family feeling, social prestige and moral propriety? I have a picture in my mind of Gauri's proud head held high as she looks on, her eyes glistening with unshed tears, determined to make up to Krishna for all the humiliation the latter had suffered, if life ever brought them face to face again. But did this ever happen? Did they ever have an opportunity to unburden themselves, exchange confidences unhampered by the obtrusive presence of others?

Somehow, I feel no sense of exhilaration at being able to understand Gauri, even though Ranjit is very complimentary and praises me for my inferential skills. The unfairness and pathos of it all eats into my soul and I do not have the heart to go back to the diaries. In office too, all the stories deal with violence against women in some form or the other and the sense of claustrophobia grows till I find it difficult to breathe.

It is in this mood of desperation that I decide to question my grandmother for I am sure she knows more than she lets on. She feels strongly about family prestige and is an adept at keeping family secrets locked in her own heart. It will not be easy to get any information out of her, but I am determined to give it my best shot.

I know she loves a cup of tea in the afternoon. Hence on a cloudy day I enter her room with two steaming mugs of fragrant tea and set them down before her. She is pleased I can see, but also a wee bit suspicious when I sit down on her large four-poster bed, put a pillow behind my back against the footboard and tuck my feet under me. Perhaps my stance is confrontational, for she decides that attack is the best defence and opens fire: 'To what do I owe this good fortune? Has the sun risen in the west that my busy granddaughter has suddenly found a few minutes for her old grandmother?'

Not to be outdone, I counter her saying, 'The granddaughter would come oftener if the grandmother had more spare time.'

'I am a lonely old woman, how can I be busy? Your mother now takes care of the household quite efficiently; after all, she is in charge now.'

I detect a note of resentment and remark hastily, 'My mother would be lost without your advice, Grandma, as would be my aunts; you know that quite well. They can do the work, but you have to take care of the planning, especially with Runa's wedding coming up.'

Runa, my aunt's daughter, is due to be married next month. She is a good, obedient girl and her marriage has been arranged as per tradition, by matching the horoscopes of the nuptial pair.

The old lady is quite disarmed now, smiles sweetly at me and asks, 'And when do I get busy with preparations for another wedding? Have you and Ranjit fixed a date yet? I do wish he would give me his date and time of birth accurately, so that I can pass them on to the family priest; but he only makes jokes when I ask him!'

In response, I turn innocently to her and ask, 'Do you really believe in horoscopes? Do you believe that if they match, the happiness of the couple is assured?'

'Well this is what this *family* has always believed. Not a single marriage has been arranged without this formality. When our marriage was arranged, the family priest said that I possessed all the signs of Lakshmi—small hands and feet, fair complexion, long hair and a soft voice. And, this helped my in-laws to make up their minds, and I must say that I lived up to my reputation, for all has gone well with the family after I came into the household.'

The note of complacency is unmistakable and I am almost sorry to puncture this bubble of self-assurance commenting, 'And, in the case of your mother-in-law, Grandma? Did they also match horoscopes when she came into the house?'

The stunned disbelief on her face assures me that my arrow has found its mark, but she recovers quickly, smiles and says, 'You mean my aunt-in-law who brought up your grandfather like a son? Yes, she was a wonderful lady and held the family together through thick and thin. I was fond of her and the entire family owes her a debt of gratitude.'

'No, Grandma, I meant my grandfather's mother; I have heard that she was as beautiful as Lakshmi Herself. She must have had a good horoscope too?'

This time she makes no attempt to keep the frost out of her voice and answers, 'A woman who could abandon her husband, home and a two-year-old son, hardly fits the bill for Lakshmi. She was a heartless, unscrupulous woman who cared nothing for family feeling or prestige, and I don't see why we should waste time discussing her.'

'But Grandma, why did she do this? Did anyone ever bother to find out?'

She lashes out at me like a whip and retorts, 'Because she had no character; she wanted more excitement; because her home was not enough for her!'

'But how do you know this? You never met her, did you? You are only repeating what others have told you. You are so intelligent Grandma, why did you not try to find out the truth?'

'What truth are you talking about Priti? Do you think I am telling you a lie? How dare you insinuate such a thing?'

I can feel that she is really angry now and decide to push it a little further. 'I am not suggesting that you would ever tell a lie consciously, but suppose what you have been led to believe is false? What surprises me is that a strong person like you would accept so tamely some malicious gossip cooked up by people who did not like her. What if those very people compelled her to leave home for reasons of their own? After all, you did not get a chance to make a personal assessment!'

There is a silence of a few moments, and when she speaks, her voice is silky and dangerously smooth. 'What I say will completely destroy these pretty fantasies you have been indulging in and in a way, I am sorry about it. The young should hang on to their dreams as long as possible, but you leave me no option. Priti, you see, I *did* meet this woman not once, but three times.'

It is now my turn to gape and splutter. 'You, you what, but then when?'

It is sickeningly evident that she has scored handsomely and that my discomfiture has pleased her no end.

She however, continues smoothly, even indulgently. 'Yes, Priti, she actually had the temerity to attempt what she called reconciliation, for she wanted to re-establish contact with her long-lost son. Suddenly, when she was no longer fit for her life of sin, she developed a strong maternal instinct! Wish you could have seen the letter, such a masterly exercise in hypocrisy!'

I however refrain from telling her that I am in possession of the letter or that I think it is one of the most moving documents I have ever come across. Instead, I decide to utilise this unbelievable opportunity to get more information and say innocently, 'And what did the letter say?'

'Oh, some nonsense about her guilt and her love, and how misunderstood she was, calculated perfectly to take in a simpleton like your grandfather.'

'And, was he taken in?'

'Oh, yes! He wanted to meet her right away, to establish the truth, just like you, Priti!'

'Then, why didn't he?'

'Because *I* wouldn't let him. Your father agreed with me. We convinced him that it would be better if we met her instead.'

'And, did you?'

'Your father and I went twice. It was not easy to make her see reason.'

'Reason?'

'That it would be best if we did not resurrect the past; that we, a respectable family, could never acknowledge her in public; that she would irreparably harm her son and his family if she forced the issue. Your father was most concerned about you Priti, your career and marriage, and impressed this upon her.'

'So, she agreed in the end?'

'Very reluctantly, as a matter of fact. At the close of the second visit, I saw your father weakening; the third time I went alone.'

There is something ominous about her words that strike a chill in my heart. I know instinctively that the third visit had put a definite end to the intercourse, but I still persist. 'You never met her again?'

'There was no need to. She recognised a closed door when she saw one.'

'And what did she look like?'

'You must remember she was an old woman when I met her, but she was still very beautiful, of course how much of it was due to make-up I have no way of knowing. These *jatra* women probably forget what their real face is like!'

The contempt and sarcasm in her voice flick me on the raw and I ask, 'Oh you met her after a show?'

'Only the first time after a performance of Draupadi. The other two meetings were in her house.'

'And how was she dressed?'

'In pristine white, like a widow, very proper, no doubt for our benefit, but the make-up was intact.'

'How do you know that she did not always dress like that?'

'Because, *jatra* women would not last long if they moped around in white!'

'You were determined to dislike her, no wonder you could see nothing good in her. You only saw what *you* wanted to see.'

'And you, my little Priti, are determined to romanticise her and see what never existed! Why, may I know?'

I realise that we have arrived at an impasse, and that she will part with no more information. Also I do not want her to suspect where my interest lies, for she would be quite implacable if she felt that the family honour was at stake. I am certain that something very crucial had happened at the third meeting, but exactly what, I would have to find out on my own. Meanwhile, I have to get back into her good books, so I fling my arms around her neck saying, 'Why are we arguing about a dead woman who means nothing to either of us? How about another round of tea and a game of chess?'

The relief is palpable on her face as she hugs me back and agrees that she would enjoy nothing better! I lose two games to her and realise that when it comes to planning moves, devising a stratagem, and keeping one's own counsel, I have a great deal to learn from her. However, I have perceived a chink in her armour, and for the time being, that is enough for me.

# 2

Somehow, this encounter with my grandmother gives me back my lost energy, resolve, determination, and I return to the diaries with renewed certainty of purpose.

Krishna's absence, for reasons unknown to me, had obviously left a gaping void in Gauri's life, for her entries after this are desultory, casual, even half-hearted, as though all her creativity had gone into writing the allegory of Krishna's story. She also seems very despondent about her own future, and a black premonition fills her heart:

*I dreamt last night that I had lost my way. I was alone in a forest amidst tall dark trees, huge snake-like creepers, thorny bushes and strange creatures—half bird, half beast. My sari was caught in some thorns and got torn into ribbons. I found it difficult to protect my body, particularly my breasts, on which round drops of blood stood out like beads. A snake came and licked the blood from my breasts, then entwined me till I could hardly breathe. I looked into its face and found it to be human; my own screams woke me up.*

On a slightly different note:

*I wanted to go to the* mela, *but my mother said I was too grown up for these frivolous pursuits; too old at fifteen? Yet, at other times, she says I am a child and should not interfere when elders speak! In the end, she relented when she found that some of our neighbours were escorting us, and we went along in a group.*

*The* mela *comes every year in the month of* Chaitra *and lasts for a month till the advent of the New Year. One of the attractions is the* nagardola *at one paisa (1\64th of a rupee) per four turns; another, the conjuror with his bag of tricks, the most awesome being the swallowing of fire; a third, the tattoo man who carves traditional designs on the upper and lower arms of boys, though for girls this is strictly forbidden; a fourth, the* bauls, *who dance and sing to their* ektaras. *The* charak *is fascinating because it is so bizarre: a special kind of tree has to be uprooted to the beat of drums. It is then shorn of all its branches and leaves, and the trunk is placed like a pole, supported by ropes fastened to pegs driven into the ground. To it are tied thicker, knotted ropes with iron hooks which are used to flagellate people who have penances to make, and strangely enough, the devotion on their faces completely belies the blood flowing from their bodies. This happens on the last day of the* mela.

*There are small shops selling odds and ends but I am most attracted by the bangles—circles of glass in every imaginable colour and the light glinting within. The* reshmi *bangles are more expensive and entirely beyond my reach; my friend's father offers to buy me some, but I do not like the look in his eyes and refuse. I also move away a little as he has constantly been reaching for my elbow, ostensibly to guide me, but his hand has been straying. Suddenly my attention is caught by a woman dancing and I move closer to the crowd gathered to watch her She is a tribal girl and is dancing on a piece of white cloth placed on a jute mat. Her movements are jerky but well planned and she never takes her eyes off her feet. At last she is done and she steps off the cloth. Two of her companions hold up the cloth and a gasp goes up from the onlookers, for clearly delineated on the cloth is a huge lotus in bright red, with several buds ranged around it. Then we realise that the mat is smeared with* sindoor, *and it is her amazingly precise movements that have created this pattern. I see in the lotus my own life, a lotus that is red with desire for life and experience, waiting to be picked up by someone who cares. Or, is it a bleeding lotus, coloured by its own blood to a point of agonised no return—a premonition of the future? Who knows?*

I can almost see the fifteen-year-old adolescent—her body at the mercy of hormones she knows nothing about; though aware of her own beauty and worth, yet entirely without hope due to the conservatism and crushing poverty of the family. Yet, she had not taken matters into her own hands like Krishna, but waited patiently for whatever life had in store for her. This certainly did not fit the image of the later Gauri. A few lines of the verse, which she had put down immediately after this entry, are characterised by poignancy and pathos rather than resentment:

*This springtime, so full of tears,*
*Has not come my way before;*
*My loneliness, the kingshook*
*Flaunts in its blood red blossoms;*
*At the entrance to my bower,*
*The chrysanthemum, clad in new leaves,*
*Is waiting,*
*Through the night and the day she waits,*
*Without fluttering an eyelid,*
*For whose arrival?*

These lines from Tagore's opera *Chitrangada,* a great favourite of mine, had never seemed so haunting or mournful before. Is this the difference between intellectual appreciation and 'feeling things on one's pulses'?

I think Gauri must have put away the diaries for some time after this for there is no entry that can be interpreted as a continuation. Perhaps she was too depressed to write or the monotony of her existence had defeated her creative urge. As she had hinted before, not to be married at fifteen was almost a blasphemous state of affairs, and the comments that accrued as a result would have been far from pleasant. With a good-looking girl like Gauri, marriage of some sort would have been easily arranged earlier, had it not been for Krishna's escapade. Did Gauri come to hate Krishna for this? Is this the reason that she never wrote of her again?

Then I stumble on an entry which I think must have been made after a silence of months and is in such sharp contrast that I am quite taken aback.

*I am sixteen and I am to be married! Guess to whom? To a prince, just as our aunt had predicted many years ago! The second son of the* zamindar, *no less, is to be my husband. It seems that Ranima saw me from her* palki *when she was on her way to a banquet in a neighbouring village and sent the proposal. The* ghatak *who came to the house said that Ranima wanted nothing from my father but me! She would accept me in a single sari and a pair of conch-shell bangles. When my father hesitated, saying that he could not afford to entertain such socially elevated people, the* ghatak *said that Ranima would pay for the wedding as well and give my father money so that he could do the honours in style. Rather sceptic, my father wondered why Ranima would do so much, for this kind of generosity from the groom's family was quite unimaginable. The* ghatak *explained that the second son was not inclined to marriage, wanted to turn a hermit, and that Ranima wanted a 'true beauty' to woo him back to family life. She had said that I was the most beautiful girl she had set her eyes on, even superior to herself or her eldest daughter-in-law who hailed from a very wealthy family! This was pure music to my ears and I gazed into the pond again and again to confirm the truth of this statement.*

This note of jubilation continues through the preparations for the approaching nuptials.

*My clothes have arrived; the wedding sari is resplendent with gold work on a deep-red silk from Benares, but my favourite is a light blue one, 'as blue as the sky, as fine as water and light as air', (a quote from Bengali classic,* Khirer Putul*) which I will wear on the night when my husband and I will be together for the first time on a flower-bedecked bed in a flower-filled room. How will it be?*

I could see it all quite clearly when I closed my eyes. The small cottage is lit up with *hajak* lanterns; in the middle of its courtyard is a special slab of stone on which the groom is standing; four banana sprouts are placed at four corners; and strings of mango leaves are festooned over the doors. Then the journey from the groom's house to Gauri's: the elders and notables in palanquins, the young and lesser folk on foot, lanterns and torches provide light, while the band from the nearest town precedes the procession playing popular waltzes, and the *shehnai* brings up the rear with plaintive *raga*s as the whole procession winds down the dark fields like a luminous, awesome snake.

I wonder what was Gauri's state of mind when the groom and his party arrived and the married women of the house blew the conch shells and performed the traditional ululation signalling their arrival? Did she feel jubilant, full of trepidation or a mix of both? Did she have misgivings about her imminent change of lifestyle and her capacity to adjust to it? Or, was she so imbued with the concept that 'women are like water and take the shape of any vessel that they are poured into' that she took it all in her stride? The problems of 'socialisation' that loom so large on the modern consciousness were not even ponderables for her. At what point did Indian women begin to lose this strength and resilience?

Apparently, the diaries travelled with Gauri, for she gives a vivid description of her welcome at her father-in-law's house.

*My* palki *stopped at a huge gate with two lions carved on the two pillars that held them aloft, and I realised that this was the* singhadwar *that I had read about in books. Here the* dhaki *set up a steady beat on his great drum as he led the way to the huge mansion that was to be my home. This is how Durga, the mother-goddess, arrives in our village every year. Ranima, in a red-bordered white silk sari and covered with gold jewellery from head to foot, helped me off the* palki *and guided me inside over a strip of red cloth that had been laid down so that my feet would not touch the ground. She pointed to a pot of milk that was boiling over a charcoal fire, a sheaf of paddy heavy with grain, a basket overflowing with vegetables, a canister piled to the brim with fragrant rice as signs of prosperity and good omens. She then told me to stand in a salver, containing milk and* alta, *while she carried out the* bauron, *the traditional welcome, which included touching three times my forehead, breasts, pelvic zone and feet with a* kulo *that contained several auspicious items, including a burning lamp. After this I walked on the white marble floor, my feet leaving red imprints on the pristine surface, all the while clutching on to the writhing live fish wrapped in a leaf that has been given to me prior to the* bauron. *This fish I knew was a sign of fertility and on this fact the quality of my future life would depend, so I gave the creature my total attention till somebody took it from me and put it in a mud vessel full of water. When it starts swimming Ranima looks pleased and says, 'A good omen; the fish is very much alive!' which gladdens me so much that tears spring to my eyes. After this my husband and I are seated on a carpet while the members of the family bless us. Everyone of them puts a sweet in my mouth and honey in my ears so that I will speak and hear only good things, and puts on me a piece of jewellery. At the end of the process, I am fighting a rising nausea with all my strength. When finally the women of the household take me to the pond at the rear of the house and allow me to bathe, the water is as soothing as my mother's arms around me; my body is cooled and I want to stay there forever.*

After this however, there is not a single entry that refers to her nuptials or her life in the great house. It is as though a deliberate veil of silence has been drawn. I wonder what the reason might have been. What did Gauri want to forget? Was it too personal to be committed to writing? What trials, tribulations, adjustments, joys lay dormant in this period? Would I ever find out? One brief cryptic statement might belong to this period but I can neither make sense of it nor see what, if anything, it is connected to! It reads like this:

*Ranima is taking me to yet another temple in which resides a very famous sadhu-baba. His blessings, it is reported, have great potency. But in our village they say, 'What is the use of cutting the roots of the plant and then pouring water on its tip?' Has Ranima never heard of this saying? Shall I enlighten her?*

When she does write again, she has arrived in Calcutta, living in a home managed by Christian missionaries. She speaks of her life there as though she has never known another, and she never looks back. But I cannot bear this silence as I want to establish some link between the two voices, the two personae, or else my project will be completely jeopardised and my frustration will get the better of me, but there is not a single clue to guide me.

Ranjit comes to the rescue as usual and we plan a trip to Bangladesh, but we need a cover story, or my family will smell a rat. Finally, we approach the editor of the paper and offer to do a feature on 'The *Grameen* Movement' as it is operating in rural Bangladesh. Since this movement has taken the whole world by storm, the editor is more than willing, particularly as we are prepared to pay for our own tickets, and he makes the necessary arrangements to procure papers and visas in record time. It is to be a five-day trip and we reckon that it is easiest to fly into Dhaka and use the local bus services.

I am busy packing when, out of the blue, one evening, my grandmother enters my room and asks me very casually, 'Which part of Bangladesh will you be visiting?'

I say I am not sure that our editor is making out an itinerary for us. Then she asks more directly, 'Will you go anywhere near the district of Barisal?'

I try to look suitably surprised and say that the idea had not occurred to me, but now that she has mentioned it, we would give it a shot.

'Do you have a particular errand in mind?' I ask.

'No, of course not! After so many years I am hardly interested. In any case, I spent only a few years in the great house, but I remember those days with great pride and joy.'

'Does the "great house" still stand?'

' No idea. We exchanged it for this house, two others and some money when the "Enemy Property Act" came through. At that point, we had heard that some Nawab had taken over our property, but this was back in the seventies. Who knows what the situation is today?'

I assure her that I will do my best to pay a visit if my busy schedule permits me to take a day off.

'Yes, a sight of your magnificent heritage may help to instil some family pride in you, a quality that seems sadly lacking in young people these days!' she comments.

The flight to Dhaka is uneventful except for a minor distraction—the passenger sitting two rows behind us puts a rather large bundle in the overhead compartment, and ten minutes after take-off, a loud and indignant squawking sound emerges from it. Necks crane, ears strain, eyes pop, stewards and stewardesses arrive at a run, but the noise stops. The gentleman to whom the bundle belongs, leans back in his seat, pulls his cap firmly over his eyes and apparently falls fast asleep. Thoroughly nonplussed, the attending staff is about to retrace their steps when the noise begins again and continues till the owner is compelled to return to terra firma. He does his best to disclaim responsibility, but the airlines tag with his name on it gives him away. When the swaddling clothes are removed, eight large fowls, their legs tied together and beaks firmly taped are revealed. One of these, more vigorous than the rest had somehow worked lose of the tape, hence the debacle!

On persistent questioning, the man finally acknowledges that this is regular practice as 'Indian chicken' has an excellent market in Bangladesh. He insists that he had hurt nobody hence, should not be penalised!

An American couple sitting across the aisle mutter, 'Everything is possible in this country,' and though I tend to agree, I cannot allow a foreigner to get away with such a remark. So I lean across and say, 'I have observed similar incidents in Los Angeles and San Francisco when people from Mexico arrive in the United States.'

Taken aback, they are honest enough to admit that such indeed is the case. I will never forget the indignant face of the man as he is led away with his chickens, protesting to the last!

On arrival in Dhaka, we spend half a day cutting through bureaucratic red tape and the next three days travelling extensively to collect evidence. We are impressed by the signs of prosperity and particularly the prominent role women are playing in popularising the *Grameen* Movement. By the afternoon of the fourth day, we are through with our assignment, but it has taken more time than we had calculated. Ranjit insists that we hire a car and set out that very evening for our destination, but we are informed at the hotel desk that there is no motor-worthy road and that we will have to take the steamer service. They say the last steamer for Barisal, the largest town near our destination, will leave at 5 p.m. After that we would have to depend on cycle rickshaws and local buses. Fortunately, we are able to secure two first-class seats on the steamer and as we make ourselves comfortable, it begins to unfasten itself from the jetty.

My grandfather had mentioned to me more than once that the *laskar*s on the steamers were the best cooks in the world and we realise the truth of this when we sit down to dinner on the open deck. With the dark waters of the Buriganga swirling around us, the stars shining as they never shine in Calcutta, plates of steaming chicken curry and rice smell and taste quite heavenly and entirely unique. Tired and hungry we fall on the food and four helpings disappear without a trace! Feeling completely replete and munching the fragrant aniseed that is offered as a digestive, we loll back in our seats and fall asleep almost immediately.

It is Ranjit who wakes me up, repeatedly tapping my shoulder. For a moment, I stare bewildered and confused; then cognition returns and I sit up stretching my limbs and pushing my hair out of my eyes. The boat is so quiet—the only sounds being snores from other passengers. A child wakes up and wails, but is hushed at his mother's breast and the steady beat of the waves against the steamer provides a gentle lullaby.

I want to go right back to sleep but Ranjit says, 'We have entered a larger river now, can't you feel the difference in the movement of the boat? I'm going out on the deck to take a look. Do you want to come?'

'Of course I want to,' I reply promptly, and he stretches out his hand and pulls me to my feet.

We creep out quietly with the help of our hooded pencil torches, arrive on the deck and lean over the guard-rails. I have travelled by boat earlier, but nothing had prepared me for the vast expanse of water that I encounter now. Like the ancient mariner, we are alone, adrift on an enchanted sea the dark depths quite unplumbable; the reflection of the stars on the water now clear, then breaking into a thousand fragments; the breeze rippling the surface and creating little waves that merge with the larger billows. The vast Meghna is a far cry from the smaller river we had crossed earlier.

I am cold and shiver almost involuntarily. Ranjit notices, takes off his jacket and puts it round my shoulders. I realise to my dismay that I am entirely at his mercy on this lonely deck! It would be so easy for a person to throw the other off the rails and the latter would disappear without trace in the tumultuous waters.

Ranjit puts his arm around my shoulders and asks, 'Scared?' I admit I am and cling to him, grateful for the support of his lithe and sturdy frame. He continues, 'Do you realise you're making the same journey that Gauri must have made in the reverse direction on her way to Calcutta, more than half a century ago?'

I do, but wonder under what circumstances the journey had been made and in what frame of mind? Suddenly I am reminded of two lines of a song by Tagore that appear at least twice or thrice in the diaries:

*Today you are on your way to a tryst*
*In the face of the storm,*
*My life-companion, my friend.*

I ponder and ask myself, 'Is this how Gauri had felt on the outward journey? Was it a tryst with a man or with destiny?'

The sky is beginning to lighten in the east, the air is less inscrutable. Ranjit and I make our way back to our seats, and prepare to disembark.

The hotel is pretty much an apology for what we had expected, but at least we have a room to deposit our backpacks. After a bath and a couple of cups of strong tea, we are prepared for what the day might bring. There is a bus that passes the village and if we hurry, we might be able to catch it. We do, by the skin of our teeth, but find seats right at the back. The bus starts with a great grinding of gears and clutch, and we are on our way. The road is a euphemism for a country track and we are jolted mercilessly from side to side, up and down. However, the noise and the movement keep at bay the curiosity of our co-passengers, for no conversation is possible! We are conscious of innumerable eyes raking our backs as we alight from the bus and move away, unbelievably towards our destination!

There is a tea-stall, a stone's throw from the bus stop, and on perceiving several elders savouring their cups, we move in their direction. I am aware that we are conspicuous in our city attire and easy camaraderie of the sexes, so I walk behind Ranjit and draw my shawl close around my body. But as my Bengali is more fluent than his, I have to do most of the talking. I explain that we are cousins and as Ranjit lives up in North India, his language is stilted. He quickly falls into the role I assign him and we find it is plain sailing thereafter. Sitting on a 'bench' that is actually a board resting on two slabs of stone, we gingerly sip the thick concoction that goes in the name of tea, but find it strangely invigorating. We also bite into toast and 'mamlet' that is surprisingly good too. After answering very politely all the questions aimed at us, we begin our own exploration.

On enquiring about the 'great house' we are told that the local landlord, perhaps a self-styled Nawab has taken it over and resides there with his large family. One of the elders remembers that it used to belong to a Hindu raja or *zamindar* before Partition and that the entire family had moved out during the exodus. On learning that we belong to that family, there is immediate warmth and lowering of guards and the eldest becomes doubly vocal. It seems that Ranima had been quite a legendary character due to her great beauty and generosity to the poor, a tradition her elder daughter-in-law had maintained till the last. But when it comes to the second lady of the house, they grow cagey and tongue-tied. They explain that she left home under mysterious circumstances and without warning, that she had gone away with a *sanyasi* who was actually a nationalist in disguise, that she had been seen with him and his group in the vicinity for over a year, but after that she had disappeared without a trace. They all look uncomfortably at each other, as though there is something that they do not know how to express, but would like to tell us. So I turn to the eldest, fold my hands and beg for information. Something about my attitude touches him perhaps, for he launches into the story without further ado.

Ranima's second son had been persuaded to marry against his inclinations, but had fallen hopelessly in love with his beautiful bride after marriage, even though she had come from a poor home and there was a scandal attached to the family. She too had done her best to keep him and the family happy and for a while all had gone smoothly. The trouble started with the fact that even after two years of marriage, she failed to produce a child. Ranima had taken her to every temple in the vicinity, but nothing had worked. The women of the house had pronounced her barren and advised Ranima to find a second bride for her son, but he had put his foot down very firmly and refused to consider such a course of action.

It was at this juncture that the tantric *sanyasi* had appeared on the scene. He was a distant acquaintance, had left home at an early age and had joined an ashram. He and a group of young sadhus had moved into the village and taken up their abode in an uninhabited, derelict building, and he was a frequent visitor to the house. It was he who had advised Ranima to hold a *Putreshti Yajna*, a ritual performed to be blessed with a son like the one carried out by King Dashrath, father of Rama, the hero in the epic Ramayana, when his three queens had proved infertile.

It was an expensive and elaborate ritual spread over nine days during which the entire village had been given food in charity. Even the untouchables who worked in the 'burning grounds' and the Muslim families had not been forgotten. Eleven Brahmins had carried out the *puja* and *hom* for eight days, but on the last day, the *sanyasi* had taken over. Nine *maunds* of dry wood had been used to build a pyre in the courtyard and one and a quarter *maunds* of ghee to lubricate the wood and feed the flames. The *hom* had started at 8 in the evening and continued late into the night, but the miracle occurred precisely at the stroke of midnight.

The *sanyasi*s chanting mantras had walked around the pyre feeding it with more and more ghee and when the flames were leaping to the sky they had stood back and cried out to the deity to appear. The whole village had seen the figure step out of fire, one made of pure light with a bowl in his hand. Gauri and her husband had prostrated themselves on the ground and the deity had put the bowl in the man's outstretched hands and disappeared into the flames. The bowl had contained *payasam* and the couple had partaken of it. Within a month, Gauri had been declared pregnant by the midwife and in the tenth month, she had borne a son as beautiful as the moon.

I thought to myself of the little boy I had seen in my dream, of my grandfather, who had been an extraordinarily handsome man, and agreed that such indeed must have been the case. Ranjit is totally mesmerised and pleads with the speaker to continue his story.

Thereafter, the *sanyasi* had become a kind of a messiah for the whole village and when it was discovered that he was involved in the nationalist movement and was working for the ouster of the British administration in the district, he assumed almost god-like proportions. Gauri's husband was his good friend and supported him in every way, and the *sanyasi* was a frequent visitor to the house.

At this stage I begin to get the impression that this is a carefully tailored story and that certain vital bits of information have been left out or reinvented, perhaps out of deference for our feelings, for, the other elders are looking at each other in surprise. So I request them to send a guide with us who can show us the house. I explain that I would like to take a few photographs back for my grandmother who had spent her youth there.

The shopkeeper calls out to Ruby, short for Rubanul, and the fresh-faced youngster comes along quite happily with us. He has many questions about India which Ranjit answers with great interest, and while they chat, I have a chance to look around.

The usual thatched cottages are now interspersed with brick, mortar and corrugated metalled structures, ruining the landscape. The ponds were still there along with the ubiquitous clumps of banana and bamboo. Graceful coconut trees sway in the breeze and their fronds reach for the sky. Little boys are fishing in the ponds with homemade fishing rods, but I do not see any girls around. I wonder whether it was on the banks of one of these ponds that Gauri and Krishna had sat on lazy afternoons and laughed at their reflections.

A twenty-minute walk brings us to the *Rajbari*. I recognise the *singhadwar* from Gauri's description right away; the lion-topped pillars still stand, but the gates have rusted and hang crooked on their hinges. What had once been the gatehouse is now a broken shelter of old brick and in it on a *charpai* sits a rheumy-eyed nonagenarian, ostensibly the gatekeeper. I am just beginning to wonder how good he is at his job, when he calls out in a sharp and clear voice, 'Hello Ruby! What brings these strangers from the city to this village?'

The suspicion in his voice is forbidding, hence I go up to him and say, 'I have come to see the house that once belonged to my ancestors.'

At this he gets off the bed, comes up to me, peers into my face and asks, 'Your ancestors? Are you a Hindu?'

When I nod, he looks at me more closely and mutters to himself, 'She is right; you must be a granddaughter of the Roy family—the features are very similar.'

My heart skips a beat but I ask as steadily as I can, 'Similar to whom?'

'To Gauri, of course,' comes the prompt reply. 'You don't have her marvellous complexion, but your features and hair indicate blood-ties.'

Ranjit can contain himself no longer and breaks in, 'Did you know Gauri?'

He turns to Ranjit and says, 'And who may you be young man? Don't tell me you are a family member too?'

I quickly intervene saying, 'He is a distant cousin and very interested in the family history.'

My voice trails off, for inexplicably the old man begins to laugh. He laughs long and with uncontrollable mirth, till a fit of coughing overtakes him, and he chokes back his laughter with tears in his eyes.

'Know Gauri? Of course I did, who did not? She was the most beautiful and spirited girl in the village. Of course we Muslims maintained a distance, but that does not mean that we did not speak when she came to fetch water or pick herbs and greens at the pond's edge.'

'And what did you talk about?' I ask hardly daring to believe in my luck.

'Oh the usual girl and boy talk. Doesn't your cousin speak in the same way to you?'

I realise that we have failed to pull the wool over his eyes and I make a direct appeal saying, 'I want to know why and how Gauri left her in-laws' house. Several people have told me different versions, but I do not believe that anyone either knows or has spoken the whole truth. Can you please help me?'

At this he looks at me directly for the first time, smiles with great sweetness despite his missing teeth and says, 'The *whole truth*? Does anyone ever know the *whole truth* about himself or anyone else? However, I will tell you a story and you can draw your own conclusions.'

According to the old man, Gauri's husband had been a peevish and bad-tempered man, very difficult to please. He had been loyal to Gauri but very possessive and hard; he had never allowed her to visit her mother's house or meet any of the old friends from her village. He had blamed her squarely for their lack of offspring. His health had been indifferent too; he had headaches and nervous attacks that left him completely drained. Gauri had served him with complete dedication like an ideal Hindu wife, but been seldom successful in pleasing him.

After the *yajna*, when his son had been born, he had been happier for some time, but a year later, the attacks had returned and with it a terrible anger against Gauri, and despite Gauri's best efforts, nothing could appease him. After the child's second birthday, which had been celebrated with great pomp, Ranima had gone on a pilgrimage to Benaras taking her elder son and daughter-in-law with her, leaving the house in Gauri's charge, and the latter had been at her wits' end with his tantrums. She had done her best to hide the bruises and wounds but, people had begun to talk. Finally, she had sent a message to the *sanyasi* to help her husband and herself. He had responded immediately and the medicines he had given seemed to help him, make him quieter and less nervous. Gauri was delighted and waited eagerly for Ranima's return, when one night all hell had broken loose. Gauri's husband got it into his head that the *sanyasi* was poisoning him and that Gauri had instructed him to do so. After beating her black and blue, he had gone for her with a kitchen knife. In her fright, she had run out of the back gate and plunged into the pond to end her life. Her husband had waited for an hour, but when she failed to surface, he had gone back, satisfied that she was dead.

Hearing about Gauri's plight, my throat is so parched, I can scarcely speak. However, regaining my strength, I manage to croak, 'And did she survive?'

The old man said that the body had not been found even though every inch of the pond had been dragged the following day, so presumably, she had escaped, but she was never seen in the vicinity again.

'Did she go away with the *sanyasi*?' I asked.

At this question, the old man is really angry and says that such stories are nothing but malicious gossip. He has no idea where she went, but has no doubts about the purity of her intentions or character. She was like a lotus without a blemish, a lotus that could only be used for a *puja* and no other purpose.

With his permission we walk up to the house and I take photographs from various angles, as much for my grandmother as an aide-memoir for myself. The white marble floor has a patina of grey on it now, but I can see the red footprints winding away into the interior quite clearly. I wonder at what point had the red auspicious dye changed to blood? An elderly lady, with fine features but casually dressed, the veil just covering the forehead, now comes forward to welcome us and offer refreshments. Ranjit says he would love a cup of tea which the lady orders. She then turns to me and asks whether I would like to see the house. So, while Ranjit sips his cup of tea on the verandah, I follow the lady down a corridor.

It opens into a central hall which I instantly recognise with a shock. The floor is patterned in black and white squares, along with majestic columns on both sides; it is unmistakably the room in which Gauri had sung and wept when I had encountered her in my dreams. I can identify the column behind which the little boy had hidden himself, but how, I wonder. Surely, Gauri had never sung in this room; then how had different images of the past amalgamated to create a picture for me?

During daytime, the women of the house inhabit the rooms to the left and the men to the right. I am taken on a tour of the female quarters. There are several rooms surrounding an open courtyard, and a verandah runs along the length of the house. From the verandah, a flight of steps leads down to the pond which the women of the house still use for bathing. I stand on the verandah and look out over the pond wondering what secrets its depths hide, when suddenly, the surface of the pond is broken and a young woman emerges, her wet clothes clinging to her supple body. She takes the hand of the little boy who has been sitting patiently on the lowest step and together they climb up the stairs. I cling to one of the pillars for support as my head suddenly swirls. The lady peers into my face, anxious and concerned.

Meanwhile, the young woman and the little boy come close to me, and the spell is broken. I explain that the heat must have got to me and am grateful for the glass of lime juice that I am given to drink. We sit in the lady's personal boudoir and discuss my ancestors, and it is heartening to find that the lady has only good things to say of her predecessors.

We return to Ranjit and just as we are about to leave, the lady comments, 'You must see Maryam Bibi before you go. She comes from this area and may know some members of your family.'

She directs Ali, the gateman, to show us her house. Ali in turn instructs Ruby. We leave after an exchange of courtesies and my last memory of the house is the lady standing at the head of the stairs and Ali at the gate, both with puzzled expressions on their faces.

We decide to have lunch first. Ruby takes us to a roadside dhaba where we invite him to share our meal. We are both confused and do not know how to reconcile the conflicting accounts we have heard. As reporters we are familiar with this problem and realise anew the hard task of historians who have to get at the truth through masses of contradictory evidence. After all, any account is necessarily filtered through the consciousness of the teller and coloured by his personal predilections and biases. As we eat the curry and rice, we wonder what Maryam Bibi would have to tell us, whether her version would again be different. Can a coin have three faces?

When we finish lunch, the shadows are beginning to lengthen and we realise that we have just an hour to catch the last bus back, and five hours to get aboard the steamer which will take us back to Dhaka. Ranjit takes a last long swig at the green coconut that is the safest drink in these parts and for which we had opted. Then we follow Ruby down a track across the fields that leads to Maryam Bibi's abode.

It is humble enough with brick walls and a thatched roof. In the front of the hut is a large courtyard, white and pristine with a fresh layer of cow dung and mud. At one end, there is a goat tied to a stake suckling two babies; a parrot in a cage is suspended from a pole and watches our approach with unblinking eyes; a creeper of jasmine has been trained over the thatch and its fragrance is maddeningly, piercingly sweet; other flowering plants have been spaced around the courtyard providing patches of muted colour. Ranjit and I look at each other with the same thought in our minds; nowhere in this village, not even at the 'great house' have we seen evidence of such simple, yet faultless artistry. Ruby calls out to the lady of the house and the parrot takes it up, screeching out the name again and again till the lady comes out wiping her hands on the ends of the *dupatta*. She goes straight to the parrot and calms him down by speaking to him gently. She turns to Ruby, smiles at him in recognition, and then she sees us and stops dead in her tracks.

That she is very old is evident. Her bent body and masses of silver white hair bear witness, but her face is one that 'neither time can touch nor age can wither'. The skin is dark, but still shiny despite the wrinkles; the nose, aquiline and sensitive; the pair of lips chiselled, and the chin dimpled, but it is the eyes that hold us mesmerised—limpid, dark pools whose depths contain a million years of experience, joy and anguished sorrow. What kind of a life must one lead to have eyes like these?

A couple of minutes lapse in total silence, then she turns to Ruby and whispers, 'Who are these people?'

As Ruby explains, comprehension dawns in those thoughtful eyes and the beginnings of a smile touch her lips.

She moves up to me and says, 'So you are related to Gauri? That explains the resemblance, of course. For a moment in the shadows, I had thought that Gauri had returned, but now I see that though you are like her, you are also quite different.'

I reply diffidently, 'I've heard that my great grandmother was very beautiful. I can never hope to be like her.' My curiosity gets the better of me and I ask directly, 'Did you know her well?'

She looks back at me quizzically in turn and says, 'Know her?' With a gentle smile she continues, 'Yes, I knew her all right, but how well I do not know. How well does one know anybody, including oneself?'

She turns to Ruby and asks him to pull up a *charpai*, and when he does, she invites the men to sit down. Then she brings a *chatai* lays it on the floor and tells me to sit down beside her. For a few moments, all is quiet. We are in the presence of very strong emotion which we cannot identify. The parrot quietly preens its feathers – a kite circles lazily above in the sun-tinged blue sky; and a single bee foraging in the jasmine hums unnaturally loud. When she begins to speak finally, the voice is very different, as though travelling from another world, over a vast distance to reach out to us.

'I knew Gauri as a child, for we were nearly of the same age. We played together when we could get away from our household chores. We often collected snails from the edge of the pond or picked greens to eke out the midday meal. We also told each other stories and shared similar dreams. Gauri was the belle of the village and we all thought that she would marry a prince, which of course she did, only that she did not live happily ever after. I was not in the village when Gauri got married. I was far away with my husband, but of course, news travels, especially when a poor girl marries a prince. I had my misgivings though about Gauri's future, for life had taught me at that early age that things are never what we expect them to be, but I rejoiced when I heard about the *yajna* and the birth of a son to Gauri. Perhaps all would yet be well? But then arrived the news of her abrupt departure. I am sure of only one thing—Gauri would never leave home voluntarily; some extreme compulsion must have driven her. Perhaps, that night she died after all!'

I hasten to assure her that this is not the case. Gauri had survived and gone to Calcutta and made a life for herself.

She smiles, takes my hand in her own, begins to count the fingers and remarks, 'The little one, the un-named one, the middle one, the admonitory one and the old one—all different, right? Now make a fist and the five will become one. We are like that too. Several people live in one body: one may die, but the others carry on. The Gauri who left home died that night, the others were different, they could not re-constitute the Gauri that was. Do you think Isa who died on the cross and the Isa who rose from the dead were the same people? No! A person can die within and still carry on with life without letting others ever know the difference. Now, I will tell you one last story about Gauri and then you must leave. This is not from first-hand knowledge, but told by a friend who was very close to both of us.

'Gauri's husband's health deteriorated steadily after Gauri left, and the best doctors could do nothing for him. It is said he called out for Gauri many times during his last days and his eyes kept searching for her endlessly. He died one late afternoon and Ranima wanted him cremated before nightfall. So the funeral procession left the house by five o'clock and wound its way down to the burning ground by the river, not too far away from Gauri's maternal home where he had come as a bridegroom only a few years before.

'It was a hot sultry day typical of *Baisakh*. Four people carried the bed on which lay the body in new clothes, smothered with flowers, the forehead and cheeks designed with *chandan* almost like a lover on his way to a tryst. All around walked family members, friends, retainers, scattering puffed rice and coins, and uttering *haribol* aloud. Saddest amongst all the mourners was Gauri's three-year-old boy, clinging to his uncle who carried him all the way. You see, the boy would have to ignite the pyre on which his father would lie. Half-way to the burning ground everyone was wilting with the heat and trudging along eyes lowered, when the little boy cried out, "Look! Look! My father is alive!" All eyes turned towards the bed, and sure enough, the body was sitting bolt upright, its eyes staring into space. Terrified, the entire party dumped the bed on the ground and took to their heels, running back to the house to inform Ranima. Only the elder brother and the little boy waited under a nearby tree. Neither of them had noticed that the sky had been darkening in the north-west, and it was only when the thunderstorm was on them that the brother took notice of it. More worried for the boy than himself, he picked up the child and walked to a cottage and asked for shelter.

'I do not know whether you have nor'westers in Calcutta, but here all fear their fury: the spiky lightning, the rolling thunder and lashing rain, trees swaying madly, and dangerously, making people firmly close all doors and windows and cower inside. Only this friend of mine, who had followed the cortege at a discreet distance, being a Muslim, was too fascinated by this phenomenon to be afraid and waited in the rain, for he felt that something momentous was about to happen.

'The rain was falling in sheets, and through this curtain of water appeared three *sanyasi*s chanting mantras, and some way behind them, was a young woman in white, with her face covered, who he swore was Gauri. The *sanyasi*s went around the body still sitting bolt upright, chanting *"Om shanti, shanti"*, and kept sprinkling the body with water, while Gauri fell on his feet and wept copiously, her long, dark hair covering his feet and her face like a veil.

'Slowly the body began to relax and the sadhus gently eased him back on the pillow, closed his staring eyes and placed two *tulsi* leaves on the eyelids. Then Gauri got up and washed the last vestiges of *sindoor* from her parting, took off the red and white conch bangles from her wrists and broke them. She put out her hand and the *sanyasi* placed a saffron robe on her upturned palm. She donned the robe, took one last look at the body, and left without a backward glance. My friend however waited till the others came back, for he did not want animals to violate the body, and when they returned, he moved away, so they never knew what had transpired.'

Ranjit, unable to contain himself, throws in a question, 'You never met her again?'

'No, never; even if I had, we would not have recognised each other, for the Gauri I knew died the night she left home. Her entry into a new identity was signalled by the donning of the saffron robe. You are Hindus, surely you know that *sanyas* means renunciation, a passing over into the spiritual phase?'

Yes, Ranjit and I have some idea of what *sanyas* means, but how did Maryam Bibi, an elderly Muslim lady, know so much? Before I can ask another question she gets up and signals that the interview is over. She mentions that it is time for *namaz*, so she must join the family. She rolls up the mat and walks towards the door, but at the threshold she stumbles and cries out in pain. I run forward and help her to right herself, and for a moment, we look into each other's eyes. She catches her breath and says, 'I am very glad I met you, a reminder of another time, another age which I had all but forgotten.'

She is about to turn away when something stronger than my will impels me to say, 'And, did you have another name then?'

At this her body grows rigid and her demeanour changes completely. She collects herself quickly and says, 'You had better go now, I am tired.' Her tone is so dismissive that I turn away. As my eyes struggle to control the welling tears, she puts her hand on my shoulder. I turn around and her smile is the apotheosis of endless regret. 'Perhaps I did,' she says, 'and who knows, that name may have been...Krishna?'

The door closes on my face as the arm pushes me beyond the threshold, and I know that I will never see her again.

~

The journey back has the unreal quality of a waking dream. We have learnt too much too quickly and most of it contradictory; we need time to sort out our thoughts before we can communicate with each other.

So it is only when we are seated on the deck again after dinner that we venture to approach what is uppermost in both our minds. The night, unlike the one before, is dark and windy; the stars are in hiding, and the vast waters of the Meghna are turbulent and rock the boat from side to side as though it were a child's toy. The captain has told us to be careful and to seek the safety of our cabins if the going gets too rough, but our thoughts are so tumultuous that we hardly notice the choppy waters or the light rain spraying us steadily.

Obviously, it is Krishna who has caught us in the solar plexus, for Ranjit's first words are, 'If Gauri was anything like Krishna, no wonder, she took the village and the *Rajbari* by storm!'

The sense of unreality is still too strong for me, hence I ask, 'She was Krishna, Ranjit? Our Krishna, I mean? Not a fake or anything? She did not seem *that* old.'

'Well, she's Gauri's twin, so she must be in her late eighties or early nineties? Fits like a glove! In any case, what would anyone gain by masquerading as Krishna?'

'Yes, and it explains Gauri's allegory perfectly—the black "wife", the chameleon, the change of colour; she was referring to religion, of course!'

'And when Partition took place and your family moved west, Krishna and her husband were able to return to the village with impunity. Priti, you did not notice perhaps, but she was looking at you with such longing. I think she would have given her right arm to hold you close once, but because you're a Hindu she didn't dare. You know, initially she thought you were Gauri, who has come back from the dead; so the resemblance must be quite strong!'

'How do you explain the weird story she told us about Gauri's husband? She obviously believes it implicitly, but do you think her so-called "friend" pulled a fast one on her? How can a dead body sit up like that?'

Ranjit smiles as though he has knowledge of something that has escaped me! 'Do you know Priti what Ruby told me?' he asks tantalisingly.

'No, how would I unless you tell me!'

'Well the gateman at the Nawab's residence Ali is Krishna's brother-in-law, and it is he who saw the entire thing happen, but he preferred to leave the telling to Krishna's discretion. He was not sure whether she would want us to know or not.'

'But how can a dead body sit up?'

'Even today, Priti, doctors fail to understand the vagaries of rigor mortis. Remember, it was a very hot day to begin with, and then the rain brought down the temperature dramatically?'

'But the *sanyasis* and Gauri?'

'There you have me beat. I can't think of any commonsense explanation at all. This is an established legend in the village and the people treat it as a part of their folklore. They expect outsiders to accept it unconditionally as they do. But do you have a choice?'

My grandmother is delighted with the photographs and they become the centrepiece for all conversations with family and outsiders for the next few weeks. She feels, I think, that she has established a fresh credibility about family prestige, now that Ranjit and I have actually seen the glories of yesteryears. She keeps asking about the village folk and their memories but she doesn't ask about Gauri directly, and I too keep away from the subject assiduously. However, now her stories make much more sense, and when she describes how she was welcomed as a bride in the great house, I am struck by the resemblance between her version and Gauri's.

I realise that I am neither wiser about Gauri's experiences after marriage or her reasons for leaving home, nor has the puzzle of her taking *sanyas* been solved, but somehow, after my encounter with Krishna, I feel I know her better, and this enables me to return to the diaries with greater confidence. However, I still do not have a time frame, or any idea of how many years elapsed between this incident and her departure to Calcutta.

It seems to me that she must have found refuge in the Loreto Convent at Entally, a lower middle-class suburb for she speaks of the sprawling compound, children playing on the lawns, young women who are training to be nuns, the orphanage, the beginnings of the slum just behind the complex that has grown to huge proportions that we see today.

I come across another entry in one of her diaries:

*People are just pouring across the border and every day I see new faces in the* bustee. *They speak my language, but they have changed beyond belief; so different from those I knew. The worst sufferers, as always, are the women, and it is difficult to recognise in these blowsy, loud-mouthed, bawdy women the demure wives and daughters whom I had known in my own land. So many of them are pregnant and they laugh in your face if you ask them who the father is. Small children with runny noses, quite uncared for, who have neither father nor mother, wail, scrabble in the garbage vats for food-scraps and compete with the street dogs who always win. I am lucky; even though I clean toilets, scrub and swab rooms, wash mountains of clothes, I get three meals a day and a space on the floor to sleep on. I have not had to sell my body, yet.*

While reading through the lines, I am reminded of a friend of my grandfather's, who began a charitable institution in the city called Matri Kalyan Ashram in the sixties. A government official himself, he had a genuine religious calling and devoted his life to the service of the downtrodden, particularly women, because his 'divine mother' had instructed him to do so. In 1971, during and after the war with Bangladesh, he had opened an abortion clinic, which had raised a storm of protest.

It is even recorded in official archives that he had said at that time, 'A woman's greatest boon and curse is her fertility which enables her to carry through the miracle of creation, but subjects her to and makes her bear the fruit of the worst kind of male intrusion.'

He had liberated hundreds of girls, young women, even children from their unwanted burdens and given them a second chance, even though this action had cost him his job and estranged him from his family. However, the problem of rehabilitation had proved insurmountable and he had been broken-hearted when he had found that many of these 'liberated' women preferred to work in brothels than pound spices or make incense sticks for a pittance. The 'red-light areas' had prospered as never before, and fathers, husbands and brothers had made a comfortable living off their women-folk. The *babu–baiji* culture prevailing in Calcutta in the early nineteenth century and which was associated with music, dance, fixed patrons called *babus*, *bilaiti* and garlands of tuberoses, had by the second half of the twentieth century, given way to country liquor and all kinds of sexual aberrations as well as sexually transmitted diseases. This easy availability of woman-flesh had caused disruption in so-called 'respectable' homes and helped to nurture the 'lost' generations that have been growing steadily, without values, moorings and hope. Such a familiar post-war syndrome coupled with social engineering on an unprecedented scale has changed the character of the city and its people beyond recognition. The process, begun during Partition, has continued unabated all over India, but the greatest sufferer has been the city of Calcutta.

As Father Harry, that crazy, impossibly idealistic, Irish Jesuit priest who worked for years in a school in Bowbazar as pastor and teacher of English once said, 'The finer points of teaching English become redundant when one is fighting tooth and nail to prevent the older boys from visiting prostitutes in the next street. The greatest problem is to offer them an alternative—intellectual excitement and spiritual awakening pale into insignificance when pitted against garish, painted faces and shamelessly flaunted bodies. Their total lack of inhibition draws these boys like a magnet and I am helpless.'

This man has given his entire life to try and retrieve some people from 'getting lost' and many a Calcuttan still remembers his famous 'retreats' and continues to wonder about the source of that indomitable energy that still keeps him going at his many projects with unabated zeal.

Leisure was rare, but whenever Gauri had a free moment she went and watched the children of the orphanage. She wrote:

*Children often live in their own world where adults cannot always enter. Today, I saw a little boy sitting on the grass and playing with two sticks and a piece of string. When I asked him what he was doing, he looked up and said, 'I want these two sticks to hold the string so that they can talk to each other, but they refuse to listen to me! Can you help me?'*

*So I took the string and tied the two ends to the sticks and gave them to him. The look of delight on his face was absolute and he gave me a quick hug before he scampered away. I can still feel his small body within my arms, against my chest and am trying to hold on to this feeling.*

In another entry, Gauri wrote:

*The little boy is becoming my friend; he loves stories and we sit under a tree almost every afternoon. I have to be very careful for he is quick to spot discrepancies. One day, when I asked him to tell me a story, he repeated the one about a sister and her seven brothers who had turned into flowers, almost word for word. Do all little boys long for stories and do they all find storytellers?*

The heartbreak is almost tangible, but never mentioned directly. I wondered was this detachment too a part of *sanyas*? Obviously, this period of relative peace did not last long. There were too many hunters on the prowl and her good looks as always were against her. She wrote:

*This man has been trying to draw my attention, making obscene gestures for some time, but I have been ignoring him steadily. One evening, when I was moving from one building to the other, I sensed a horrible, liquor-stained, hot breath on the nape of my neck and a pair of strong arms catching hold of mine and twisting them behind my back. He had mistaken me for a city-bred girl who is defenceless, and so my backward kick in his crotch took him by surprise and caused him to howl with pain. I took advantage of his momentary weakness, twisted myself free and ran shouting for help. How he had got over the wall I do not know, but the other servants gave him the beating of his life and he never came back.*

This is the convent from which Mother Teresa had observed the teeming, hopeless slums, and decided that she had to do something to help these people, and one fine morning, had stepped out into the unknown. She had neither money nor too many friends, only indomitable determination and complete faith that 'God would provide'. In later years, she too had called herself a *sanyasin*.

There is an obvious interval between this entry and the next, for it is evident that the fatigue is getting to her and that the prospect of endless, and fruitless labour is beginning to prove daunting. She wrote:

*This evening I have a few minutes off before I am called to roll out a million chapattis in the kitchen. Yes, a new chore has been piled on me, for the girl who worked in the kitchen has run away with a man from the nearby slum. I try to take a look at my face in a glass pane for mirrors are forbidden here, and I hardly am able to recognise the hollow-faced creature who stares back at me—the hair, so dark and lustrous once is now brown with dirt and neglect, the collar bones stick out through the flesh marring a once-perfect throat, the arms are thin and the flesh hangs loose. I turn away to look at my hands and the callousness and broken fingernails make tears spring to my eyes. Is this then the price of virtue? This endless penance was undertaken for whose benefit? What sins have I committed that I must continue to pay and pay? The* sanyasi *told me that one pays through physical denial to attain spiritual purity, but I can only feel resentment, anger and pain; can this be the right path? I don't want spiritual peace at this cost. I want a full meal, decent clothes, some rest, protection; if something does not happen quickly, I may not be able to hold on to my resolve.*

Had the God she had been taught to pray to since childhood looked on and not provided succour? Or, had He responded to her need as Lord Krishna had to Draupadi at the gaming session when Yudhistir had pawned her, his wife, in the epic Mahabharata? Perhaps He had, for suddenly there is a note of hope:

*Who says there is no God? I will never forgive myself for my moment of weakness and doubt a few weeks ago. Today, the matron told us that a rich widow is looking out for someone to take care of her physical needs and keep her company. She is coming today to see us. Perhaps she will select me? But will she recognise the real 'me' through this 'rag-doll' that she will see? I must clean up myself and try to look respectable!*

All of a sudden, I find that I can no longer see the pages of the diaries open before me—the words are so blurred that I cannot make them out. It is only when a drop or two fall from my eyes onto the page that I realise that I am weeping. I mop up the drops carefully with a piece of blotting paper, push the diaries away and relieve myself by crying out profusely for some time. The paroxysm over, I understand that it is not her predicament that has touched me, it is after all a familiar story; it is her courage and her pathetic faith in virtue and the 'God' that the *sanyasi* had conveyed a vision of, that is so heart-breaking. Gauri had continued to put her trust in life even though it had betrayed her again and again. How could the family treat such a woman so callously? How could my grandmother, who had never known a day's want in her entire life, speak so insultingly of her? For the first time, a doubt arises in my mind about my grandfather; to me the thought is sacrilegious and I try to push it away, but the questions linger persistently at the back of my mind. Had he been too weak or just had not fought hard enough to attain justice for his mother?

When I go back to the diaries, the next day, I find Gauri assailed by myriad problems, doubts and questions.

*What shall I wear? How will I clean myself? How will I wash this huge coil of hair that I cannot bear the weight of? I must speak to Lakshmi; she does not speak my language but is very resourceful and clever. At night I manage to get a few moments alone with her and she gives me advice that takes me back to my childhood. Soap had always been a luxury and I had learnt to use it freely only after marriage. What my mother would do is to get some soft mud from the edge of the pond, dry it, pulverise it and then strain it through an old sieve. This powder she would knead with some water, oil, pounded turmeric and make into small cakes. Whenever she wanted us to have a 'proper bath', she would give us one of these cakes. We would smear it all over our faces and bodies, Krishna and I would rub it into our hair and let it dry. After an hour, when the mud began to flake, we would rub ourselves down vigorously and plunge into the pond. When we came out, we would be so 'clean' that we hardly would recognise each other! We would then hold hands and dance around on the edge of the pond chanting:*

*Today we are clean,*
*Today we are pretty,*
*But no one will see us,*
*Which is a pity!*

*Tomorrow the groom will come*
*But we will be dark,*
*And on his mind*
*Not leave a mark!*

*What should we do then*
*Will you tell us pray?*
*Why, have a bath of course,*
*Every single day!*

*I have not thought of Krishna for a long time, but today I can see her so clearly!*

*So in the early morning, when no one is yet astir, I go out to the old tank at the end of the lawn and take a mud bath. I also clean my only whole sari and blouse in the same way and put them on the grass to dry. When I join the group of girls and women who hope to be selected, they all look askance at me, and I realise that some sort of transformation has taken place.*

*One young woman, not bad looking herself, says cattily to the others at large, 'It is a pity that an old lady and not a young man is coming to inspect us; otherwise, what chance would we have against Gauri?'*

*An older woman snaps back saying, 'None of you young ones will get selected; the lady will choose someone of good character, not man-eaters like you!'*

*The young woman laughs and replies, 'With your looks, Aunt, you have no chance of losing your character!'*

*A gale of laughter greets this witticism, but dies down like magic when we perceive the matron escorting a tall, dignified, aristocratic old lady who reminds me strongly of my mother-in-law. She is dressed in spotless white, wears no jewellery and holds herself erect with the help of an ivory-headed cane. We are standing in line and she passes slowly scrutinising our faces, bodies and postures. At the end of the line, she retraces her steps and stops in front of me.*

*'What is your name?' she says in a mellow but authoritarian voice.*

*I somehow manage to pronounce my name, for my heart is pounding so hard that I feel choked.*

*The lady turns to the matron and says, 'I would like a few words in private with Gauri.'*

*Within minutes, I find myself at the door of the matron's room. The lady surprisingly does not draw away when I bend down to touch her feet, but actually puts her hand on my head in a brief blessing. She says something quietly to the matron who moves out of the room rather unwillingly, and I am left standing alone before her staring at the ground.*

*'Sit down child,' she commands in a firm but gentle voice. So I do, on the floor at her feet. She looks closely at the parting in my hair, examines my earlobes, wrists, fingers and throat very carefully, and then makes a pronouncement, 'You were married into a well-to-do family and lived there for many years; why did you leave and how did you get here?'*

*I look up at her in amazement and manage to stammer, 'How did you know?' But my voice trails off and I turn awkwardly from those penetrating, all-pervasive eyes.*

*'Your parting still has signs of the* sindoor *you once wore, for the dye gets into the skin and it is impossible to get it out. You also have the same tell-tale mark on your forehead where you once marked it with* sindoor. *Your ears, throat, wrists and hands show clearly that you wore a lot of jewellery, regularly. Also, although you are very slim, I think you must have borne at least one child. Come, if you want to go home with me, you must tell me the truth.'*

*I think furiously for a few moments; telling the truth is out of the question, but lying to this lady will not be easy. Also, I desperately want to get out of this place; so I decide to spin her a tale that is the truth yet not the whole truth. I tell her that I had indeed been married into an aristocratic home and borne a son, but after my widowhood, had been forced to leave due to property disputes. My own family had not wanted me back, so I had been compelled to work as a maid. Then Partition had taken place and I had been swept along by the general exodus and found refuge in this place.*

*The story is a familiar one and seems to satisfy her, but she suddenly asks, 'Where is your son?'*

*I tell her truthfully that I have no idea for my mother-in-law had held him back, and I have had no news of him or the family since I had left home.*

*After this, things happen very quickly. I put my few meagre possessions in a plastic bag, am given a homily by the matron on my good luck and need for good behaviour, some papers are signed, and I am seated in a motor car for the first time in my life and whisked away to an unknown destination. My only regret is that I have not had an opportunity to say goodbye to my little friend. When he comes for my story session and finds no storyteller, how will he feel? Will this be his first lesson in betrayal? Then I think that this is a lesson we all have to learn, so better perhaps sooner than later?*

*The car twists and turns with incredible speed through a maze of alleys and streets till we stop in front of a shop where the lady buys some cheap but respectable clothes. Then from another shop she purchases a silver chain and two bangles, and a pair of slippers from a third one. All this she puts in my lap and says, 'These are for you.'*

*This munificence takes me so much by surprise that I just stare at her dumbly, unable to find words to express my gratitude; but at the back of my mind lurks the bitter irony of fate, that I who had worn twenty-five to thirty* tolas *of gold on a regular basis should be grateful for this cheap finery. Perhaps the conflict shows in my face, for the lady turns away without another word and says to the driver, 'Turn right.'*

*He looks back, amazement writ large on his face and stammers, 'You mean on the main street?'*

*'No, next turning,' she answers firmly.*

*Without further ado, the driver swerves the car into a narrow lane lined with cheap and poor dwellings. I have been in such lanes before I came to the convent, but here there is a difference. Girls and young women in cheap but showy clothes, garish, false jewellery and lots of make-up on their faces line the verandahs, waiting for whom? Heads turn inquisitively as the car rolls along at a snail's pace avoiding garbage and potholes, and finally, comes to a stop at a command from the lady. The young women in this house fall back when they see who the chief inmate is, but continue to stare at me askance, even though their faces are averted. The driver blows twice on the horn and an elderly woman hurries out wiping her hands on the end of her sari. She folds her hands, bows low, does not touch the car, and very humbly awaits orders, but I can see her eyes darting in my direction.*

*The lady turns to me and asks, 'Do you wish to disembark here?' As I stare at her in disbelief, she continues: 'You are a young widow, your desires are very much alive; if you cannot control them, this is where you will end, for there is no alternative for women such as you. If that be the case, I will leave you here today and Mashi will take care of you, for you will fetch her many customers.'*

*By this time, tears of shame are slowly coursing down my cheeks, my loins stirring unmistakably. Is it that I am totally depraved or am I just a healthy young woman who has been starved for a very long time? Moments flit by, the wetness increases, tears continue to fall on my breasts that are taut with expectancy. My head begins to swim and I continue to stare at the handsome but ruthless face inches from mine, mesmerised by my own inner turmoil.*

*The lady reads my mind like writing on a sheet of glass and says implacably, 'Choose, once and for all; in life there are no second chances.'*

*A fly is buzzing against the glass trapped by an invisible barrier, sharing my predicament. The driver swipes it with a swatter and it falls to the floor, a tangle of broken legs, body and eyes, lies still and suddenly I realise that there is no choice, never has been, and my flaming body is stilled. I fold my hands and say to her very simply, 'Please take me home with you.'*

*The driver turns to look at his mistress, she nods once and the car jerks into life as though impatient to get away. I carry with me a memory that will haunt me for days—pairs of eyes staring hungrily as a victim gets away—a mix of chagrin, frustration, envy, but also perhaps vindication, though vicarious.*

When I look away from the diaries finally, I find that I have been sitting on the edge of the chair, and my fists are so firmly clenched that the nails are digging into the palm. When I finally open them the dark, red-half moon bear mute testimony to the tension I have undergone, as though my entire theory of vindication depended on her decision, which of course it did in a way. But somehow, I am not satisfied; there are too many unanswered questions for my liking, too many nuances beyond my comprehension, my sense of rationality, a dichotomy that I can neither resolve nor comprehend.

Ranjit, however, finds fault with me rather than Gauri's narrative, for he feels that I am trying to fit Gauri into a preconceived mould, an image that *I want* her to have.

'Be careful Priti so that Gauri does not become your Gauri, because you are so keen to vindicate her. You must be dispassionate and objective or the truth will elude you. If in the end, you have to admit that your grandmother is right after all, you must have the courage to face that eventuality. You must never read into her discourse what you want to hear, but make every attempt to hear the true voice, the actual thoughts and feelings, even though they may be unpalatable to you.'

At this point, I throw a light paperweight at him and tell him to stop being didactic and boring.

He catches the paperweight in mid-air and says, 'Don't evade the issue, you know that I'm right! The cardinal rule of investigative journalism is: no distortion due to personal bias. Remember our professor drumming this and other dicta into our heads?'

Although I shrug off his advice cheekily, I know in my heart of hearts that I am getting too involved emotionally with Gauri, and that I need to steer clear of erring signposts erected by my own predilections. I also realise that I have arrived at a watershed, a line of demarcation beyond which the narrative will take a different turn, and where both the deconstruction and reconstruction will have to be accurate and unbiased if I am ever to lay the ghost that is haunting me to rest.

It is perhaps this sense of inadequacy that keeps me away from the diaries. I need time and space to arrive at an untainted perspective. Ranjit is always right; damn him! I turn to other things—do some reading, send off a reminder to my friend in Banibon so that his interest does not flag, talk more to my grandmother though in a conciliatory tone, hoping to pick up snippets of information she may have held back consciously or otherwise. So absorbed have I been with my task that I have not noticed how time has flown, and it is with a shock that I realise that a whole year has gone by and the household as well as the city is preparing for the annual Durga Puja. Last year there had been no festivity or observance due to my grandfather's passing away, so this year the preparations are all the more intense, as though to mark the passage from mourning to renewal.

The first day of the Pujas is *Mahalaya*, a day on which respect is paid to the dead and offerings of food, water and clothes are made with the help of the priest who takes the family through the ritual with the appropriate mantras. This year, the ritual takes on special significance as my father will offer and place the oblations for the first time on this occasion for his father. My grandmother wants it to be a memorable event and so no expense is spared. The extended family and close friends are invited, for after my father completes his prayers, other members of the family, including myself, will follow suit.

The ceremony takes place on the terrace where a protective awning has been erected to keep out the sun. Several sets of utensils, copper and brass, containing rice, vegetables, fruit, betel leaves and nuts, clothes and silver coins have been laid out to be offered by various family members. The fragrance of incense sticks burning in large numbers intermingle with sweet-smelling flowers, mainly, the tuberose, jasmine and lotus that are ranged either in bouquets and garlands or in loose but tidy heaps. The priests, dressed in the traditional *dhoti* and *chadar* are seated on woollen mats putting finishing touches to the offerings. Large quantities of sandalwood paste will be required, so I diligently rub the piece of wood on a round, flat stone and continue to sprinkle water on it. Slowly a paste is formed, thick and fragrant, which I put in a small silver bowl. Then I sprinkle more water and continue rubbing. One of the priests who has been watching me for he has known me from my childhood, suddenly says, 'Do you realise that what you are doing is a metaphor for life?'

When I tell him that I do not understand, he smiles and says, 'Do you know that it is not only the sandalwood that produces this concoction with water, that the wood of the bel tree will also do the same thing if similarly rubbed? A thicker paste as a matter of fact! The only difference is that in the latter, there is no fragrance at all. Men and women too are ground down in the course of their lives and must come to the funeral pyre, but some scatter fragrance, all through, while others just live!'

It is an interesting analogy and for no reason at all, I am reminded of Gauri. Was her fragrance deliberately masked by other people? For whatever reason, I cannot get her image out of my mind. When the priest announces that the essence of this ritual is *shraddha* and that one must believe in the real presence of the spirits of the departed who are summoned through the mantras, a chill goes down my spine. Will Gauri come if I beseech her to accompany her son? Will the collective hostility of other family members keep her away? I am determined to make the attempt.

My father is the first and the chief votary and I can see that he is genuinely moved, that his innate scepticism is fighting a losing battle with his desire for faith. He wants to believe so that the ceremony may become meaningful to him. Every eye is moist as he begins his prayers, and my grandfather's memories are so overwhelming that they conjure up a very real presence, indeed. I close my eyes and my long and wonderful association with him forms an indelible montage on the screen of my mind. I feel I can reach out and touch him, and clasp his strong warm hands as I always had done when I needed reassurance.

When my grandmother comes and puts her hand on my head and says, 'It is your turn now,' I bring myself back to the present with an effort. Now that the moment has arrived, I have terrible qualms about the course of action I have decided on. Will my attempt trivialise the purpose of the ceremony and detract from my devotion to my grandfather? Then I remember the urgency of his letter, his passionate appeal, and my fears are stilled. If anything, my grandfather would be pleased that at least one member of his family had made the attempt to invoke his mother's spirit—one who had been repulsed and maligned in her lifetime by this very family.

I cannot sit on my father's mat as his is a special one—made of *kusha* that can only be used by men; so I sit docilely on a woollen one, cross-legged in the lotus pose and fold my hands. I have eaten nothing since morning and my head is swimming. Ranjit who is sitting on the other side, amongst the invitees, smiles encouragingly at me but looks anxious. I wonder whether he has an inkling of my plan?

I have to wear a ring made of *durba*, repeat the mantras after the priest and pour water from a fish-shaped copper vessel called a *kosha* into a bowl also made of copper, with the completion of each mantra. Slowly, a spacescape is created for me with the chanting—the soul travels through space that is infinite; there is no shade, no refuge, no resting place; in thirst there is no water, in hunger there is no food, in rain there is no shelter, in fatigue there is no rest. Footsore and weary, the soul may never stop, never weep, never wince in weariness; for this is the way to *moksha*, to *nirvana*.

The soul must also cross River Vaitarni, which is believed to separate this world from the next, overcoming its monumental waves, its slippery, stony bed, the gaping crocodiles, and the merciless wind that whips its waters in vicious fury. I can see it all so clearly—the beloved figure, battling the elements, moving ahead, bent almost double in fatigue, but without reprieve. I continued with the chanting of the mantras.

'It is for this reason that I, your granddaughter Priti, offer you food for your hunger, water for your thirst, clothes for your nakedness, a stick to support you on your unending way, an umbrella to protect you against the elements, and flowers and sandalwood to make your path fragrant. Please accept my offerings and give me your blessings.'

I feel as though my moorings in this present world are loosened and the hands that hold me are slackened. So great is the attraction of this other world that has risen before my eyes, so great the desire to be with my grandfather that I can feel myself slipping away. Dimly I can see a flight of stairs before me and I begin to climb steadily not heeding the voices that wish to detain me, not looking back once.

At the head of this flight is a landing where stairs bifurcate and I realise I have to make a choice. On one side is the figure of my grandfather. I know it is he even though his back is turned towards me. He gives no sign, makes no attempt to establish contact, but so great is his loneliness that it emanates in waves towards me and draws me inexorably. I am on the verge of moving towards him, about to cross the threshold when something detains me and I look to the other side—a woman in saffron robes stands before me, her long hair streaming across her face preventing recognition, but her gesture is unmistakable. She holds up her right hand, the index finger extended in admonition, and shakes it from side to side indicating that I should not follow him, but return the way I have come. There is something so authoritative about her stance that I obey unquestioningly and stumble down the stairs almost against my will. When I finally turn around, the stairs, the figures, and the choice are no more!

The priest is still chanting, 'Go in peace to the land where there is no love, no hate, no friend, no foe, no rain, no sunshine, no light, no darkness, no fear, no pain, no desire, no attraction, but only joy illimitable. Perhaps you will face rebirth, perhaps you will know human suffering again, but ultimately, you will achieve *moksha*, that is, peace, or *nirvana*, that is God.'

I repeat the words dutifully after him and experience a strange sense of release—freedom from mourning that has pursued me throughout the year. I feel as though I can establish contact with him any time, that some invisible barrier has been lifted, and then darkness engulfs me.

Drops of water falling on my face cause me to open my eyes. I find my mother looking into my face anxiously; my grandmother saying, 'The strain has been too great for her'; my father insisting, 'Not a good idea to fast so long'; and Ranjit staring at me with consternation on his face.

Only the head priest smiles and says, 'I think Priti was very close to her grandfather and this has been a strange but meaningful experience for her; one she will not forget easily.'

'How does he know? Was he a spectator throughout?' I wonder. I find it difficult to come to terms with this 'vision' or to share it with anyone, even Ranjit; but the more I think about it, the more convinced I am that the woman was Gauri, telling me in no uncertain terms to return to life, to fight both for myself and justice for her, that it is harder to live life than to slip away from it. Had I invoked her spirit by thinking of her or had she come of her own volition?

However, as time passes, I begin to believe that she had come out of her need to communicate, to revitalise my sense of mission, to remind me of my promise to her son and that I was guilty of tardiness, that I must pick up the threads and continue to weave till the tapestry is complete. If I do not carry out her behest will a curse fall on me like on the Lady of Shalott? This may sound fanciful in retrospect, but I think I believed in it at that time; so strong an impression had been created by that persona.

So I waste no time and return to the diaries. But as I peruse the pages afresh, I realise with a shock that its resources are coming to an end. Most of the entries have been read and used and only a handful remain. How will I proceed after this? The newspaper cuttings contain some valuable information, but hold no clues to the mystery of her death; will all the 'whys' remain unanswered at the end of all this effort? But before the depression can weigh me down, a saying flies out of nowhere: 'Sufficient unto the day is the knowledge thereof.' Bewildered but strangely comforted, I return to my task with peace in my heart.

The house to which Gauri was taken was perhaps in the Shovabazar area, for she spoke often of the river and its proximity. She wrote:

*The car comes to a halt before a large mansion and I am struck by the tall flight of white marble steps that leads from the short entry path to the broad verandah that runs along the length of the house. Tall trees fringe the railing that edges the road in front and the water body behind the house. On leaning forward, I can see a glint of water between the trees, behind the house and wonder whether it is a pond or the river. A tall, yellow jasmine creeper at the entrance has laid a carpet of yellow-stalked, sweet-smelling white flowers on the steps and the fragrance takes me way back to my childhood.*

*I get off the car still clutching on to my belongings but bend to pick up a handful of flowers and hold them to my face. In a moment, I am drawn back to memories of my paternal house, the courtyard with the* tulsi-manch, *Krishna and I making Shiva* lingas *with mud and decorating them with garlands made of yellow jasmine. Perhaps the lady sees a wayward tear, for she puts her hand on my shoulder and gently propels me up the steps, through the heavy, shuttered doors into the cool, dark interior.*

Another entry reads:

*The house is even larger than my in-laws', also more opulent; the heavy velvet curtains, portraits in heavy gilt frames, the furniture made of heavy, dark mahogany intricately carved, huge mirrors in heavy ebony frames, doors and windows of heavy, solid teak—the emphasis is on heaviness and solidity throughout. Very few people live in this house—the lady whom everyone calls 'Ma'; her two sons, Rajat and Rajiv; their wives Kamala and Nirupama, respectively; Rajat's sons Gaurav and Sourav, aged twenty and eighteen; and Rajiv's daughter Tilottama, who is sixteen and a paragon of beauty. Her grandmother says affectionately that she has seldom seen such affinity between name and person! Tilottama and her mother are friendly and kind to me but Kamala maintains a steady distance.*

*I have specific jobs—after a dip in the Hoogly which is a stone's throw away from the back of the house, I return in my wet clothes, change, and pick flowers from the garden for the daily worship, then I clean the* puja-*room, scrub the heavy copper, brass, silver utensils and leave them in readiness for the family priest who comes in every morning. I then wake up Ma with a cup of tea and help her to bathe and dress. After breakfast I help out in the kitchen and after lunch, press Ma's feet till she falls asleep; late afternoon and early evening I read from the scriptures while she listens and dozes. Late evening, the family sits together while I retire to my room—a small one adjacent to Ma's and read or sew.*

*Sometimes Tilottama comes in for a game of chess or a chat. It is during one of these sessions that Tilottama discovers that I can sing and tells her grandmother that I have a good voice and that she would like me to sit and learn with her when her music teacher comes. Nirupama is also enthusiastic and reluctantly, Ma gives in. Kamala is openly contemptuous of what she calls the 'new-fangled nonsense of treating servants like family members', but I take no notice, for I love music and cannot believe that I will actually have a chance to learn.*

*Tilottama has a melodious and sweet voice but I have greater range and power, so says the teacher, and we make a fine pair. Slowly we build our repertoire: Ramprasadi,* kirtan *and Rabindra Sangeet. The teacher is very dedicated and says we might be able to learn some* ghazals *and* geets, *provided we get the pronunciation and intonation correct. The bi-weekly lessons constitute the highlight of my life and I look forward to them with impatient eagerness.*

*I look in the mirror sometimes and find that I am beginning to look more like myself. My complexion has cleared; the hair has lost its rusty look and is dark and glossy; my body is regaining its curves. I am very careful to cover myself head to foot, keep my eyes lowered and avoid the male members of the family assiduously, but cannot help noticing that the boys look often in my direction as do their fathers.*

I close the diary I was reading with a snap! I wonder in apprehension: Will Gauri fall prey to lust? Will she be forced to pay for the sin of others in the tradition of the nineteenth-century novel? Will she disappoint and turn out to be as clichéd as the other 'pure-at-heart' heroines? I analyse the facts in my mind to reconsider if I had misunderstood Gauri and in the end decide to proceed no further with my investigations.

When I communicate my fears to Ranjit, he looks at me quizzically and comments, 'You see Priti, you still want her to fit the model you have created for her and cannot bear any lapses. So what if Gauri went through a liaison? She was deprived enough; in what way does it detract from her total personality? After all, the transition from a "servant", however glorified, to the owner of a *jatra* company could not have been made without compromise. However strong one's spirit may be, the flesh inevitably has a part to play!'

I have to admit that this must indeed have been the case, but I cannot reconcile the Gauri of Krishna's story with a woman who bought her way to fame and security with her body, and it is with a heavy heart that I return to the diaries.

There is an entry that seems to have slipped my attention, for surely, this should have appeared earlier in the discourse I am trying to construct. It goes like this:

*This family is so affluent, but how do they make their money? On the surface, they are in the jute business. Behind the house is a jetty at which boats arrive periodically loaded with bales of jute which are stored in the warehouse next to the river, and then sent in lorries to the wholesale market in Posta; but does that fetch so much money? Also, next to the warehouse are extended servants quarters where many men live, but they never come into the house. They wear the uniform of the family business, but unlike others, carry arms—daggers, staves, even guns. I had assumed that they were security staff, but am beginning to wonder whether they are otherwise employed. I must find out.*

This is in such startling contrast to the benign portrait of the family I have encountered so far, that I am completely fascinated and search frantically for a sequel. But there is nothing; the trail just disappears into thin air. Whatever it is that she found out, if anything, she did not commit her findings to paper—I wonder why. However, there is another entry, which again tantalises me, but leads nowhere.

*I wake up in the middle of the night, my heart beating wildly, for I hear men shouting and women crying. But as I sit up in bed, the sound slowly dies down. It is raining steadily, the river is in high tide, the water has flowed into the compound as it does at such times and is lapping around the house. It must have risen half-way up the marble steps at this point in time, though by the time we get up in the morning, the water will have receded leaving behind debris on the steps. I decide that I must see what the river has brought before anyone else does, for once I had found a silver bangle. I had taken it and kept it carefully hidden. But I wonder who is shouting and crying; is it a nightmare? But why is the sound so real and why is it still ringing in my ears? I cannot go back to sleep, so I sit up and repeat to myself the mantras that the* sanyasi *had taught me, again and again, till the turbulence within me is stilled. I lie down and look steadily at the windowpanes waiting for the sky to lighten, so that I can investigate the steps before the house is astir. But when I step quietly through the door, there is someone walking in the direction of the steps before me, and with a shock I realise it is Ma. The tapping of the ivory-headed cane is too distinctive to be mistaken for any other sound, and with her is Brojoda the major-domo, the main servant of the house, who has been with the family for thirty years, but has never allowed the mask of the perfect servant to slip. I keep to the shadows and follow at a discreet distance for I know instinctively that my presence will not be welcome.*

*Finally, the huge portal opens with a groaning of the hinges and Ma stands clearly outlined against the dawn. She is standing at the head of the steps now. Brojoda goes down the stairs and returns with something cradled in his arms. It looks like a bundle of old clothes, but when he holds it up I gasp in horror. Amongst the clothes is a baby – very small and dead! The tableau is stark. The white-bearded, old servant holds up the dead baby for inspection; the water from the old clothes steadily dripping on the white floor; the stately old lady averting her tired eyes and whispering to herself as much as to Brojoda: 'Always they return, always to point a finger at me. Will this volley of accusation ever end? Will I ever get my release?' Then she turns to Brojoda, reverting to her usual autocratic self, and says without a tremor, 'Throw this filth back where it belongs and then go back to your room!'*

*I have already started retreating and am in my room curled up in bed when the door opens and Ma looks in. Satisfied that I am asleep, she withdraws and I am glad that she has not heard the tumultuous beating of my heart. The word 'always' is ringing in my ears. I understand then that this is not an isolated incident but one of many. Does the river regularly lay down dead babies on the marble steps of this house? But why?*

I find myself importunately echoing Gauri's query, for the incident described is bizarre enough to whet the curiosity of even a jaded journalist like me; but again, there is no follow-up. Was she afraid to investigate further? The next entry concerns her own predicament and is a passionate outburst against injustice.

*Is it my fault that I am good-looking, that God gave a straight nose and even teeth? Now Kamala has gone and complained to Ma that I am making eyes at her sons and that I should be sent away.*

*Ma realises of course that I have done nothing of the kind, that the boys look on me as their older sister, and that Kamala is basically concerned about her husband who is thoroughly depraved anyway. But Ma has to do something for she is the head of the house and cannot ignore such a serious appeal. What will she do? Will she send me back to where I came from? Suddenly, I remember the terrible house where the car had stopped on its outward journey; how is it that Ma knows about such houses? Is it because she has sent errant girls like me there, before?*

*The thought takes root and in my desperation I turn to Nirupama who has always been kind to me and has no fears about her own husband. She recognises my urgency but pleads helplessness.*

*Finally, it is Tilottama who has a brainwave and appeals to our teacher, Shankarda. 'Can you help us out? Gauri and I are in great trouble,' she tells him.*

*Thoroughly nonplussed, he wants details; so I take over and spin a tale about wanting to stand on my own feet and better my prospects. He is sympathetic, says he appreciates my sentiments and that he will make enquiries and get back to us within a week.*

*The week lengthens into ten days; Kamala is getting more importunate in direct proportion to the roving of her husband's eyes, and I am almost at my wits' end when Shankarda comes up with what could be construed as good news—a* jatra *company is looking for a young woman who is pleasant-looking and can sing and dance. Obviously, I fit the first two requirements but not the third; however, Shankarda is confident that I will 'learn' easily since I have a strong sense of rhythm.*

*The idea is broached to Ma who is obviously relieved, but says that she must meet the owner and assure herself that this will be a 'safe option' for me, and that is how I meet Mr Sikdar for the first time.*

*As for the 'owner of a* jatra *company' I had a clichéd image of a man in* kurta *and* pajama *or* churidar, nagra *slippers, even though I thought the spindly legs would warrant less courageous wear, and a mouthful of* paan *with the red juice running down the corners of the mouth, leering and lascivious!*

*But the man I encounter is in such sharp contrast to the image I had that I am almost dismayed. He is tall and possibly in his early fifties. With strong features and humour in his eyes, he looks more like a college professor than a man connected with the stage. He is in the drawing room speaking with Ma in a low voice, while Brojoda is serving tea.*

*Meanwhile, Tilottama and I peep through the curtains and try to make sense of the moving lips of both parties, but fail. Finally, when I am sent for, I am so nervous that I pull Tilo along with me, and as though to make the difference between us perfectly clear, Ma asks Tilo to sit down next to her while I remain standing.*

*It is Mr Sikdar who indicates a chair and says 'Please sit down,' in a deep but pleasant voice that matches his personality perfectly.*

*As he begins to question me I can see that he is trying to 'place' me but does not quite succeed, so I spin him the same tale that I had told Ma two years ago, and then I can see comprehension dawning in his eyes for he had obviously expected a different 'class' of girl.*

*After a short silence, he says something that no one has said to me before. 'Do you want me to make enquiries about your family or your in-laws? I have many contacts and I know a lot of people in Bangladesh. Perhaps it may be possible to send you back?'*

*For one moment, my heart leaps! I have scarcely allowed myself to think of the past for I am afraid to experience the overwhelming nostalgia that will result. Also, I have known that to return would require resources that I could never muster, but now that this kind-*

*faced man is making the offer, I am terribly tempted to return to the old cottage, my mother, the flowering trees, the pond, perhaps Krishna—to be a child again, to put aside the knowledge and experiences of the last few years, to unburden myself and to retrace time. Can it be done? Then the fruitlessness of these yearnings rises like gall, and my throat is bitter. They, my people, would probably not even open the door to look at my tarnished face!*

*Mr Sikdar has been watching me intently, and now says, 'So the answer is in the negative; I assume therefore that you would not like to return?'*

*Ma quickly breaks in, 'Don't you think, Mr Sikdar, that I would have sent her back if it had been possible?'*

*He looks at her, then at me, perhaps reads the disbelief my face registers at these words, then says courteously but with a touch of irony, 'Of course, I do realise, you must have made every effort and failed.'*

*Ma hastily changes the subject and asks whether he would like to hear me sing, but he declines the offer saying that his friend Shankar's accolade is assurance enough for him. He then says that he will give himself and me seven days to take a decision and Ma signals that the interview is over, and that we may leave. I find however, that Mr Sikdar spends another half an hour in conversation with Ma. What are they discussing?*

*Tilo and I talk late into the night weighing the pros and cons of my staying back in the house versus Mr Sikdar's proposal, which means virtually taking a leap in the dark. Tilo does not want me to go, but realises that once she is married I will have no friend left in this house, that Kamala will become increasingly spiteful and Ma irate in proportion, that such an offer may not come my way again. In the end, we both decide that if Mr Sikdar makes a respectable offer,*

*I will accept it. Two days later, Mr Sikdar returns and Ma calls me in to discuss the 'terms'.*

*I will board and lodge with the other women who work for him in a small building adjacent to his house and be paid rupees ten a month to begin with. Later, if I prove useful, my salary will rise and my clothes, daily needs and medical care will be provided for. I, who have never had five rupees to call my own, think this offer unbelievably rich and agree enthusiastically. He looks at me with something akin to pity and asks whether I can read and write. When I nod my head, he produces a piece of paper which he calls a 'contract', and tells me to read it.*

*Ma, Tilo and I peruse it together and find that it states clearly what the company will do for me; also that I must serve them for a minimum period of five years, after which the contract will be renewed if I have managed to prove myself. Ma nods in agreement, tells me to write my name in the blank space and sign at the bottom. Mr Sikdar affixes his signature below mine and the die is cast. How would I look back on this moment five years later?*

*Mr Sikdar says he will send Shova, the manager of the company, to fetch me next Sunday, and again Tilo and I leave the room.*

*I did not find out till many years later that Mr Sikdar had paid Ma five hundred rupees for this transaction.*

This is the last substantial entry in the diaries. After this, for whatever reason, the diaries take a back seat and entries became sporadic, disjointed and enigmatic. A number of songs and some lines of poetry are entered at random without a clue to their context—nothing that I can decipher to enable me to construct a sequential narrative.

I explain to Ranjit that my biggest problem is with the period of transition, for the newspaper cuttings give us some idea of her popularity, fame, success, also the controversy that her shows gave rise to, but how did this essentially simple, village girl turn first into an actor of such great merit, then a hard-drinking, foul-mouthed but very successful director, and then finally, the owner of the company remains a mystery. Also, when and why did she change her name to Gauri Sikdar? I wonder at what stage she gave up the values she had learnt during *sanyas* and to which she had clung with pathetic tenacity through thick and thin. Ranjit disagrees totally and says that she never gave up her values to espouse money and success, but merely remodelled them to suit a different lifestyle. He tells me that I am being quixotic; that my romanticism is taking the edge off my critical faculties, that idealism, inevitably, goes to the wall when it clashes with the prospect of material success. Why should Gauri be different? And why should I expect her to be?

But I have a counter point to these questions. We had expected Gauri to become the proverbial 'victim' and survive in Ma's household with its questionable morals by making compromises. Contrary to expectation, she had not only survived with dignity but had actually managed to create a future for herself, launch herself into a career where she would make a living by exploiting the talents which had received no nurture till a short while before this time. Did this square with a woman who would 'buy success at any cost'?

Ranjit concedes that I have a point, but also says that since we have little further information at our disposal, we must try and piece together the news items and the disjointed entries in the diaries to create a credible design. This is the first time he has offered active help and I am delighted. He also warns me that he will be totally unsentimental and completely analytical, but I am convinced that he is planning to participate because he cannot bear to hold aloof any longer!

The first thing to do is to sort out and file the news items in keeping with our newly acquired information, for my grandfather had put them in chronological order in his own methodical way, and to this end, Ranjit and I spend an entire Sunday afternoon as well as evening in my study. We tell the family that we are working on an important 'story' and for this we require peace, quiet and innumerable cups of coffee!

My mother places a flask and two mugs on a tray and sends it to our room, but a little later, my grandmother looks in with a jar of biscuits. I wonder if she is still suspicious. The cuttings are lying on the table and if she looks closely, we can be in serious trouble. But newspaper snippets are so much a part of our lives that she casts only a cursory glance at them.

Instead, she turns to us and says tongue-in-cheek, 'I hope you will concentrate on these cuttings more than you will on each other, so I brought some cookies to go with the coffee and keep you occupied!'

Ranjit is always at his most charming with her, for he has identified her as the 'chief enemy' a long time ago, and still has the highest respect for her sharp eyes and brain. He gets up, gives her a quick hug and says, 'I still have not made up my mind who I love more, the grandmother or the granddaughter!'

Thoroughly disarmed, almost purring with satisfaction, she withdraws. When her footsteps die down, Ranjit closes the door firmly and points at a cutting lying on the table, with 'Gauri Sikdar' printed on it in bold letters, which has been staring at us in the face all the time! The cuttings are old and fragile, and cannot be filed; so we arrange them by date and content and then proceed to paste them down on the pages of an exercise book. So absorbed are we that it is past six o'clock when we take our first coffee break and go through the biscuits ravenously. Then I step out, inform my mother that Ranjit will stay to dinner, and go back to work. The last bit is glued down when there is a knock on the door. It is my father this time to tell us that dinner is served, and I triumphantly hold up the book and flip the pages cursorily and at safe distance, to show him how busy we have been. Ranjit returns polite rejoinders to his casual queries while I lock the book securely in my cupboard.

From the cuttings it appears that Harish Sikdar had been quite a name in the world of Bengali theatre and *jatra*, for the first few items concern him mainly. For instance, a news item from *Alik Nazar Patrika,* a well-known Bengali daily, dated 11 October 1952, Behrampore, states:

*Harish Sikdar is doing his usual round of the* mofussil *towns before he returns to Calcutta and its suburbs for the Pujas. This year the main attractions are 'Sita', 'Shakuntala', 'Mirabai' and 'Maharaj Harishchandra'. In the last play, Sikdar himself plays the title role, and people who have seen him once flock to the other shows again and again.*

Again, another English daily, *Suhas Bazaar Patrika*, dated 29 September 1954, at Nadia, reports:

*This year Sikdar has concentrated on the epic of Krishna, the avatar of Vishnu, and all plays revolve around the various aspects of his life, the destruction of Kalia, Putana and Kangsa, all embodiments of evil, and of course, the eternally green love story of Radha and Krishna. Sikdar and his wife Ratna are getting on in age, but their art, if anything, gains perfection with maturity. There have been many encore shows.*

This is news to Ranjit and me. We had not known that Ratna Sikdar was an artist of such stature, or that they had performed so consistently together. There is a photograph too, blurred by time, of the pair in their Radha-Krishna attire, their aquiline faces alive with emotion.

In the next entry, there is a brief mention of Gauri. The name of the paper is not given, but it is in Bengali and the date and venue is clear: 4 December 1956, at Krishnanagar:

*This year there is a definite shift in focus in Sikdar's plays. The themes are mythological but they are cleverly moulded to convey strong social and political messages, and for this purpose, Sikdar has concentrated on the Mahabharata, the wonderful medley of myth, war, politics, statecraft, love and philosophy that lends itself so easily to adaptation.*

*This time Ratna plays Ganga, Gandhari and Kunti, the main female characters of the epic, while a newcomer by the name of Gauri plays Draupadi. She has a lot to learn, but shows great promise. Her striking good looks and wonderful voice will go a long way towards assuring popularity.*

We begin to realise that Sikdar had performed at an interval of two years—beginning before Durga Puja, continuing through the winter and winding up after Holi. The next item is an excerpt from the *Alik Nazar Patrika* dated 16 February 1958, at Chinsurah:

*This year, Sikdar has surpassed himself; he has continued to concentrate on the Mahabharata, and the current political turmoil is clearly reflected in the Pandav–Kaurav struggle for power. Also, there is greater emphasis on the social role of woman in a male-dominated society, and the highlight of the show is the gambling scene where Draupadi is betted upon and lost. While her five husbands look on in effete silence, the Kauravs insult her in every way possible, and finally, try to disrobe her. It is at this juncture that her own* stree-shakti, *aided by her friend Krishna, comes to her rescue. The role is played with great fire by Gauri, who has definitely come of age artistically. Kunti, played by Ratna, and her passionate denunciation of her sons is entirely Sikdar's creation. Although there is no such scene in the original epic, it is the most memorable part of the play.*

Then again another report in *The Politician*, dated 3 January 1960, at Howrah, states:

*In a complete volte-face, Sikdar has concentrated on Tagore this time and this is serious theatre, not* jatra. *He has focused on two plays—*Muktadhara *and* Chitrangada, *one political and another concerned with the woman question. In the first play, Sikdar plays Dhananjay Bairagi, a seer, and is quite unforgettable in this role. His wonderful voice takes the hearts of people by storm as does his unique rendition of this inimitable character. In the second, he plays Arjun, Ratna plays the real Chitrangada while Gauri plays the make-believe one. It is impossible to decide on respective merit, for they are all outstanding. One cannot help thinking that this play seems to reflect Sikdar's private life, caught between the waning and rising suns.*

This explains why the songs from the two plays had found such pride of place in the Gauri's diaries. Dhananjay Bairagi, the man who has broken all shackles of convention, desire and karma, sees in fire the symbol of his freedom:

*Thou fire, art my brother, my friend,*
*I sing thy victory, praise without end,*
*Thy unshackled exuberance,*
*Thy red and gold flamboyance,*
*Is a blinding revelation, my friend!*

Chitrangada, who has been repulsed by Arjun due to her lack of beauty, feels that her womanhood has betrayed her and prays to Madana for a year's reprieve. He grants her the boon and in her new image she feels:

*Every limb,*
*Every atom of my being*
*Is replete with the music*
*Of the flute...*

But a year later, tired of the uninterrupted idyll, Chitrangada realises that she is a monarch, the protector of her people and she tells Arjun that she will be his partner only if he can accept her true self:

*I am Chitrangada*
*daughter of a king,*
*Not a goddess, not a mere woman,*
*Neither to be worshipped, nor neglected;*
*If I am acceptable as an equal*
*Through danger and prosperity,*
*Then, I repeat,*
*I am Chitrangada, of regal birth...*

It seems however, that Sikdar disliked predictability and refused to be 'labelled'. The next item from *Suhas Bazar Patrika*, dated 4 November 1962, Burdwan proves this:

*This year Sikdar has focused on famous women in Indian history: Razia Sultan, Rani Lakshmibai, Nur Jehan, the politically significant queens, and has reverted to pure* jatra *with its emphasis on song, dance, action, melodrama. Audio-visually magnificent, particularly with Gauri playing the lead roles, his shows have broken all records of popularity and ticket sales. Perhaps, Gauri lacks Ratna's sophistication, but her complete identification with the roles she plays, the raw power of her emotions capture the hearts of her audiences and hold them riveted to their seats. Quite a find for Sikdar!*

After this there is a gap of three years, but instead of the news items we have come to expect, there is a black-bordered obituary notice that had appeared in the prestigious Bengali magazine *Swadesh*, dated 1 July 1965, and runs like this:

*Ratna Sikdar b.1910; d. 1965*

*Ratna Sikdar, née Ghosh, was born into a respectable, conservative Brahmo family and received her education at Brahmo Girl's School. She also had considerable training in Indian classical music. She met Sikdar at the Brahmo Samaj and their love of music and theatre brought them together. Their marriage, though childless, was happy, and they gave to their Sikdar Natyashala the love and nurture they might have lavished on their children. Few people who have seen Ratna in her most memorable roles are likely to forget her wonderful voice, the classical purity of her movements and her sensitive rendition of characters—tragic, comic, pathetic or melodramatic. It is no secret that Sikdar, for all his creativity, might have been a non-starter if it had not been for Ratna. As he said, Ratna was his greatest inspiration and strength.*

*All her admirers are cordially invited to the prayer meeting at the Mahajati Sadan on 15 July at 4 p.m. May her soul rest in peace.*

The following excerpt dated 15 March 1966 is from the same magazine. A report on the fortunes of the Sikdar Natyashala says:

*One wonders whether the Sikdar Natyashala will survive the passing of Ratna, for Sikdar has gone into a depression so deep that it is doubtful whether he will return to active work. Although not yet sixty and physically fit, he seems to have lost all interest. One hears that there is terrible infighting amongst the staff and that one or two members are trying to take over the company.*

*One can only pray that such a distinguished institution will not collapse so ignominiously.*

Vaguely something stirs in my memory—a piece of information that I perhaps had gleaned in Banibon—my friend saying that Sikdar's wife had died after a prolonged illness, that Sikdar had given his entire attention to her, and that the company had survived at that crucial juncture only because of Gauri, that she had even done some shows on her own to keep the money flowing. How, I wonder, had she survived the internecine struggle for control? How had she brought Sikdar back on an even keel? And most crucial, at what point, why and how had she become Gauri Sikdar?

Ranjit comments, 'Several scenarios rise to my mind—each more clichéd than the other. The first scenario is that Sikdar had fallen in love with Gauri even in Ratna's life time and this had precipitated her illness and hastened her end. After a suitable interval, the two had married. The second scenario is that the disconsolate widower had turned to Gauri for comfort and she had met him more than halfway. The third scenario is that Gauri had schemed the whole thing, slow-poisoned Ratna, and blackmailed Sikdar into marrying her and so assumed control of the company. And the fourth scenario is…'

I do not give Ranjit a chance to continue and tell him to change his vocation and become a scriptwriter for a *jatra* company, for he is wasting his fertile imagination working for a newspaper! He laughingly agrees that none of these denouements square with our conception of Gauri and that the truth lies elsewhere.

So, we are back to square one and turn again to the newspaper clippings. The next item in the order of chronology is an advertisement occupying half a page in *Alik Nazar Patrika* and the writing in bold letters goes like this:

*Good news! Good news! Good news!*
*The Natyashala is back in action.*
*Under the able direction of Harish and Gauri Sikdar,*
*the company strides from strength to strength!*
*Gauri will play the lead roles in:*
Savitri Satyavan
Sita in Lanka
Rani Durgavati
Jahanara
*Tour begins: 15 September 1967 at Bishnupur.*
*Book tickets early!*

The shows had apparently created quite a stir and were rated a positive review in the prestigious English daily, *The Politician*, dated April 1968, at Calcutta:

*The Sikdars have recently wound up their tour after an unqualified success. Their tour lasting six months and comprising over fifty-five shows have broken all records at the box-office. Not a single vacant seat was to be found. I have seen all four shows in complete fascination. Not only does Gauri play her roles with total fidelity, there is a force emanating from within that touches each character with fire as though*

*Gauri is vindicating her womanhood through these guises. One has no idea of her antecedents, but cannot help wondering what her life has been. What is the source of this passionate conviction?*

I suddenly realise that I have a point of reference on the timeline! In 1968, my grandfather was climbing the heights of his career; my father had just joined his professional course in college; my aunt was about to be married; and my grandmother was well on her way to becoming the *grand dame* we see today. Since she did not have a mother-in-law to contend with, she had been the mistress of the house ever since her arrival in Calcutta. Her aunt-in-law, the lady who had raised my grandfather, had lived in another house with her two sons and daughters-in-law.

When in the fifties, the Enemy Property Act had come into force and compensation been paid, three houses had been bought and this abode had been registered in my grandfather's name. The house, a large one with a garden, is worth a fortune today, and my grandmother never lets us forget her role in securing it by giving her husband good advice at the point of registration. It was she who had insisted that it be registered under a single name rather than as a piece of family property, for while she trusted her aunt-in-law completely, she did not have the same faith in the latter's sons. After all, as the only son of his father, my grandfather's share should be 'equal' to the share of others. This point had been hammered home by her. This explains why our house is larger and has better amenities than any one of the other family houses. It also explains the slight frostiness that underlies the apparent cordiality between the two families.

So, how old had Gauri been in 1968, I wondered. She said she was married at sixteen and assuming her son was born two years later, she would have been in her late fifties that year. Ranjit and I stare at each other in amazement. To us Gauri has been always young, a fighter, challenging fate constantly, defying misfortune, determined to live and not give up. There has been nothing to indicate that she had turned middle-aged, even old, and the staff reporter, raving about her performance, did not sound as though he were speaking of an elderly woman. Had *sanyas* endowed her with eternal youth? Or, had she struck a bargain with the devil somewhere along the line?

On closer analysis, Ranjit and I realise that this impression of her enduring youth has been created by the quality of Gauri's entries in her diaries. It is as though time has stood still for her and she has moved along this fixed dimension, witnessing change but not changing herself. When she had lived in the convent she would have been in her late thirties, but her reactions and reflections had been those of a much younger woman. She had struck up a friendship with a three–four-year-old boy obviously because she was trying to establish contact with her son vicariously, but she had sought out someone close to her son's age when she had left him rather than someone who would be closer to her son's age at that time, about nine or ten.

Suddenly, Krishna's words echo in both our minds: 'The Gauri I knew died the night she left home and her entry into a new identity was signalled by the donning of the saffron robe. You are Hindus, surely you know that *sanyas* stands for renunciation and passing over into the spiritual phase?'

But what exactly did all this amount to? Was there a rational explanation? Would we ever understand? Can we ever bring ourselves to accept the concept of a human being who defies time? Was this the Gauri who had appeared in my vision?

From the year 1968 onwards, the Natyashala tours every year. There is a significant change in the repertoire and the scope of travel broadens. There are shows in Lucknow, Allahabad, Agra, Delhi and Fatehpur Sikri. It is evident that Gauri tries to adapt the themes and personae to the place of performance; hence, Mumtaz Mahal within the premises of Taj Mahal, Shah Jehan and Jehanara in the Red Fort, Ganga and Shantanu in Allahabad, Mirabai and Padmini in Chittorgarh, Salim and Anarkali in Fatehpur Sikri in the courtyard beyond the Buland Darwaza. Although she speaks in Bengali, people of all languages flock to see her and are mesmerised by her wonderful voice and histrionic talents. Harish Sikdar fades into the background while Gauri holds centre stage in every sense.

The *Swadesh* dated 15 December 1970, comments at length on what it terms, 'The Sikdar Miracle':

*Gauri is like a shooting star in the theatrical firmament; the speed of her ascent and her histrionic brilliance find few parallels in thespian history. Now she has added other skills to her repertoire—authorial and directorial—and the plays produced by the Natyashala are written by the husband–wife duo and directed jointly. The plays are changing qualitatively as well; careful to maintain the* jatra *tradition, they focus more pointedly on current social and political issues. The Naxalbari movement, in particular, has spawned some memorable items and proved an irritant in certain quarters. The Sikdars should be more cautious.*

*The Natyashala has always been famous for its consciousness about the woman question and Ratna Sikdar had been the living icon of this aspect, but the approach had been romantic, even idealistic. Now the treatment is more direct, explicit, and even brutal at times. The terrible exploitation that began with Partition continues unabated, if one is to believe the Sikdars, and one must, for they base their plays on actual happenings and newspaper stories, which are dramatised, but thinly veiled. There have been occasions when their performances have been disturbed by the local goons in the pay of political leaders and once, by the police. This of course, has only heightened their popularity and imparted a crusade-like dimension to their efforts. Other units also explore social and political issues but are careful to align their philosophy to that of the 'powers that be'; only the Sikdars, it seems, do not care to be politically correct. More power to this fearless couple; may the God of Justice protect them!*

1968–71 were the years of the Naxalite Revolution, marked by police brutality, and 'the knock on the door after dark'. These years swept away a significant number of the youthful intelligentsia, too honest and committed to see the chasm at their feet. I have heard much about this movement that began in the sixties and spilled over into the seventies, from my father who was a student at that time. He had lost many of his friends and had himself escaped imprisonment narrowly. He insists that the intellectual void of the eighties was a result of this loss.

My mother's family lived in Dum Dum, a suburb of Calcutta, and she recalls how Pandey, the rickshaw-puller who took her and her sister to school, would take separate routes on different days. When my maternal grandmother questioned him, my mother heard him say sotto voce, 'I take them through routes where there are no dead bodies lying in ditches and gutters with deep gashes on their heads and their guts spilling into the water. I do not think you would want innocent children to see these things?' My mother says that their schooling would have come to a standstill if it had not been for Pandey. Once he had taken them on a circuitous route, a distance of nearly five miles, to prevent the children from seeing bodies stabbed and buses burning, but had not charged a penny extra. Much later, they found out that he had lost both his sons at that time. He had no idea whether they were absconding or were in permanent exile. Pandey had left his native land, Bihar, to raise his family in the peripheries of Calcutta, 'the city where no one starves'.

No wonder the echoes of these years reverberated Gauri's experiences at the grassroots on the stage of the Natyashala through a language that courageously revealed the unspeakable. Not surprising then that the 'Sikdar tours' caused considerable unease in high places.

Out of the blue, Ranjit has a brilliant idea.

'Let us talk to your Dad, Priti. He has such vivid memories of those years. How can he not remember the Sikdars and their immense contribution?'

I have no doubt that my father remembers perfectly, but whether he will discuss them is another matter. However, we decide to give it a try.

It is Lakshmi Puja, a very important event in our house, particularly for my grandmother and part of a tradition carried over from the ancestral home. She had brought with her, from the great house, the silver image of Lakshmi and the silver urn in which the auspicious mango leaves are placed. Over the leaves lies the green coconut, with its long, green tip intact. The offerings are laid out in the silver utensils and the huge silver 'lamp' that holds thirty-five wicks is used for illumination and rituals. The family prays to Goddess Lakshmi. This annual *puja* occurs on the night of the full moon in October, but the *puja* is also performed on every third Thursday of the month. The annual event is a lavish one with a large number of invitees, but the monthly worship is a family affair.

While the priest carries out the rituals, my grandmother reads the book sacred to the Goddess, and my mother and I listen dutifully. Two things strike me as I listen to the prayers: *Amar santan jeno thakey dhudhe bhate* ('May my children have their daily share of milk and rice throughout their lives') reminiscent of the Lord's Prayer, 'give us this day our daily bread.' This ubiquity of the staple diet in prayer is striking; but more significant is the image of the woman who is dear to Lakshmi. 'Beautiful, gentle, soft and sweet spoken, unquestioningly obedient, dedicating her life to the service of elders and respected members of the family, care of children, hard-working, sparing of speech, never questioning the commands of seniors including her husband, content in all circumstances… in such a woman Lakhsmi resides eternally.' No doubt, this image of the ideal woman has been created by man but as it is the women who read the book and listen, not the men, it has been endorsed by generations of women to retain control of their households. I wonder if one does not conform, does one get rejected completely, like Gauri?

Suddenly I feel suffocated, as though the smell of the incense, heavy with hypocrisy, was choking me. I utter an excuse to my mother and leave. I can feel my grandmother's eyes boring into my back, but I rejoice in the fact that she cannot leave the room till the ritual is over.

My father is with Ranjit in the sitting room chatting desultorily when I enter. I realise that they are discussing the escalating violence in the districts, those essentially induced by political parties during pre-election times. I make up my mind to tackle him directly. I sit down, turn to him and say, 'Dad, does this remind you of your student days?'

Slightly taken aback, he replies, 'Well on a smaller scale—that was a much wider movement.'

Ranjit has realised my intentions and comes in on cue.

'Sir, have you seen in the papers that a *jatra* company is planning a show on the fundamentalists in Kashmir and their subversive activities, but the government has intervened? The government feels that this can cause unfortunate repercussions in Bangladesh and amongst the local population as the first show is planned to open in Murshidabad, a Muslim stronghold.'

My father recollects that he has heard and read about this and mourns the fact that 'art' must be politically correct if it is to have an audience.

Ranjit continues, 'You know, Sir, I was looking through some archival material in the Records Office, and I found a parallel in the sixties and seventies. The Natyashala, directed by a man called Harish Sikdar, apparently ran into a lot of opposition—political and otherwise—because they attempted to highlight various kinds of corruption rampant at that time. Do you remember anything about them?'

I carefully wipe my face clean of all emotions and look at him innocently. There is nothing but genuine curiosity on Ranjit's face.

My father has no idea whether I have any knowledge of Gauri, for my grandmother has kept the information of my various encounters with her on the subject, completely private. He has no idea of the real purpose of our trip to Bangladesh, and he can hardly deny all knowledge. Although the fan is on at full speed, he perspires profusely but I mercilessly repeat Ranjit's question, 'Dad, don't you remember anything?'

He takes himself in hand with obvious effort and replies hesitantly, 'Yes, yes, of course, the Natyashala was quite famous; they did shows all over North India.' His voice trails off.

Ranjit continues, 'I also found that even though Sikdar died in the mid-seventies, the company continued to function very efficiently under the direction of his wife, but increasingly ran into trouble with local dignitaries and the police. Have you any idea, why?'

My father mumbles that he believes the company had been targeting specific political names and this was construed as blackmail by the authorities.

Ranjit shoots his question directly thereafter, 'What is your personal opinion, Sir?'

My father is slowly beginning to regain control. He replies now more steadily, 'Well, I'm sure you realise that all this was a long time ago, and since then much water has flown under the bridge. I don't know if I am qualified to pass an opinion.'

Before he is completely back on an even keel, Ranjit makes a last effort and comments, 'We have heard that Mrs Sikdar wrote quite a few plays which were acted out by the company, and some were pending publications. Have you...'

Before he can complete the sentence, my father breaks in as though anxious to bring this discussion to a close.

'Oh, I suppose you are referring to the manuscripts that disappeared at the time of her death and were never traced? I remember because it was part of the police enquiry; and now that I have told you all I remember, shall we speak of more pleasant things?' he says smiling brightly at us.

And not a moment too soon, for my grandmother appears in the room with fruits and sweets on a silver plate, ready for distribution. How much has she overheard? Later, when Ranjit and I can speak freely, we hug ourselves and each other in glee, for without his cognisance, my father has provided us with an invaluable clue—the veritable missing link! Why would the missing manuscripts be part of a police enquiry if they were not fatally incriminating for someone? In any case, why should the manuscripts disappear in the first place? I have no doubt that these pages contain the answers to the questions that have been dogging us since the beginning. Ranjit thinks that they might even hold the vital clue that could explain Gauri's mysterious death.

After the first euphoria is over, however, we tell each other that we are no nearer to solving the problem, for we have no idea where the manuscripts are. We don't even know whether they are still in existence. What if someone has deliberately destroyed them in a determined attempt to obliterate evidence? An image of a pair of diabolical hands shredding and burning the pages rise before our eyes!

But Ranjit refuses to be discouraged and undauntedly he comments, 'Your grandfather was too intelligent and pragmatic to set you off on a wild goose chase. He would never expect you to undertake a project unless there was a fair chance of success. Remember Priti, how fanatical he was about fair play?'

I admit that I do. When I was a child and he initiated me to the intricacies of carom, he would always play with his left hand and give me two chances to his one. He guided me so skilfully through the mazes of chess that it became a life-long passion. I will never forget his joy when I managed to corner him for the first time. No, Ranjit is right; grandfather would always give me even chances, and I owe it to him to see that the dice loaded against his mother is restored to equilibrium. We toss ideas back and forth about our next plans till, for a change, I come up with a good one.

I suggest to Ranjit, 'Why don't we make the "lie" a truth? You told my father that you had acquired information about

Sikdars from the records office and he had no way of knowing that you were referring to our newspaper records office! But now, why don't you get your boss to speak to the police commissioner to grant you permission to examine their files about the Sikdars, particularly records of the enquiries made when Gauri was killed or committed suicide?'

Ranjit jumps up; his eyes shinning like a cat's in excitement. 'You are a whiz, Priti! Why didn't I think of this? Of course! The files will have all the information, not only about the murder, but also of the occasions when the police were ordered to intervene and break up their shows, or were called in to restrain the goons. Priti, you had better come with me to the boss in your Sunday best. Make sure you wear green, it's your colour, and make eyes at him till he gives in!'

Our boss is unexpectedly cooperative, particularly as he smells a story that could make headlines, and gives us a written introduction. He also says that he will have a chat with the commissioner on the phone. We consult him about the line we should take, and he says, 'Tell him the truth—that you are a pair of journalists carrying out an independent investigation only to resolve an old mystery; that you have no personal axe to grind.'

As we leave the office after thanking him profusely, we ponder to ourselves on the many faces of 'truth'.

Before we approach the commissioner, we decide to take another good look at the news items on the case that we have found in the suitcase and pasted in the book. Were all of these put together by my grandfather over time or were some of them 'sent' to him as well? The mysterious dispatcher, who had mailed the diaries to him, might well have sent some of these cuttings later. I veer towards the latter theory as there are news items from Bengali newspapers that do not find entry in our house like *Bhabishyat* and *Purakaal*. Predictably, the case had aroused great interest amongst the Bengalis, and newspapers, perceiving the sensational nature of the events, had capitalised on this to the fullest. *Bhabishyat*, dated 17 September 1977, states:

*The Natyashala has become more incendiary ever since Harish Sikdar passed away last year. It seems that Gauri, in her urgency to get the message across and expose corruption in high places, has thrown caution to the winds! This play,* Lankadahan*, seemed innocuous enough when it opened. Hanuman, the leader of the forest-dwellers who helped Ram in his battle, went over to Lanka to discover the secrets that would enable Ram to destroy Ravana, the demon who had abducted Sita, Ram's wife. But once in Lanka, his tactics assumed the qualities of a police inspector investigating a crime. Because he could make himself invisible, he gained entry to places where the authorities would never allow his presence. He found out that Ravana was not the real villain but a dupe of his underlings. The money he disbursed lavishly for 'the people', particularly for those who sought refuge on his shores, never reached them, but helped his officers to build larger houses, buy better cars and educate their scions abroad. The stage has two spot-lit areas and the scenes are played out in stark contrast—an osmotic process where exploitation in one area directly fuels glaring prosperity in the other. When Hanuman informs Ram of this, the latter joins the underlings to place Ravana in a state of siege. The final betrayal is by Mandodari, Ravana's wife who shows Ram where the magic arrow, the only instrument that can kill Ravana, is kept. In the last scene Ram, with his arm around Mandodari's waist, pierces Ravana's heart with an arrow. As he leaves the stage in triumph followed by his entourage, the only mourners on the stage are the 'people', Sita and Hanuman. The play ends with Sita's lamentation.*

*The indictment and the expose of officials in charge of disbursement of public funds, particularly meant for those crossing the border, leaves very little to the imagination. Not surprising that it ran to packed audiences but only three times; the fourth show was broken up by the police. They say that Gauri who played both the female roles was superb, and people did not know which was greater, their hatred of Mandodari or compassion for Sita.*

Other paper cuttings tell us that there were a few more productions in a similar vein: a play about an aristocratic family who lived in a palatial residence near River Hoogly and who patronised music, art, theatre, and looked after the poor in their locality but were, in fact, labour contractors and made their money through heartless exploitation. The play is called *The Well*, as the dead bodies of rebellious labourers, men and women, were thrown into this dry well and smothered in quicklime, while unwanted babies were just tossed into the river. Strangely enough, it is the matriarch of the family who orchestrated these nefarious activities. This play, because of its stark portrayal of vice in high places, was very well attended and was running to packed houses when a group of hooligans invaded the stage, smashed the props, beat up the actors including Gauri, and left. Appeals to the police proved to be of little avail and the goons were never identified. Local people, however, swore that they were outsiders, who had come and departed by train, and their language had indicated that they had come from Calcutta. Obviously, the play had found its mark.

Gauri's arm had been broken but this did not quench her spirit; there were reports in the papers recording the fact that she had continued to breathe fire and brimstone with her arm in a cast. The shows had not stopped. In desperation, the police had approached Gauri, pleaded with her to be careful, and offered protection. She had welcomed the protection but refused to tone down her performances.

Finally, tragedy had struck on 10 December 1981. She had been found in her apartment by her servants who had broken down the door to reach her. Although an attempt had been made to make her death look like suicide, no one had been deceived.

Her obituary in *Swadesh*, dated 15 December 1981 states:

*Gauri's appearance on the* jatra *scene had been sudden and dazzling. No one till date has any idea of her antecedents. It is rumoured that she was not an actress by profession, but had been recruited by Sikdar because of her good looks and lyrical voice. There were many hints of a* ménage à trois, *but it is incontestable that Gauri and Ratna were good friends and worked amicably together. Her marriage to Sikdar came as a surprise to many and it is believed that Sikdar went through the forms to give her legal rights in the company. If so, the stratagem worked, for Gauri took charge and breathed new life into the institution. Her character also started to change at this point. She drank more, became increasingly harsh and abusive. Perhaps the strain was beginning to tell at last? However, nothing touched her stage presence. She remained till the last, magnificent, incomparable and quite unique.*

*Her will indicated that she had left all her money to the members of the company, her servants, and a particularly large bequest to her dresser Abdul. Abdul, however, had disappeared two days before her demise and had not turned up to claim his legacy. The police, naturally suspicious, had made every attempt to trace him, but failed. Gauri's lawyers have placed the money in a fixed deposit account in a bank. Will Abdul ever return to claim his money?*

*So Gauri had lived and died, had gone from the unknown to the unknown, remaining an enigma till the last—exquisite, anachronistic and inscrutable!*

*People who attended her funeral were amazed at the peace and tranquillity on her face. Except for the bullet hole in her temple, and her blood-clotted hair, there was nothing to indicate that she had met a brutal end. She looked more asleep than dead and ever so young and beautiful; more like a young girl who has fallen asleep than an old woman who has died a violent death.*

*The most striking feature was the complete innocence and purity of her expression, untouched by vice, sorrow and contamination of any kind. Was this also another aspect of the 'Gauri Sikdar miracle'? May her soul rest in peace!*

Despite the letter of introduction from our boss, the police commissioner does not appear happy to see us, nor is he at all forthcoming about the details of the case. As a matter of fact, he waxes sarcastic about 'investigative journalism', saying that it is merely another name for sensationalism and does more harm than good. '*Kyon garhe murde ukharna chahte ho?*' (Why do you wish to exhume dead bodies buried long ago?) he asks us. Ranjit tries to speak of 'justice for the dead', 'getting at the truth', etc., but the commissioner gives him short shrift and remarks, 'These are all clichés, that's all. Everyone uses these catch words. You know very well that you are trying to manufacture a story where none exists. What is your interest—money or fame, or both? Who cares how or why the owner of a *jatra* company died? There are millions of them. In any case, the woman was notorious enough!'

But Ranjit is not so easily cowed and he says, 'Sir you must have been very young at that time, just might have joined the force, perhaps. Surely, you would have first-hand knowledge?'

'And what if I do?' the answer comes as quick as a whiplash, 'I don't have to share the information with you, do I?'

We look at each other completely at a loss. We hadn't expected such hostility.

Then Ranjit makes up his mind, gets up, turns decisively to me and says, 'Come Priti, we are wasting our time here. We will try elsewhere.'

The commissioner turns to me and says, 'Are you not Mr___'s daughter? And, is he aware that you are involved in this so-called "investigation"?'

He has caught me on the wrong foot and he knows it! But Ranjit, cold as frost, cuts in smoothly and replies, 'If I know Mr___, he will never interfere. Priti, you should inform him immediately. We have nothing to hide.'

He sounds so confident that the commissioner is taken aback. For a moment, he weighs bravado against genuine confidence, looks at both of us by turns, then most unexpectedly, smiles for the first time.

Expansively he now says, 'Young people are so hasty, so quick to take offence! Sit down, sit down, let me order some coffee, then we can discuss matters amicably.'

We smile back rather uncertainly. He makes small talk. He is rather good at it for he has a sense of humour. The coffee arrives, there is more small talk. The clock is ticking away. Finally, Ranjit breaks in.

'Sir, we have taken up much of your valuable time and we are none the wiser! Maybe you can put us to someone who could help us—an inspector perhaps?'

Smooth as cream comes the reply, 'Of course. I will make enquiries and find someone who was part of the team at that point, and let you know as quickly as I can. It may take a little time of course, twenty years is quite an interval, but I will do my best.'

Then, as we are about to leave he says, 'So, how is your grandmother young lady? I have met her only a few times, but I have the greatest respect for her. Your grandfather's untimely death was such a tragedy. Please do convey my salaams to her, and tell her and your father that I'll pay them a visit one of these days.' He escorts us to the door and closes it firmly behind us.

Like the sudden illumination of a landscape in a sheet of lightning, the scenario becomes clear to both of us, and we realise anew the length and strength of the tentacles of control my family extends.

Ranjit says urgently, 'There is not a moment to lose. I have no doubt that he will get on the phone to your father at the earliest opportunity. So before he can do that we will have to reach someone else.'

He makes a quick call to our boss, tells him of the failure but not the reason for it, and begs to be put on to someone more helpful. Our boss knows the chief at the records office and promises to call him. We are advised by him to proceed there without delay.

In the car, speeding towards our new destination, Ranjit says, 'Don't forget Priti, you come from a family of *zamindar*s, past masters in the art of intrigue and conspiracy. They needed brain as well as brawn to maintain themselves in power generation after generation, and old habits die hard! In this battle of wits with your grandmother, I am afraid you are at a distinct disadvantage!'

I too can understand certain coincidences after racking my brains and agree with Ranjit. 'She must have overheard part of our conversation with Dad the other evening and drawn her own conclusions. Then she must have instructed him to get on the phone to the commissioner, just in case we had similar ideas! But I am not going to give up! We have to get a break some time!'

'I agree Priti,' says Ranjit soberly, 'and don't forget that we have Gauri and her son on our side to counter the mother-son duo on the other!'

The chief of the records office is waiting impatiently for our arrival. Apparently, our boss had caught him just as he was about to leave for a meeting. He greets us kindly, turns to an officer who is also in the room and says, 'Inspector Sharma will help you. I see no objection to your going through the papers of a case that was closed almost twenty years ago. Do you seriously hope for a reversal of verdict after all this time?'

I assure him that we expect nothing so dramatic, only a 'fresh angle' to the case. He smiles and tells the Inspector Sharma to take over, but as we leave we hear him mutter: 'Bloody journalists!'

Inspector Sharma, however, is much younger and more sympathetic, less jaded and more enthusiastic than his seniors. Our sob story strikes an instant chord of sympathy in him and he takes genuine trouble to locate the file.We wait in an anteroom that opens into the archives and peer around us. The rooms are dark, cavernous, ill lit and smothered in dust. I draw my finger along the surface of a table and the dark wood stares at me almost like an accusation. The files are piled on top of each other in what appears to be complete disarray, and the comparative shades of sepia that the once white papers have turned to, is the only indication of age or passage of time. The windowpanes too are very dusty, and the occasional patches of clarity look to me like faces peering in.

When I mention this to Ranjit, he says, 'Have you any idea how many ghosts haunt this room, Priti? Each file has a story to tell and its own pet spectre. Among them is Gauri. Perhaps, she will only leave this place if we are successful in our mission.'

The wait seems endless. Somehow, neither of us is inclined to speak. The air is so laden with dust or memories that it seems sacrilegious to disturb it. I feel that if I breathe too heavily, a storm will blow up and we will be smothered. Like the traveller in De La Mare's *The Listeners*, we have disturbed the silence of years which has receded temporarily only to surge back when we are gone. Without volition, my fingers move over the dust on the table. At last we can hear footsteps from the interior and we find Inspector Sharma, with a file under his arm, beckoning to us. Before we leave, I look down at the table and find that I have drawn a temple with a woman seated on its steps, praying, with her back to us! I wonder why I have drawn it. I certainly have no memory of doing so consciously, or with intention. Has this impulse risen from my subconscious, or is there an external agency at work? Also, as Ranjit points out later, how have I drawn so well? Drawing has never been my forte!

The file is sparse in its contents—a routine police enquiry containing affidavits from various members of the company, evidence given by neighbours and acquaintances, an inventory of the belongings found in her rooms, an account of her yearly expenses, and a copy of her will—objects that are impersonal and bereft of life. There are no letters or personal photographs, no memorabilia, no suicide note. The gun, a cheap pistol of which no registration number was traced, had been found inches away from her body; no fingerprints on it except her own. Since the doors and windows had been closed from inside, suicide had seemed the obvious solution, but some police officers, particularly the man in charge of the investigation had stood out strenuously against it. It seemed that six points had been cited against the suicide theory in the last report:

First, the angle of the gunshot wound had pointed downward, as though fired from a height. Had Gauri killed herself, the shot would have been straight or even pointed downward.

Second, there were no powder burns on the skin, as would have been the case if the gun had been held close to the temple.

Third, only the lower bolt of the door had been in place, not the upper one. The lock had been a self-locking one. Anyone could have shot Gauri, left the lower bolt trailing and pulled the door shut. The bolt would have automatically fallen into its groove.

Fourth, Gauri had been in her nightclothes. A woman with her sense of propriety would never have allowed herself in such a dishevelled state, even in death.

Fifth, although there was a considerable amount of jewellery and twenty thousand rupees in cash in her cupboard, nothing had been taken. However, papers had been strewn all over the room, books lying open, drawers turned out, as though a frantic search had been made for certain documents, obviously incriminating in some way to someone.

Finally, Gauri had been planning a grand tour for the Natyashala. She had been rehearsing for months to make it a success. It was rumoured that she had written an entirely new repertoire of plays. Hence it was hardly the ideal preamble to suicide!

Inspector Sharma, who has been reading the file with us comments, 'Have you noticed that there are some interesting sidelights? For instance, although she was reputed to be a hard drinker, no liquor was found in her room or on her breath? Yet an old half-opened bottle of brandy was found stowed away in her *puja* room, covered with dust.'

Ranjit counters replying, 'I think the alcohol was a form of window dressing, and went with the image of a hard-headed, hard-hitting business woman. Maybe she drank socially to endorse this image, but never developed a liking for it or drank on her own. I don't think she wanted any form of control, certainly not enslavement to liquor.'

Inspector Sharma continues, 'Apparently, the week before her death had been rather troubled. Her servants and neighbours had testified that various people in groups of twos or threes had visited her, and that the encounters had been stormy, acrimonious and loud. On one occasion, Gauri had called her security guard and asked him to throw out two men. They had gone, but had threatened to return.'

I interpose saying, 'It seems there was also a woman, very respectable but alone, who had visited her, and that a particular meeting had been tearful rather than bitter? The maid had overheard her saying, "My fate is in your hands, I can only beg for mercy," and Gauri's rather uncompromising reply had been "You must deserve mercy, before you beg for it".'

I am taking a wild chance based on my exchange with my grandmother, but Inspector Sharma takes it in his stride and says, 'You will have to admit, there was cause to suspect Abdul, who disappeared just two days before her death. Every effort to trace him failed. His family knew nothing and he never turned up to claim his legacy.'

Ranjit breaks in. 'Maybe he too was killed? Knew too much and had to be silenced like Gauri?'

Inspector Sharma looks sceptical. 'The body, Sir, the body! Contrary to popular belief and some detective novels, a large male human body is very difficult to dispose of! In any case, "bodies" were less common then, than they are today, it would have turned up somewhere.'

'Maybe it did, but the police never made the connection,' I add.

Inspector Sharma shakes his head and says, 'I don't think Abdul died or was killed. There are two alternatives—either he knew that something was about to happen to Gauri and got out while the going was good, or he went with her consent and with a particular purpose in my mind. Maybe Gauri sent him away to carry out a particular mission.'

Ranjit who has been listening intently now breaks in excitedly, 'Perhaps he carried away what the murderers were looking for! Gauri may have entrusted these papers to him and sent him away with them!'

I can contain myself no longer. 'Ranjit do you remember what my Dad had said? Gauri had hit out at specific targets. So what if Gauri's grand tour was meant to rip the façade off certain faces who could not afford the exposure at any cost? What would they look for after killing Gauri?'

Inspector Sharma has been listening to this interchange very intently and now exclaims, 'God dammit! You are right! Sometimes amateurs have a fresher vision than so-called "experts"! They would look for the manuscripts of her plays of course for the evidence lay in their pages. They were searching for these manuscripts to destroy them once and for all.'

Ranjit nods his head with great deliberation and comments, 'But Gauri was too clever for them. She anticipated the worst and got the manuscripts out of the way with Abdul. She must have been sure that he would guard them with his life; and having been satisfied with the arrangements she had made, she calmly waited for the axe to fall.'

I say, 'And that explains why Abdul never turned up to claim his legacy. That would have been too dangerous and defeated the purpose of the mission completely.'

For a few moments, we sit quietly, busy with our respective thoughts, convinced that we are right, yet wondering whether the explanation is too pat or too convenient. Can it be true that we have stumbled onto the solution which had eluded the police at that point in time, when the evidence was still fresh and immediate?

Then Ranjit turns his head, squares his shoulders and asks Inspector Sharma, 'Is it Sir that we have more insight or is it that the police deliberately turned a blind eye to the obvious because they were under pressure at that point? It seems absurd that the police knew that the manuscript was highly inflammable, yet did not put two and two together!'

Inspector Sharma has the grace to look abashed and stammers that such a contingency is entirely possible. But then he makes a comment that highlights his own insight and perspicacity. 'You must admit,' he says to both of us, 'that the image of Gauri that has emerged through my conversation with you is a very different one from that delineated in the police files. It seems that you have special knowledge and detailed information that was denied to us. Some of your comments indicate that you have had personal intercourse with her, but how is that possible? You are both too young to have known her personally.'

Realising that we are on dangerous ground, I break in on his surmises saying, 'Sir, you forget that we are reporters, and can give free reign to our imaginations to substantiate conjecture. That is how we spin our "stories", but that luxury is denied to you for you must deal only with actual evidence.'

But he is not easily sidetracked. 'You mean that you've been working on this case for some time? What are your other sources of information? How…?'

Ranjit comes to my rescue and gives him his spiel about record office, and gradually the bulldog stops sniffing; but he is not done yet.

'What are your future plans? I don't believe that you will stop now, having come so far; you will not rest till you have got to the bottom of the mystery. How are you planning to proceed?' Inspector Sharma asks.

I can see that it is not idle curiosity that prompts his question; that he is genuinely interested in the human angle of the story is evident; and then, there is the natural repugnance of the investigator for an unsolved problem. So I look straight at him and say, 'Would you extend your cooperation if we ask for it? Would you advise us on how to proceed? Believe us, this could be the most important assignment of our lives, professionally.'

He raises his brows and asks ironically, 'Is it only professional interest? I get the impression young lady that the last word was an afterthought. Look, I will make a deal with you. You have an interest in this case and that is rooted in emotion.'

I attempt to break in but he raises his hand, stops me from intervening and continues, 'Let me finish. Sure, there is the intellectual excitement of resolving an unresolved question; that is obvious. But there is something else about this affair that pulls at your heartstrings. Am I right?'

His eyes, boring into mine are trained to separate the grain from the chaff, and I realise that any attempt at prevarication would be futile.

So I turn to Ranjit and ask simply, 'What should I do?'

Ranjit, I think, has been making up his mind for some time, for he merely says, 'Will you tell him, or shall I?'

At a nod from me, he plunges in headfirst. I have to admit that he does a fine job. In ten minutes, he updates Inspector Sharma on reasons, events, strategies, taboos, reservations, clues, and action taken. Inspector Sharma makes rapid jottings on the pad before him but never takes his eyes off Ranjit's face. It is obvious that he's looking for discrepancies. When Ranjit comes to a halt, he continues to write for some time, goes over his notes, puts down his pen, and looks at us with something like respect.

Rather unexpectedly, he says, 'I am a Christian, not a Hindu, and a Bengali, not a North Indian, Sen-Sharma as a matter of fact, but like you, I believe in the immortality of the soul. My grandmother, however, was a Hindu. When she decided to marry my grandfather Laurence D'Souza, she was disowned by her family, even though she never converted and remained true to her creed till the end. She used to tell us stories about her father's house, her family, especially during the Durga Puja. I can still recapture the heartbreak that lay behind these simple reminiscences. But do you know, before she died she told her husband to bury her as a Christian and insisted on being baptised on her deathbed? So he had her body cremated, gave part of her ashes a regular Christian burial with a funeral service, and scattered the rest in the Hoogly, her beloved river. As a child, she had bathed in it with her family at the Kasi Mitra Ghat. He always swore that as the ashes touched the ripples of the river, he had a clear vision of her as a young girl, her face lit up with joy, walking away on the surface of the water till she disappeared from sight. Only once did she turn back to look at him and beckon. You will be surprised to know that he survived her by just six months!'

It is apparent that Inspector Sharma is greatly moved, and we wait in complete silence as he collects his thoughts.

Finally, he smiles and says, 'So you see, I have a weakness for grandmothers and will help you in your quest. But I warn you that the truth, when you finally arrive at it, might be as unpalatable to you as it is to your family. Are you sure you want to go on? It is obvious that you have your image of Gauri pretty clear in your mind. Can you bear to see it destroyed? Perhaps your family is in possession of facts of which you have no knowledge?'

Ranjit has warned me of this often enough and I am not really taken aback by the inspector's words. I can clearly recall the pleading in my grandfather's eyes when he put the key into my hands, the words of appeal in his letter are burnt into my brain. If he could risk it, so can I.

Looking steadily into the officer's eyes, I say, 'I have nothing to fear. Please tell us how to proceed.'

Every inch a policeman now, he looks down at his jottings and tells us to take down directions.

'One, tell your friend in Banibon to put advertisements in the Bengali newspapers requesting information about Abdul and his relatives. He should insert a reward clause for a fairly large sum. Say, ten thousand rupees. Two, give out handbills to as many *jatra* companies as possible. Say that you are prepared to pay two thousand rupees each for copies of her plays, preferably handwritten. Three, get in touch with a well-known film director, someone who has done features on women and gender issues, and enlist his or her support. Persuade this person to authorise you to put a large number of classified advertisements in all leading newspapers, saying that a series of features will be done on "Women in *Jatra*", and that the first will be on Ratna and Gauri Sikdar. Ratna's life is well documented but little is known of Gauri's antecedents. Anyone who knew her personally and has genuine information to offer, will not only be rewarded, but will also have an opportunity to appear in the proposed film to be documented; hopefully that will attract a greater audience. Then sit back and watch. Don't hope for miracles, but something will come of it in the end, I'm sure. But you'll have to be patient.'

'How often should the ads appear?' I ask.

'Once, every week, till you get a bite.'

'What if we don't? How long should we continue?'

'Now, now, young lady,' he wags an admonitory finger at me and continues, '"The quality of patience is not strained", if I may misquote Shakespeare, and it is of the essence. We know that in our work, sometimes it turns out to be a battle of wills between the criminal and us. Mostly, the former makes the first mistake because he lacks the will power and staying capacity that we have!'

'When can we come again?' asks Ranjit.

Inspector Sharma smiles whole-heartedly at us for the first time and I realise that the incipient wrinkles on his face are of the right sort, not of anger. I also wonder how often he gets an opportunity to smile.

'Keep in touch,' he says. 'On this card you have my mobile number which will put a trace on me, day or night. I know you are too intelligent to misuse this facility, but do get in touch as soon as you have something concrete to report. You can also call once a fortnight. Today is the 10th; I'll expect a call from you on the 24th.'

Gracious till the last, he sees us out of his room and we find ourselves back in the musty corridors of staid officialdom.

The following two weeks we work like maniacs to carry out the tasks assigned to us. The ads are easily done, the handbills printed and distributed, but the film project is not easy to execute. The film industry in West Bengal has been in the grip of a depression for some time and producers are loath to invest money in 'interesting' but non-commercial ventures. One or two directors do realise that the 'story' has possibilities, but are hamstrung by financial difficulties. Our first report to Inspector Sharma is, therefore, very tame; no leads at all!

He is not at all surprised, and says, 'People are always wary of the unusual and are slow to even look at, leave alone accept or respond to them. However, as Kabir says, "If you keep rubbing on a piece of stone with a strong rope, the friction will wear away the rope, but after several such have been worn away, there will be a permanent impression on the stone." So, keep working and God will be with you.' He hangs up, and not for the first time, we wonder about the hidden attributes of this very correct police officer.

# 3

A month passes by. Ten more days, and then a postcard arrives. We had given a post-box address which is monitored by Ranjit. The letter is written in Bengali, in a shabby, crabbed handwriting with thoroughly misspelt words. The writer claims to have a manuscript by Gauri in his possession; but he wants to be sure of the money before he lets us look at it. The address is scribbled in one corner of the card. Ranjit writes back curtly, saying that no money will change hands till he is sure of the authenticity of the item. Finally, a rendezvous is arranged in a seedy restaurant in Free School Street. Ranjit decides to meet him alone.

We inform Inspector Sharma, and he sets the stage with meticulous care. It is rather like being on the sets of a film, waiting for the action to begin. Only this time we are both audience and participant, and more excited than we ever have been before!

It is impossible for me to stay away altogether. So Inspector Sharma has instructed the police constable in plain clothes who is driving my car, to cruise around the area and to pass the restaurant as unobtrusively as possible. In any case, the traffic at 7 p.m. in that locality is impassable, and we are reduced to a series of staccato jolts that passes for movement in the busy streets and alleys of Calcutta, in the evening hours. Ranjit is punctual and by 7 p.m., he is seated with a drink at a table near the big glass windows facing the street. He picks up a cheap magazine and pretends to be absorbed in its tawdry pages, while maintaining a thorough surveillance of all entrants. As arranged, he's wearing a blue shirt and a navy-blue striped tie. His jacket hangs on the back of his chair.

We have circled the block twice and are about to move away again when the light turns red. I sit well back in the shadows but can hardly contain a gasp when a man walks in, looks around, spots Ranjit, and stops in his tracks. He is obviously nervous and looks ready to run at the least hint of trouble. Ranjit, catching sight of him, smiles his most charming smile and gets up to shake hands. The man smiles uncertainly and withdraws his own hand quickly from Ranjit's grasp. Inevitably, the light turns green and we jerk forward, out of range.

When we return, Ranjit is waiting on the kerb; he slides into the car even before it has come to a halt and the trained driver changes gears and picks up speed as though there has been no interruption at all! Before I can say a word, he presses my arm to caution me. I have to hold my horses till we get home.

My grandmother, delighted to see Ranjit, insists that he stay for a cup of tea. She sends for my parents, and the 'cup of tea' becomes high tea. Ranjit and my father are soon in the throes of a political argument that threatens to be endless. I am ready to cry with frustration, but no one seems to notice.

Ranjit is on duty at the office and has to leave by nine at night. He looks at me and smiles mischievously, says polite goodnights all round, then turns casually to me and enquires, 'Walk me to the car?' I nod wordlessly.

When the others are safely out of earshot, he whispers, 'The man did not say much. I'll tell you in office tomorrow, but he has given me a couple of handwritten sheets that seem of the right vintage. Only *you* can decide whether they are genuine or not. He says that there are plenty more of the same kind and he will part with them at a price.'

As we see my father standing clearly silhouetted against the light above the front door, Ranjit gives me a quick hug, and in the process, thrusts some sheets of paper into my hand. He then starts the car, reverses it in one swift motion and is gone before I have time to collect my thoughts or my father has time for second thoughts. I roll up the sheets very carefully, and return slowly to the house.

Ranjit has good reason to leave the final decision to me. Bengali is not his language, and the stylistic nuances that characterise individual writing are difficult to grasp, even for a specialist, which I am not. And I have to go by all the sheets to check if the style and content match with the diaries.

There are three sheets, clearly selected at random. The first two are connected, but the third is just a fragment. I inspect the first one closely. It is a soliloquy by someone called Rashmi:

*'I, like the row of coconut trees on the bank of the river, think to myself, does the river remember all those who enter its depths? Or does it turn its thoughts away to the next arrival? Who, then, keeps an account of those men and women who plumb the river's depths to attain everlasting peace? Or are they completely forgotten? How long do memories remain to haunt those who survive?*

*'I too was tempted once to let the cool waters wash over me, to let the burning cease. But I held back, why?*

*'Today, the soil around my roots is eroded. Chunks fall into the swirling waters; time for me to go. Should I have gone before? What purpose was served by delaying the inevitable?'*

It is so easy to read personal history into a fragment of narrative like this one. It reminds me of Gauri's sojourn at the riverside house before she met Sikdar. Her experiences there could easily have been woven into the fabric of a play later, though there is no proof that this was done. Also, there were no distinctive features of style to indicate authenticity. With an inward sigh, I turn to the second piece.

This is neither philosophical in tone nor reminiscent of her life in any way. It portrays the conflict between man and wife over the future of their daughter. It is sharp, down-to-earth, and even brutal. The language is in a dialect of rural East Bengal, so it is impossible for me to do justice in translation, but I try my best.

*Shankar: If you could stop producing daughters, we would not be in this mess today.*

*Shefali: And if you could behave less like a pig on heat and more like a man, I would not have produced so many children.*

*Shankar: I have no objection to producing children, only daughters...*

*Shefali: Why? Do I produce them alone? Aren't you your daughters' father? What am I, then? A whore?*

*Shankar: Shut up!*

*Shefali: What will you do? Hit me? Pull my hair? Knock me down? Go on! I've been through it before!*

*Shankar: Suppose I turn you out, and your daughters?*

*Shefali: Don't make me laugh! We can look after ourselves. In any case, what makes you think that the boys will side with you?*

*Shankar: They are my sons. They carry my name!*

*Shefali: Your name? (cackles hysterically) And what use is that? Can you eat it? Wear it? You can't even sell it? Not a single buyer! Hawk it around the marketplace and find out for yourself!*

*Shankar: You…bitch…I…I…*

*Shefali: Stammer away, you impotent fool! A man—so-called head of the family! You are worse than a piece of dung!*

*Shankar picks up a glowing piece of wood out of the fire and goes for Shefali. She throws a bucket of water in his face, stunning him, and runs out of their hut.*

I move on to the next sheet.

*Scene 5:*

*Narrator: That night, the men held a conclave. They came in twos and threes, their faces and heads covered, and met under the ashwatha tree.*

*First man: This has gone far enough, Shankar. Your wife is a bad influence.*

*Second man: Yes, our wives too are beginning to murmur. At this rate…*

*Shankar: I've done my best. But she has no fear. She says she can only die once.*

*Third man: She will die if no other solution can be found. How did she get out of hand? You should have been more careful.*

*Shankar: It's those social workers who distributed sewing machines and taught our women how to use them. We did not object then. The extra money was useful. But now…*

*First man: What?*

*Shankar: Shefali has taught the girls how to use the machine. Between them, they earn much more than I do.*

*First man: So?*

*Shankar: I needed money to buy a cow. So I wanted to marry the eldest girl off.*

*Third man: I don't see the connection.*

*Shankar: Well, the groom is sixty-three, with grown-up children from previous wives. He's rich. He offered me ten thousand rupees for my daughter. Shefali won't accept the deal.*

*Second man: What rubbish! Why?*

*Shankar: She said she would buy me the cow if I waited a year.*

*Third man: So wait; what's the problem?*

*Shankar: The groom has put up the price to fifteen thousand, and with that amount of money I can buy a cow and a goat.*

*First man: Hmm…that's worth considering, certainly.*

*Second man: It's only a girl! Besides, you have many daughters, too many, as a matter of fact!*

*Shankar: Exactly!*

*A small boy runs up to Shankar and gives him a piece of paper. One of the men holds up his torch and Shankar reads aloud:*

*You are the Krishna of Kaliyug.*
*You have put the good Krishna to shame,*
*He had sixteen thousand women.*
*But you have greater fame.*
*You fornicate by hill and dale.*
*You waylay village belles,*
*You love your daughter greatly,*
*For she's a product that sells!*
*You are brave when beating women,*
*But hide when a man appears.*
*So watch while your manly wife*
*Reduces you to tears!*
*We are leaving you alone*
*To enjoy your hearth and home,*
*And may the wife you marry next,*
*Wear you to the bone!*

At this crucial point the fragment abruptly ends and I am left wondering about the aftermath of this tragicomedy. However, the rhyme at the end dispels my doubts. It is clearly of the tone I had encountered in the diaries—the ironic, tongue-in-cheek humour is unmistakable! Besides, the 'woman question' as the central theme adds to the authenticity as does the East Bengal dialect; we are finally on the right track!

Inspector Sharma is pleased when we convey the news, but feels that the man who had parted with these pages, having once tasted money, will only provide with more papers in dribbles. So, it's important to trace the source of the documents and deal with him directly.

I am terrified that the man will bolt leaving us high and dry. I don't mind waiting and paying, but Ranjit and Inspector Sharma do not agree. After much discussion, we decide to arrange another meeting, and Ranjit writes to him to that effect.

This time the man agrees to bring an entire play. The price is high. He will settle for nothing less than ten thousand rupees. Ranjit bargains with him, so as not to make him suspicious, and actually brings the price down by fifteen hundred rupees. On this occasion, the venue is a Chinese joint on a quiet lane in South Calcutta.

It is a dark, moonless night with a hint of rain in the air. The street lamps burn low and stand at long intervals. The trees, bushes and clumps of grass echo with the chattering of cricket. An occasional flash of lightning leaves the briefly illuminated scene in greater darkness than before.

Tonight we have dispensed with cars and decided to walk. However, there is a car with armed men hidden in the shadows of a lane that is adjacent to the restaurant. As planned, the two policemen in plain clothes waiting inside the restaurant will follow the quarry should our visitor decide to take a taxi.

This time I'm not allowed to participate. Ranjit has put his foot down with characteristic vigour and Inspector Sharma has backed him the whole way. So I see them off reluctantly at the head of the lane and walk home. Inspector Sharma, hopefully, will not be recognised in plain clothes. He is to sit in an adjacent room in the restaurant and keep an eye on the proceedings.

We seem to have taken care of every contingency but as I walk on, a sense of foreboding creeps up my legs, enters the pit of my stomach, and clutches at my heart, almost stifling me. Ranjit is out there risking his life. What will I say to his parents if something were to go drastically wrong? How will I survive one day without him? I am tempted to go back, but realise the truth of Ranjit's argument: that I am one pawn in the game who could be used by the enemy against us, and end up doing more harm than good. I shiver helplessly, and to distract myself, look around for company.

There are a few people on the road, but when I try to keep step with any of them, they look at me, and unaccountably, either speed forward or fall behind. I quicken and slow my pace alternately, but still find myself moving in a pool of isolation as though caught in a time warp. Home is still half a mile away and strangely, I am terrified of crossing a dark stretch of the road overshadowed by dense foliage. I have my mobile with me and could call my father, but that would give the whole game away. Suddenly, Gauri's account of her life in the convent and her unprotected status there comes back to me with aching poignancy. With what courage she had fought the intruder! I realise with a failing heart that I do not have her stamina or determination, and still hesitate at the edge of the darkness when a young woman walks up to me and says, 'Scared?'

I look up quickly. Her face is in shadow and her long hair falling over it does not help. Normally, I would rather die than admit defeat, but something in her attitude—completely empathetic and totally without condescension—makes me nod wordlessly.

'Just keep walking and be assured that I will be right behind you. Don't look back, for if you do, people around you will sense your fear, and that will never work. Let's go.'

Almost without volition, I move forward. I can sense her presence at my heels and it is strangely reassuring. Not once does logic intrude to ask what use another young girl would be in an emergency. Would she not be as vulnerable as I if danger were to strike? The shadowy patch seems unusually long and I keep walking like an automaton, long after it has been replaced by half-light. It is only when a very vigorous street light shines right into my eyes that I'm jerked back to consciousness. When I look back, there is no one behind me! I look around, sorry that I've not had the chance to thank my kind deliverer. Yet, I feel in my heart of hearts that she would not expect gratitude. To help people in need, in her code, constitutes the daily substance of living. I am quite amazed at my own insight about someone I have not even seen properly, so I will myself to get home before I am caught up in more fanciful thoughts, but try as I might, a line from T.S. Eliot's *Wasteland* keeps reverberating in my head:

*Who is the third who always walks beside you?*
*When I count, there are only you and I together*
*But when I look ahead up the white road*
*There is always another…*
*Gliding, wrapped in brown mantle, hooded…*

My grandmother opens the door, looks pointedly at her watch and enquires, 'Why so late and alone?'

The frost and outrage in her voice are clear, so I throw my arms around her neck and tell her how exhausted I am. The effect is magical and she is immediately very concerned and affectionate. I am taken to my room, told to put my feet up, and given a cup of steaming chicken soup. I have to admit that when it comes to taking care of people my grandmother has few equals.

When she leaves me to 'rest' and so to my thoughts, I immediately try to reach Ranjit, but I find his mobile switched off. I have no luck with Inspector Sharma either. After several attempts, I feel the anxiety again mushrooming within like a nuclear cloud and spilling over to my muscles and joints. So I bury my face in my trusty pillow and try to calm myself.

It is almost two in the morning when my mobile rings sharply. In a taut voice, Ranjit informs me that the police have managed to put a trace on the 'resource person' and, if all goes well, we might have our hands on the entire repertoire in a week's time. Though the news seems positive, I wonder why Ranjit sounds less than elated. When asked he cuts me short, saying he's in a hurry, and rings off. When I try to call again, the disembodied voice is back, telling me that the phone is switched off. I'm ready to cry with frustration.

In an effort to regain control, I sit cross-legged on my bed and stare out into the dark but now luminous night, shades of grey fading into the palest black with diamond drops scattered at irregular intervals, some clusters, others solitaire. I can see a woman on a secret mission moving stealthily towards the Akash Ganga to find the bridge that will take her across the swirling stars to the land of the mysterious caves, in one of which Truth lurks like a beleaguered animal, wounded and bleeding. The way is strewn with stones, woven with thorns; there are demon sentinels at both ends of the bridge. How will she manage? With every attempt, her garments are rent, her limbs and breasts lacerated, her face mutilated, till the landscape begins to redden with blood. The redness spreads steadily, moving from the east to fill the sky, and the woman is drowned, choking in the life-giving fluid that emanates from her. Moments pass with agonising lassitude. At last the blood begins to fade—purple, pink, lilac, violet, indigo, and finally, the sweet, healing blue of early dawn; clearly outlined against the blue, stands Goddess Durga, clad and armed in perfect gold. I wonder if it's a vision or a waking dream as tears roll down my cheek.

Ranjit is unaccountably absent from office, and I learn the whole truth only when I meet Inspector Sharma at three in the afternoon. While Ranjit and his quarry had been deep in conversation, a third man had turned up and claimed that he possessed the original documents while the other was nothing but a sneak and a thief. In the ensuing argument, the second man had pulled a knife and lunged at Ranjit's wallet, not realising that the money was in a pouch on his belt. A well-directed kick in the groin from Ranjit had sent him sprawling, but he had managed to slash Ranjit in the ribs. At this point, the police had moved in and taken both men into custody. However, they had refused to speak, and Inspector Sharma felt that they would inevitably have to use third-degree methods to elicit information.

I ask for a glass of water and am hastily told that Ranjit is in no danger. He's resting in a nursing home as he has lost a fair amount of blood. His family has been told that he had to rush out of town on an important mission. I can go and see him whenever I want.

With the recent uproar against 'police brutality' and as third-degree methods are bound by serious restrictions in actual fact, Inspector Sharma is doubly cautious. What they will actually do is prevent the men in custody from sleeping and carry on with the interrogation monotonously, hour after hour, till the suspect makes a slip. These men prove tough and even after three days, the police are no wiser.

Ranjit is back at work. He wears a jacket to mask his bandages. As a special concession, he is allowed to join the interrogating team. On the sixth day, one of the men, in total nervous exhaustion, drops a name—'Abdul'. Then he clams up and they can get no further information from him.

~

It is Sunday morning—chilly, sunny, exquisite, and I'm unwilling to give up my warm bed. As a matter of fact, I'm falling off to sleep again, when an argument beneath my window draws my attention. One of the voices is my mother's, while the other belongs to a woman I don't know. She is asking for 'Didi' and will not speak to anyone else. Fortunately, my grandmother is in the *puja* room and will not be able to enter the fray for a while, so I throw a shawl around me and rush downstairs.

The nose-stud, the clothes, and particularly, the tattoo-marks on the chin and wrists indicate that she's Muslim. My hopes soar. Can it be that after all our travails, the vital clue has walked to our doorstep? I ask her if I am the 'Didi' she is looking for.

Delving into the recesses of her *burkha* she pulls out a grubby photograph, looks at it and then at me with fierce concentration, and says, 'Could be. There is definitely a resemblance.'

'Let me see,' my mother puts out her hand first.

My legs turn to jelly and I hang on to the door for support.

'Look, Priti, there is certainly an uncanny resemblance, but of course, it's not *your* photograph. Here, look!'

I am staring down at a face that, given a chance, as Tennyson says, 'would have launched a thousand ships'. She is older, more mature, and incredibly lovely, classical in proportion and feature, ethereal in spirit, feline in grace—a face that might change from goddess to demon in the twinkling of an eye. And yes, in a strange way, one could call me a shadow of this unique original. I remember Krishna's reaction when she had first seen me, and my last doubt disappears. This is Gauri I'm looking at.

My mother, fortunately, still does not see the connection, and I step in before she can start questioning the girl.

'You must have come a long way. Have a cup of tea,' I say.

As I had anticipated, my mother looks doubtful at the prospect of a Muslim stranger being entertained indoors, and I proceed to solve the problem by offering to take her to the tea-shop round the corner. Having changed in record time, I rush out before too many enquiries are made. As we turn onto the road, my grandmother comes out on the verandah and stares after us.

The tea-shop is a few benches and a brazier with earthenware cups laid out on a ramshackle table. It is too early for the regular crowd, so we have the place mostly to ourselves. Though many trees in the area have been cleared to make way for apartment blocks, a silk-cotton and a laburnum have somehow escaped the ubiquitous bulldozer. They hold up their branches against the azure sky in a misshapen medley of black and brown, with hints of bright red and yellow incipient clusters of buds at their tips.

The girl is still very anxious and I make small talk till the tea arrives. She wolfs down the *samosa*s, takes a long draught from the cup, and says warily, 'If the photograph is yours, how is it that you look so much younger?'

I square my shoulders and ask sternly how she had got hold of the picture.

Jerked out of her complacency, she mumbles that she had taken it out of her grand-uncle's collection.

'Collection? What collection?' I ask.

'Collection of books, magazines, papers, photos.'

'Does your grand-uncle live with you?'

'He has recently come to stay with us.'

'Why?'

'I don't know.'

'I think you do. Why?'

'He said his home in the village wasn't safe.'

'Why?'

'Why do you ask so many questions? Don't you want the photo? If you want it, you will have to pay for it.'

'How much?'

'A hundred rupees.'

'Why should I pay so much for an old photo?'

'You said you would.'

'To whom?'

'In the papers. You said you would pay lots of money for information.'

'I have said nothing of the kind.'

She looks crestfallen for a moment, and then more shrewdly says, 'Give it back and I will leave.'

I take out the photograph and hand it to her.

'Okay, give me fifty, then.'

'I will give you a hundred and a lot more if you will speak the truth and give me the information I want.'

'But I'm afraid.'

'Of whom?'

'I can't take names.'

'Aslam and Arjun?'

She stares at me and whispers, 'How did you know?'

'Because they are in police custody. They can't harm you.'

'But there are others in the gang. Ismail and Nakul. If they find out about the police, they will kill us.'

'That is all the more reason for you to tell me everything. Then I can arrange police protection for you and your family. Don't hesitate. You are wasting time and giving them an opportunity to get at you.'

Gradually, the story tumbles out in a torrent of incoherent, disjointed words.

According to Sameen, for that is the girl's name, Abdul was given a large sum of money by Gauri to look after the manuscripts and keep them safe. He had gone away to his village and for many years all had been well, as long as the money had lasted, to be precise. Abdul had two sons, never-do-wells, who had been happy enough to sponge on their father with their families, but when the money had begun to dwindle, they had not loved their father quite as much as before.

Heart-broken and disillusioned, Abdul had turned up at Sameen's grandfather's house in Rajabazaar. The old man, who was Abdul's brother, advised him to put the remaining money in a bank which would bring him a small income for the rest of his life. Part of this income went to Sameen's family and Abdul settled down comfortably in his brother's household. He had a room to himself, and in it, along with his sparse belongings, he kept a small trunk, permanently locked. Whenever Abdul left the premises, he carefully locked his room after closing both windows and took the key with him. This had caused a lot of curiosity to begin with, but Abdul had said that the case merely contained papers that had to do with his life in the theatre, and so, people had soon lost interest. In fact, he had shown his brother some posters of the *jatra*s where he had worked. After a while, Abdul had found employment with a company that put up road-shows and the salary he made had been a welcome addition to the family coffers.

Today's Rajabazaar bears no affinity to its grand name, hailing from the time when the Nawabs of Calcutta had shopped exclusively in this 'king's market'. With the economic decline of the Muslim aristocracy, at the turn of the century, the clientele had gradually lost buying power and the area had become the preserve of the lower middle class with their modest cottages and small shops. The refugee influx of 1947 and the steady trickle of humanity, thereafter, has turned the area into a sprawling, festering slum that winds almost into one of the canals that cross the city at regular intervals. Once distributaries of the River Vidyadhari, these natural outlets of waste water to the River Hoogly have gradually been converted into sewers with the incredible human congestion that has choked them with filth. So desperate are human beings for shelter that they live in shanties that lean into the evil-smelling mess cheek by jowl with the pigs who thrive and proliferate in the muck. This area has also become a convenient hideout for criminals who manage to remain anonymous in the faceless crowd and carry on their nefarious activities with impunity. Abdul too had managed to evade detection here until he had offered one of the scripts in his possession to the road-show company for whom he worked.

A play about slum children and the plight of the girl child in particular, it had proved an instant hit with the players who hailed from similar contexts, and because they had identified so completely with their roles, they had played with conviction, passion and fire. They had played all over Calcutta, its suburbs, and finally throughout West Bengal. Then they had been invited to Bangladesh by a wing of the Government, The Cultural Commission, and all the newspapers had featured them. I remember writing about them myself, and wonder anew at the quirks of fate. Abdul had been handsomely remunerated by the Cultural Commission and others who had used the plays and was asked whether he had more such plays in his possession. He had also been questioned closely about the authorship of the play, but he had maintained a stubborn silence.

It was at this juncture that our advertisements had appeared, and Abdul had been toying with the idea of approaching us when 'the gang', having put two and two together, turned up at his doorstep demanding that they be allowed to play intermediary for a 'suitable commission'. Abdul however, had been clever enough to see the enormous economic potential of the contents of his trunk and managed to hide most of the papers, hence the fragments we had seen. He had kept with him two complete works in order to deflect suspicion though, and one of these was meant to be handed over to Ranjit by Aslam, when Arjun had suddenly appeared on the scene and messed up the deal. Ismail and Nakul had gone underground immediately, but Sameen felt that they had their spies who were keeping a watchful eye on the family. Hence, she had come as an emissary to me, hoping that any woman in a *burkha* is indistinguishable from another woman similarly attired. Sameen has stopped speaking for some time and I have a clear picture of the sequence of events in my mind now, but there is something that is still bothering me, and I cannot put my finger on it; like a flicker of lightning in an otherwise clear sky, it eludes perception and detection.

Sameen, in the meanwhile, has put her head down on the table and dozed off, the precious photo still clutched in her right hand. I gently prise her fingers open, ease it out and take a long careful look at it. The proud set of the head, the aquiline features, the faint, enigmatic smile combine to create perfection of form and tone, but the spirit that illuminates the eyes defies interpretation, classification or recognition. Suddenly I find that my carefully constructed and nurtured image of Gauri is disintegrating into fragments, and that I am as far away as ever from the true picture. Gauri and I are approaching each other from opposite ends of a long, dark, seemingly unending tunnel; when we meet, will we recognise each other?

As though in answer to this question, I suddenly realise that it is the photograph and Sameen's words that have been worrying me! Who had told her that I resembled Gauri? Why had she been so insistent on meeting the 'Didi' and no one else?

I jerk Sameen's arm; she sits up, rubbing the sleep out of her eyes.

When she is fully awake, I pose my question, 'Who told you that I resemble this photograph, and how did that person know my address?'

'My grand-uncle, of course! Who else?'

'And how did he come to know these bits of information?'

'Members of the gang told him your name and address.'

'And about the resemblance?'

'I am not sure.'

'Still, you may have some idea?'

'I think the message came from somewhere through an unknown person.'

'What did the message say?'

'That the young woman who has put the notices in the papers was a relative of the *jatra* lady and resembles her a great deal.'

'You have no idea where this person came from?'

'Not really. However, I think it was soon after a group of people who had smuggled themselves out of Bangladesh, came to our area.'

'Bangladesh!'—the ground shifts under my feet as though alive, for I realise immediately that the only person who could have sent such a message is Krishna. She has seen me and she knew that I wanted information about Gauri. But in the name of all that is wonderful, how had she established contact with Abdul? There is obviously a network in place, of which we are completely unaware. Does Inspector Sharma know of this organisation? Very likely, but he never volunteers information.

Sameen is still looking expectantly at me, so I put a hundred-rupee-note into her hand and tell her to go home; before she leaves however, I call up Inspector Sharma on my cell phone so that he can have her followed. She is immediately suspicious, and wants to know why I am putting the police on her trail. I assure her that it is only for her own protection and keep her busy with inconsequential conversation till the car with the known driver at the wheel, and his mate Afzal, comes into view. Then I walk her to the bus stop, note the route of the bus she boards, 235, and the number of the bus, WB 02-6441. Then I walk home at a leisurely pace. As I enter, I find my grandmother rocking gently on her favourite chair in the verandah, with her eyes half-closed, just like a spider at the centre of its web, seemingly motionless, but totally alert.

I know better than to attempt evasion, so I go up to her and say, 'I have brought for you some of the *samosa*s that you like so much.'

'And did your new friend like them too?' she asked in a voice like cold silk.

'Yes, she did. As a matter of fact, she ate four of them!'

'And are these then the left-overs?'

'How can you say such things, Grandma? I bought these after I had washed my hands very carefully. Don't I know how particular you are?'

Slightly mollified, she opens her eyes, looks at me almost wistfully and says, 'Priti, I wish I were less fond of you.'

I move behind her chair, place my hands on her shoulders, look down into her face and ask, 'Why?'

'Because I don't like to see you thwarted, I want you to get everything you want out of life.'

'Except?'

'Except…'

The war that has been latent for so many months is declared now. I feel rather sorry for the old lady, for I realise I have an unfair advantage over her in my knowledge of recent developments of which she has no idea. So I give her a quick hug, put the *samosa*s on a table beside her and go into the house. I look back briefly. The eyes are still half-closed but the smile is too benign.

I only realise the extent of this benignity when I get a frantic phone call from Inspector Sharma two hours later to say that

Sameen has disappeared without a trace! When Inspector Sharma, Ranjit and I meet in his office, it is late afternoon and the shadows are just beginning to lengthen. All of us share an uncomfortable feeling that we have completed a full circle, having come back to the starting point without achieving anything concrete. On just such an afternoon, we had ventured out with such great hope, and today, a mere couple of months later, the taste of defeat is bitter in our mouths. We realise that we had underestimated our adversaries whose ingenuity is far greater than we had anticipated and whose network has proved to be vaster and more efficient than ours. We will have to be more vigilant in future and cover our tracks with greater care if we wish to outwit them.

Inspector Sharma explains that his man had carefully followed the bus to Scaldah where several *burkha*-clad women had alighted, but Sameen had not been among them, for her distinctive green apparel would have stood out amongst the more traditional black ones. The next stop had been Rajabazar, but again, Sameen could not be spotted. Then the bus had taken a turn to the right, for the route runs the entire length of Rajabazar, but every stop had proved a disappointment. The man had followed the bus to its distant terminus, but the girl was nowhere to be seen. He was absolutely certain that he had not lost sight of the bus or its occupants for a single moment, and was therefore at a complete loss as to the nature of this strange phenomenon.

Ranjit, who has been listening with complete concentration, now breaks in saying, 'There is more here than what meets the eye; this is not a straightforward conflict between Arjun's gang and us. There is a third party involved of whom we have no knowledge, and one who is utilising us to get to Abdul. I am absolutely certain that they have abducted Sameen, and if we cannot reach her within the next few hours, we will lose every advantage we have gained and might never get our hands on that precious collection of papers.'

I now speak up and say, 'I have a confession to make, but the idea is so preposterous that I am hesitant to put it into words.'

I am vociferously encouraged by both men and so I recount to them what had happened on that afternoon.

At lunch my grandmother had been extra sweet, piling my plate with all the things I love; when I had protested, she had asked in a voice dripping with honey whether the *samosa*s had taken my appetite away. My father had been surprised and wondered why he had not been offered a share of the delicacy, but before my mother or I could speak, she had gone into a long spiel about my taking a 'friend'; the word was carefully emphasised, to the shop for breakfast and returning 'after a long time' with *samosa*s for the family. She told my father, particularly, that I had been too late for a mid-morning snack, and so, she would have to serve them at tea. My father had naturally wanted to know about this 'friend', and I had to invent a story about a newspaper item that sounded flimsy even to me. Fortunately, the rich food had taken its toll and my father had not been as alert as usual, so I had got off lightly, but the look of bitter disappointment on the old lady's face had been unmistakable, and I knew that she would rake the matter up at the earliest opportunity.

Out of the blue, I remember an entry in one of Gauri's diaries about a childhood experience:

*Tomorrow they will take down the big hive on the* bakul *tree near the well. Most of the honey will be sold as my father needs the money, but we might get a few drops to sweeten our daily bowl of* muri. *Krishna and I will make sure that we are around when they bring the hive to our courtyard and place it upside down on a large earthenware vessel to drain out the honey.*

*This morning, my father and cousins lit torches made of bamboo, one end wrapped in old cloth and dipped in oil, to create a lot of heat and smoke; they pushed the flames so close to the hive that the wax began to melt and drip; some bees were burnt to death in the hive, but others managed to escape; they buzzed around angrily but helplessly as their home with its golden treasure was carried off before their eyes! How did they feel? They got their revenge however, although they did not know it, for when we examined the honey, it was not bright gold but dark brown, not sweet but bitter, bitter as the* karela*! We later found out that most of the honey had been collected from neem flowers. We were disappointed but my father sold it for a good price to the hakim, who would use it to make medicine for asthma. I think to myself,*

*Honey gold is sweet,*
*Honey brown is sweeter,*
*So sweet on the tongue*
*It tastes bitter, bitter.*
*People who look fair*
*Are often dark inside,*
*And their fair face doth*
*A black, dark heart hide.*

Had Gauri looked into the future and described her daughter-in-law? At the end of the narrative, I voice my opinion diffidently to Ranjit and Inspector Sharma, 'I think my grandmother is the third player in the game.'

Ranjit looks at me with a half-smile, for he knows her well, but to my surprise, Inspector Sharma takes me quite seriously and says, 'It is entirely possible that a network of women is involved in this business, and that your grandmother is in touch with them. She does enjoy quite a reputation for ingenuity and resourcefulness, you know that don't you? One such organisation spans Bangladesh and India and carries on a very fair business. It also has many branches. The *burkha*-clad women in the picture who have taken Sameen away, strengthen my conviction that this is indeed the case.'

When Ranjit enquires about their line of business, he cheerfully replies, 'Oh, drugs, food, medicines, woman-flesh, cosmetics, religious relics—the list is endless. These women are on very good terms with the personnel of the BSF and get away with blue murder on a commission basis. Don't you often hear of people who have been stopped at the border by the BSF? Well, these are the folk who have failed to pay the stipulated amount, and so become living monuments to the zeal of the security forces. And of course, the *burkha* is a real boon to these women and hides a multitude of sins literally!'

While I have been listening to him, an idea has been taking shape at the back of my mind, and I now enquire whether it is possible to send for the driver of the car that had followed Sameen to have a word with him. Fortunately, the man is still around and enters the room a few minutes later, looking sheepish and harassed. I, in the meanwhile, have spoken to Ranjit, for I want him to interrogate the man.

Ranjit starts with the interrogation and asks Raju, the driver, 'You are absolutely certain that Sameen did not get off the bus at Sealdah?

'Believe me Sir, I would have never missed her if she had; after all, I am trained to keep people under surveillance,' replies Raju.

'Did you have a second man along with you to help you?'

'You mean Afzal, Sir? Yes, we always work in pairs.'

'So, while you were concentrating on the driving, Afzal was carrying out the surveillance?'

'Only where the traffic was very heavy otherwise I kept a sharp lookout as well.'

'You travelled along Circular Road and got caught in the traffic snarl at Sealdah. Is that right?'

'Even before that, Sir. We stopped for a good five minutes at a traffic light in Moulali, and that is when two taxis forced their way between our car and the bus that we were following.'

'Did you tell Inspector Sharma about these two taxis?'

'He certainly did not,' says Inspector Sharma. 'But why?' he asks extremely curious.

'Well, it did not seem important at the time,' replies Raju rather embarrassed.

'Now think carefully and tell me, did these taxis try to get ahead of the bus?' asks Ranjit.

'Well, the lights turned green and the bus lunged forward, and so did our car.'

'And the taxis?' asks Ranjit impatiently.

'One managed to get ahead of the bus but the other remained between the bus and our car.'

'Where did you stop next?' asks Ranjit.

'At the foot of the flyover, and that is where the women in black *burkha*s got off the bus.

'And you are sure there was no green *burkha* among them?' asks Ranjit to reassure himself.

'No Sir, I am sure of that. And then, the bus began to move and so did the taxi. And thereafter, suddenly, Afzal cried out "Look out Raju!"'

'Why?' asks Ranjit.

'Because a fruit vendor, with a laden basket on his head, had decided to cross the street right in front of our car! I would have hit him if Afzal had not warned me!'

'Where was the traffic police?'

'A constable came running up to the vendor, but by that time I had raced forward in pursuit of the bus.'

'Did you get a glimpse of these women at all?'

Raju, wrinkling his forehead in an effort to remember says, 'May I call Afzal Sir? He will remember more than I do!'

Inspector Sharma strikes the bell on his desk and tells the man on duty to send Afzal in, but the man is nowhere to be found. Apparently he has gone off to visit a sick relative in hospital on the completion of his duty hours. So Ranjit exhorts Raju afresh to try and recapture the details of the incident to see if he has omitted a relevant incident. Obediently, Raju closes his eyes and leans back in his chair. The lines on his forehead deepen with concentration. It is evident from the expressions on his face which pass in quick succession that he is going back step by step, retracing his experiences as he has been trained to do. After about five minutes, he relaxes visibly and sits up, eyes still closed. The clock ticking away on the inspector's desk is almost deafening in the perfect silence of the room, and the constant hum of activity in the courtyard several floors below is strangely muted. I do my best to take away my eyes from Raju's face, but find it impossible to keep my own face averted.

Gradually, the lines on his forehead fade away; he opens his eyes and looks at us with new-found confidence and says, 'The taxi during the debacle with the fruit-seller had fallen behind us and two of the *burkha*-clad women had got into the taxi; one of them was so fat that that the other one had to help her to get into the taxi before she got in herself!' His voice trails off on a new note of uncertainty.

Ranjit asks, 'But Raju, how could you see all this, in the rear-view mirror?'

'I looked into the side-view one too for the vendor had forced me into the lane on the extreme left. And now, when I think about it carefully, I realise that there was something distinctly odd about one of these women.'

Before Ranjit can speak Inspector Sharma breaks in impatiently, 'Come on man, tell us what you saw, we have no time to lose!'

'Well, please don't laugh, but I think one of the women was a "*churail*"!'

Inspector Sharma and I are totally at a loss, for the word does not exist in the Bengali lexicon, but Ranjit's eyes, we find, are shining like a cat's!

'Why do you say this? Come on, tell us. This could be of vital importance!' Ranjit insists.

But Raju is looking doubtful again, and his recent confidence seems to be oozing out of him.

He mutters, 'Better not to speak of these things, Sir. These creatures can cause great harm to people they dislike; and in any case, this woman is not important.'

And from this position, it is impossible to budge him. Ranjit is the most frustrated, for he had hoped for instant corroboration of his ideas, but all his powers of persuasion fail as Raju sits as immoveable as stone, with a stubborn, bovine look on his face.

We are just about to let him go, when there is a knock on the door and Afzal is ushered into the room. He says apologetically, 'I am extremely sorry Sir to be away when you needed me, but Raju knows everything as well as I do, if not better.'

Before Raju can say anything, Ranjit breaks in swiftly. 'Raju was telling us about the women who got into the taxi, the fat and the thin one, and that he thinks that one of them is a "*churail*". However, he refuses to help us any further for whatever reasons. Can you throw some light on the matter?'

Afzal throws back his head and laughs in a characteristic manner that is very engaging and says with faint contempt in his voice, 'Unlike Raju, we believe in Allah and have no belief in superstitions. What he means to say is that although he saw two women, he saw three pairs of feet, one of which were pointing backwards, away from the body. Now tell me Sir, how is this possible? Raju has taken to day-dreaming and should not be entrusted with important missions in future.'

This criticism galvanises Raju into action and at the cost of future peril, he breaks into a torrent of speech affirming the truth of his experiences.

'I tell you Sir, I saw it all so clearly—two feet in red slippers pointing backwards! How is it possible for this creature to be human? And now that I have told you this, God knows what she will do to me!'

*Churail*s, I found out from Ranjit later, are she-demons who inhabit tall trees and take innocent, unsuspecting men unawares. They may take different forms, but their feet always point backwards, making it easy for victims to recognise them, though not always in time to be saved. At the moment however, it is the mention of 'red slippers' that triggers a memory of Sameen, sitting at the tea shop, enjoying her cup of tea and the *samosa*s, swinging her pretty, slim feet in red slippers, to and fro, to and fro.

So I turn to Ranjit and say, 'But Sameen *was* wearing red slippers this morning! Do you think...?'

Before I can complete my sentence, we hear a sharp intake of breath and turn to find Afzal with an ashen face staring at us. Then he begins to sidle towards the door, but Raju, all fear gone, lunges at him and holds him in an iron grip. They struggle hard, but when another orderly moves into the fray, Afzal realises that he has no chance of escape and goes limp in Raju's arms.

Ranjit says triumphantly, 'I felt all along that the *burkha* had played a key role in the entire affair. It would be simple enough to clap a handkerchief soaked in chloroform on Sameen's nose and then pretend that she had fainted. The older woman would then claim kinship and take her into the folds of her own *burkha*. Other passengers, men and women, would respect her concern and refrain from interference. The two women then got off the bus dragging the inert Sameen with them, her distinctive green *burkha* hidden under the voluminous black one. The only thing they could do nothing about were Sameen's red sandals that would drag, toes pointing backwards.'

Now Raju turns on Afzal balefully and says, 'So, the fruit vendor jaywalking in front of the car was arranged to divert my attention from what was happening behind me? No wonder, you pointed him out to me so thoughtfully! Just you wait you devil till I get my hands on you!'

And suddenly he bends sideways and twists Afzal's arm so hard that he cries out in pain.

The denouement of this entire affair is managed most efficiently by Inspector Sharma. As Afzal is aware of Sameen's whereabouts and knows Abdul's address, he is likely to prove a wonderful shortcut. Knowing this Inspector Sharma enforces severe professional pressure and compels Afzal to be the official informer. Afzal agrees as this is the lesser evil for him and within an hour we are on our way to Rajabazaar, with Afzal safely ensconced between Inspector Sharma and Raju who never lets go off his hand.

The shantytown, bound by the foul-smelling canal on one side and the forbidding high walls of a factory on the other, is a bewildering maze of shelters made of bamboo, corrugated tin, sheets of plastic and pieces of asbestos. However, some habitations of a less ephemeral nature are also present; low rooms, dark and airless, passing as houses. To one of these, Afzal guides us. The lanes are too narrow to permit the passage of a car, and we have to pick our way on foot, single-file, avoiding potholes, puddles, animal and human excreta.

As we approach our destination, the crowds seem to thicken and become more vociferous; as a matter of fact, there is an all-pervading hum of conversation, and although individual sounds are indecipherable, there is an ominous ring to the sound in general, that is unmistakable; whether the hostility is directed at the police only or Ranjit and I as well, we have no way of ascertaining, but it adds to the discomfort. Inspector Sharma uses his authority freely, and his uncompromising attitude coupled with the gun in his hand, keeps the onlookers slightly at bay and carves out a path for us. We finally arrive to find several local elders, quite distraught, standing before a locked door; an old-fashioned one, with a chain and staple, secured firmly on the outside by a stout padlock.

On enquiry, a tall, bearded gentleman comes forward and introduces himself as Abdul's brother and Sameen's grandfather. On seeing me, he stops short and in a voice quivering with apprehension, asks whether she ever got to me, and if she did, why she is not with us. Inspector Sharma however, cuts short this conversation and assures the old man that Sameen is safe and will join us shortly. His main thrust is Abdul and his whereabouts, for he knows that precious time has been lost due to Afzal's unauthorised absence from the police station and then due to his prevarications. The setting is bizarre enough; the sun is about to go down and there is a miasma rising from the canal that shrouds us in an evil haze. Above the haze, the rays of the setting sun create a devil's playground, banked with dark clouds and a floor of fire, hinting at strange inhabitants engaged in forbidden activities. Suddenly, a lone ray breaks away from its prison to fall at my feet, and in the faint illumination, I perceive a dark liquid flowing out under the locked door, forming a viscous pool on the worn stone of the steps. Having seen this, iron crowbars are brought and strong men go into action. Before their combined onslaught, the door yields and we look in to find Abdul lying on the floor; a neat bullet hole in his back around which the blood is beginning to congeal. The cupboard has been broken and cleared; the trunk is gone!

By the time a stretcher is improvised and Abdul is placed in the ambulance summoned on Inspector Sharma's mobile, his breathing has become shallow and laboured. The doctor says he has been shot at point-blank range and that the bullet must have missed his heart by the fraction of an inch. We race behind the ambulance as it speeds towards Nilratan Hospital in Sealdah. The sky is dark now and the garish illumination on the giant hoardings en route, only highlight the absurd disparities of urban life that surround us. When we finally leave the hospital well after midnight, Abdul has been placed on the life-support systems and is fighting desperately to hang onto the tenuous thread we call 'life'.

The time for secrecy is over. When Ranjit and I get home we find the entire family waiting for us in the sitting room and we launch into our story, beginning with my grandfather's request to me. As we recapitulate, however, we find that a factual account is easy enough to render, if the emotional register remains untapped. I cannot and do not try to convey my feelings on meeting Krishna, my responses to the poignant entries in Gauri's diaries, or for the want of a better word, my 'mystic' experiences. Whatever the shortcomings in my discourse are, I certainly cannot complain of lack of attention on the part of my audience—my father, hands on knees, drinks in every word; my mother, leans forward, gives me her total attention; my grandmother, severely upright, with her back uncompromisingly straight, clenches and unclenches her fists by turns, while her emotions chase each other across her aquiline, sensitive, mobile face like dappled shadows on a sunlit lawn. Her face turns grey as mist when I mention of Sameen's disappearance, but when she realises that I will not betray her, the relief and gratitude in her demeanor is almost palpable. When she learns that Abdul has been shot and that the trunk has disappeared, she finds it difficult to conceal her jubilation and maintain her customary mask of inscrutability, but when she learns that he is in hospital and has a twenty-five per cent chance of survival, 'the fit is upon her again'.

A flood of questions from the family greets us which we do our best to answer and parry alternately. It becomes increasingly clear that for mother and son the main focus is Abdul, and the apprehension that he might survive and speak after all.

When my mother says, 'I do hope the man recovers and speaks, or all the hard work Priti and Ranjit have put in will go to waste,' the old lady turns on her ferociously and in a voice sharper than a rapier lashes out, 'Work? You call this work? This digging into the past with no thought for family prestige, dignity, honour? I call it ghoulish, downright indecent, completely vindictive!' Her bosom heaving with passion, she is about to launch into another tirade, when my father cuts in and says reproachfully to me, 'Really Priti, you and Ranjit might have consulted us before going out on a limb like this.'

Before I can speak, Ranjit moves in smoothly. 'And would you have helped us, Sir, if Priti had consulted you? Would you not have advised her to "let sleeping dogs lie and let the past bury its dead?"'

These glib phrases, favourites with him, echoing in the quiet room, make my father distinctly uncomfortable and he has the grace to blush, but his mother has no such compunction, and her voice is like a whiplash when she speaks, 'My son has been brought up to honour and respect the family name and heritage, not cast aspersions on it. Why would he want you to waste your valuable time and effort digging up the antecedents of a woman who has only brought shame to him and his forbears?'

I can contain myself no longer and turn to look at her full in the face and say, 'Tell me if she was so vicious, why would a man like your husband, a man who never committed a dishonourable act in his life, entrust *me* with this mission? Why was it so important to him that I find out the *truth* about his mother? And most importantly, why could *he* not institute the search *himself*?'

Her voice cuts through mine with the viciousness of a sharp knife. 'That was because he was afraid of what he would find! Because he knew in his heart of hearts that she was rotten to the core! Because he...'

This time I interrupt.

'So he left it to his granddaughter to wallow in filth? Was he that kind of a man Grandma? You know better than anybody else how much he cared for me, how he could never bear to see me hurt? Would he ever expose me to a situation where my sensibilities and values would be compromised? No, a thousand times no! He wanted me to expiate his guilt in neglecting his duty. He trusted me so implicitly and confidently, because he knew she was completely innocent of the charges laid against her. He wanted me to prove once and for all, that she was honourable and clean, as clean as yourself, and I will not rest till I have carried out his behest!'

I think she would have struck me physically, if the phone had not rung at this dramatic point. Before anyone can move, Ranjit picks up the receiver and listens intently, thanks the speaker for the good news he has given, turns to us with a radiant smile and informs us, 'That was Inspector Sharma to tell us that Abdul has pulled through and is out of danger. He should be able to speak to us in a day or two!'

The long, golden fingers of dawn are just beginning to touch the tops of trees and buildings; the grey sky is turning pink; the sparrows are calling sleepily to each other, hailing yet another day. We are on the balcony watching this daily miracle, hand in hand, and I turn away from Ranjit just in time to see my grandmother's white saree vanishing through the door.

The doctors have been over-confident. Abdul's recovery takes longer than expected. It is a month before he can think and speak coherently, a month and a week before he can partially recapture the past, and two months before he can take the journey that will provide us with a clue to the final solution. We are not very hopeful, for the trunk has not been recovered, and though Sameen has returned, outwardly unharmed, she has no idea of who the killer or thief might be. The men under interrogation who have finally yielded to pressure, have individually assured the authorities that none of their gang members are responsible. They claim that their activities do not include murder. Afzal thinks it to be the handiwork of a member of the network, but the organisation is so strictly compartmentalised, that he cannot put a name or face to the perpetrator.

My grandmother does not speak with me these days and keeps mainly to her own and the *puja* room; my father is distinctly cool, but finds it difficult to dislike me permanently! Speaking with Abdul is also a frustrating experience, for 'time' and 'place' are two points of reference he is most confused about, and the memories of the fateful day seem to have escaped him completely. We really seem to have hit an all-time low.

Inspector Sharma however, has not been idle. By subjecting Afzal to intense and searching interrogation, he has managed to elicit a lot of information about the organisation that operates so easily across the border. It seems there are two groups within the network with conflicting aims: one group wishes to eliminate Abdul so that the entire issue may die with him; the other group however is desperate that he survives, but their purpose in desiring this is not known. Neither of them has any connection with Aslam's gang, who constitute the third group that lies outside the network and look on the entire network as 'bloody interlopers'.

Inspector Sharma has realised that the triple involvement involves high stakes and his professional expertise is considerably challenged. He finally says to us, 'This is no longer the preserve of a pair of romantic reporters chasing shadows in the past; these appear to be deep waters with international implications and stakes are high enough to cause murder. We will have to get to the bottom of the matter, or the Home Department will start asking awkward questions.' As an afterthought, he adds, 'Thanks for bringing it to our notice!'

Abdul is released from hospital after four weeks, while our impatience 'to know' keeps mounting. However, he is not allowed to return home. He is placed in a police 'safe house' under round-the-clock surveillance, and only special people are allowed to visit him; among these are Sameen, her grandfather, Ranjit and I. He still requires medical attention so there is a nurse in constant attendance, and only we know that she is a policewoman with hospital training, and that she carries a gun with its safety-catch off. Inspector Sharma feels that some attempt will be made either to contact or to harm him, and this will give us the lead we are waiting for.

I sit with Abdul as often as possible, and with Sameen's help try to engage him in conversation. At times his memory is lucid, connected and he speaks fluently, even animatedly, about his life in the village, the selfishness of his sons, his little granddaughter, Rukaiya, whom he obviously misses; or of his travels with the Natyashala all over India, the crowds, the accolade, the excitement. But the moment we speak about 'plays', the 'trunk', the 'gang' or the 'attack' on him, his eyes glaze and become unfocussed, his speech slurs, he loses coherence of thought and expression, and it becomes impossible to get a meaningful sentence out of him. He also looks at me with great interest but in a bewildered manner, as though trying to establish a connection between the two images—Gauri and Priti, but as the connection continues to elude him, he becomes frustrated and ceases to communicate.

The house in which he has been placed is an old converted warehouse on the fringes of Rajabazaar. It is a tall, narrow three-storied building with blind walls on three sides and a single entrance in front, heavily guarded at all times. Inspector Sharma feels that the house is impregnable, and for that reason, he is fairly certain that an attempt will be made to contact him through a letter. He has left minute instructions for this contingency, but fifteen days pass by without an incident and we begin to wonder whether the enemy has given up or is merely biding his time. This period of waiting is one of mental attrition, and instead of relaxing, we find our nerves completely on the edge. There is also a growing sense of defeat which threatens to overwhelm us at times.

The attack when it does come is so unexpected and ingenious that it leaves the police gasping! The old-fashioned iron spiral staircase at the back of the building, typical of colonial India and usually meant to be used by the domestic helpers, is so rickety that it has been out of commission for the last fifteen years, and the door that it leads to has been chained, firmly padlocked and forgotten. However, the iron stanchion to which the staircase is anchored is as strong as it ever was, a fact that the police seem to have overlooked. Two men throw a rope ladder over this structure, secure it firmly and climb up; they then place some explosive against the door, light the fuse and depart; a few minutes later the blast rocks the building like a house of straw and the door is blown in. Before the guards have even located the source of damage, two masked men enter Abdul's room and attempt to abduct him, and would have succeeded had it not been for the nurse who shoots one man in the thigh bringing him down. The other man lunges at her gun and she shoots him through the heart, killing him instantaneously. The wounded man however, tries to turn his gun on Abdul but she covers him and takes the bullet in her shoulder instead, and shoots the gun out of the attacker's hand.

All this comes out when we attend the felicitation ceremony at which the policewoman receives a medal and citation for 'honourable discharge of duty', a month later. At that moment however, she has to be rushed to hospital as does the witness, for they are both bleeding heavily.

This man proves a valuable though limited source and leads Inspector Sharma to break up a drug joint, rescue some women from a respectable politician's home in an elite area of the city, confiscate consignments of illicit liquor, but he fails to get through to the 'bosses' who continue to function with impunity. Reports of the 'nine days' wonder' flood the newspapers and then recede quietly, without having made a real impact, but earn Inspector Sharma considerable recognition and accolade.

After this incident, however, there is a subtle change in attitude. Inspector Sharma feels that he has got all he needs from Abdul and that it is time for him to move to a different location, assume a new identity and begin life or what is left of it, afresh. With the prime witness out of the way, Inspector Sharma infers that the enemy will relax and he will have a better chance of netting the big fish. In direct ratio, Gauri's case is losing importance for him.

Ranjit and I are at our wit's end and plead with him to grant us a fifteen-day reprieve; if by that time we fail to elicit further information from Abdul, we promise to withdraw from the case. He agrees, but makes it clear that there will be no sixteenth day.

After much discussion, we decide to go back to the doctors, one of them, a young psychiatrist, in particular, seems to be more innovative than the others. He is very straightforward and asks us bluntly what kind of information we want, how far we wish Abdul to go back, why we are interested and what our purpose is. He makes it very clear to us that if we want his help, we will have to be completely frank with him. So Ranjit and I spin him a story based on half-truths that maintains privacy, yet is tantalising enough to capture his interest. Surprisingly however, he has heard of the Natyashala and its famous Prima Donna, and when he sees the photograph he is completely hooked! He takes it away with him to study it and devise a plan of action.

Two days later, I am just preparing to crawl into bed, dog-tired and world weary, when I find my mobile blinking furiously at me. The message shows a lion and a leopard, hand in hand, gazing longingly at a lone gazelle. Translated, it means that Ranjit and the doctor are onto a good thing and need to talk to me urgently. I realise that he is trying to cheer me up, but I am too dispirited. My grandmother's obvious elation at our failure has not been easy to bear, and I don't have the heart to devise a witty reply. So I merely leave a message for Ranjit telling him to set up a meeting in the doctor's chamber at four in the afternoon, the next day.

It is obvious that the doctor is really excited, and the first question he asks me the following day is, 'What kind of songs did Gauri enjoy and sing?'

Quite taken aback, I enquire whether he means privately or professionally, and quick as a striking hamadryad he asks how I know about her personal preferences! I have no intention of showing the diaries to him, and prevaricate smoothly saying, 'I have heard people say that Tagore was her favourite.'

He accepts, shrugs and says, 'It figures that she was performing when he was at the height of his popularity.'

'And before his copyright with Viswa Bharati ran out!' I add.

'So, if we use music as an aid to memory, it will have to be authentic, is that what you're saying?' he looks at me quizzically.

This is the first inkling I have of the use he intends to put music to, but I just nod knowingly and wait for him to continue. He turns to Ranjit and says, 'I have a plan; it is rather unorthodox and may or may not work. Do you want to hear about it?'

Ranjit says, 'You gave me an outline and I called Priti because I thought it sounded promising. Will you please let us have the complete details?'

It seems what he has in mind is a combination of hypnosis and a recreation of the ambience and situation that are reminiscent of the past. He will induce in Abdul a state of semi-hypnosis and place him in a situation which will take him back to his time with Gauri. This perhaps will make him more receptive to external stimulus and so enable him to respond to questions easily and independently.

I am a little doubtful; somehow it sounds melodramatic and unreal to me. Such tricks seem to succeed in movies and bestsellers, but in real life? So I say, rather hesitantly, 'Are you sure it will work? What if this experiment sets him further back?'

The doctor faces both of us squarely and says, 'Do you have a choice? In any case there is little likelihood that his condition will improve in the next few days, and after that you will lose touch with him permanently. I think you have to take a decision now.'

He sounds distinctly nettled. But before I can speak, Ranjit makes up my mind for me. 'We will go ahead,' he says confidently, 'for this is the only course of action that promises success. We are grateful to you Sir, for all the thought and effort you have expended on this project. I personally think your idea is quite ingenious.'

His words sound like flattery to me, but the doctor looks much more cheerful, and I realise that he is really going out on a limb to assist us. If this venture succeeds, it will be an astounding success for him professionally, but this can also turn out to be a flop and make a laughing-stock of him amongst his colleagues. Not for the first time do I bow to Ranjit's superior wisdom and feel grateful and humble.

After a detailed discussion of many hours, the modus operandi is worked out and the die is cast. It is planned that we will go into action on Saturday evening, when we all have time to spare, for the doctor says that the process can take hours or may even yield results within minutes!

I have tried to set down below a minute by minute, word for word account of the evening's events and conversation, and I do not think I have made too many mistakes, for even today I only have to close my eyes and think, and the entire sequence passes before me like a montage, clear in every detail.

The room is in semi-darkness; the only source of illumination is a lamp suspended from the ceiling casting a pool of light—umbra and penumbra—on a polished circular table. In the corner is a CD player which I must operate on cue, but I can hardly be seen; Ranjit sits in the other corner, still as a statue; Abdul leans back in an armchair, expectant, yet relaxed; at the opposite end of the circular table sits the doctor in an upright chair hands on knees, conversing easily with him.

Gradually, the doctor's voice becomes slow and monotonous, takes on the sing-song quality of a chant and we hear him saying, 'Abdul, you think you are asleep, but actually you can hear and understand what I am saying to you. This is true and you know it. This is true and you know it. This is...'

After about fifteen repetitions, I can see Abdul breathing easily and regularly like a man peacefully asleep, but his eyes are open and there is a half-smile on his lips that I have never noticed before.

Suddenly, the doctor's voice changes and he asks more decisively and authoritatively, 'Abdul, can you hear me?'

'Yes.'

'Can you understand what I am saying?'

'Yes.'

'I am taking you on a journey to your boyhood, taking you back, b-a-c-k, b-a-c-k-, b—a—c—k--; can you remember what happened then?'

'Yes.'

'You are about eighteen years old and you work as a dresser for the Natyashala, right?'

'Yes.'

'Who is kindest to you in this place?'

'Ma.'

'You mean Gauri Sikdar?'

'Yes.'

'How does she help you?'

'With food, money, clothes...'

The doctor intervenes asking, 'Do the other people in the institution like her?'

'Yes, but some people are jealous of her...'

Though Abdul cannot complete the sentence, the doctor continues insisting, 'How do you know this?'

'Because they tell lies about her.'

'What kind of lies?'

'That she is a drunkard!'

Ranjit and I look at each other anxiously. This point, rather inconsistent, has troubled us all along.

'And is she?' asks the doctor.

'No, of course not!' Adbul replies in vehement protest.

'But it is true, that liquor is always kept in her room?' asks the doctor.

'Yes, true, but it is for her *puja*, not for her own consumption. People will say anything to create a sensation!'

'*Puja*? This is a new angle!' the doctor comments sarcastically.

'And one that very few people know about. She had a guru, a tantric. He taught her to pray with skulls and liquor.'

'How did this work?'

'She had four skulls at four corners of her prayer-mat and one in front,' Abdul starts describing.

'And?'

'She poured liquor into their gaping mouths and they drank greedily.'

'And then?'

'They do whatever *she* told them to do.'

'The skulls?' asks the doctor extremely curious.

Abdul retorts saying, 'You are really ignorant; not the skulls but their spirits, whom her guru controlled absolutely.'

'And you, a Muslim, actually believed this?'

A bit irritated at the doctor, Abdul counter questions him, 'Would you have me deny the evidence of my own experiences?'

As a Muslim, we realise that Abdul is mystified about this aspect, but goes along strongly with this practice due to his unshakable faith and belief in his Ma.

The doctor quickly reverts to his earlier question and asks, 'Who were her other enemies?'

'I don't know, people outside the Natyashala.'

'What was the cause of their enmity?'

'Ma knew a lot of things about a lot of people, and they were afraid that she might speak out…'

The doctor interrupts Abdul and asks, 'How long did you work in the Natyashala?'

'For about ten years.'

'Why did you leave?'

'Ma asked me to go away.'

'Why? Was she displeased with you for some reason?'

'Not at all! She sent me away because she trusted me!' There is a touch of genuine indignation in his voice.

'That does not make sense!'

Abdul evidently upset at the doctor's remark replies, 'Yes, it does. She wanted me to take away some precious items and keep them safe for her. There were not many people she could trust, and her enemies were very powerful.'

'Why you? She could have gone to the police!'

'Please don't make me laugh! The police? It would have been easier to hand them over to her enemies!'

A lot of pieces of the jigsaw now begin to fall into place for Ranjit and me with the mention of the police and their negative attitude.

Still persisting to squeeze out more information, the doctor asks, 'And so she decided to trust you?'

'She gave me this box full of her writings, and told me to take them away to my village.'

'And is this the box you brought with you to your brother's house?' asks the doctor holding the box in front of Abdul.

'Y-e-s.'

'Are you sure?'

Abdul re-confirms.

'And was this box taken away by the robbers?'

'Yes.'

'Did you get a look at the man who shot you?'

'No.'

'How come?'

'Because it was a woman who shot me!'

Taken aback with the answer, the doctor asks, 'A woman? But did you not catch a glimpse of her face?'

'How could I? She wore a *burkha*!'

'So, now then do we have any way of laying our hands on these writings?'

'No, you don't; they are gone, lost forever!'

Abdul stirs uneasily, as though trying to break out of the trance he is in, but the doctor speaks to him in a soothing tone and he gradually relaxes and leans back in the chair.

The doctor then raises his hand in a pre-arranged signal and I press the 'play' button on the CD player. Strains of Tagore's song, the one I had encountered in my dream and in Gauri's diaries, fill the air:

*When my life is lost in aridity,*
*Come to me as a stream of compassion,*
*My Lord…*

Abdul shivers, his eyes widen, whether in fear or anticipation, I do not know, but he presses his hands together as though in the grip of some strong emotion.

The doctor picks up the thread smoothly as though there has been no interruption and says, 'Abdul, can you hear what I hear?'

'Yes, a song.'

'Have you heard it before?'

'Many times.'

'When?'

'A long time ago.'

'Did someone dear to you sing this song?'

'Very dear.'

'Who was the person?'

'Ma, of course; it was her favourite song.'

'Abdul, would you like to meet Ma again? In person?'

'Yes, but it is not possible.'

'Why?'

'Because she is dead and her ashes are scattered.'

'How do you know this? You were not in the vicinity when she died, were you?'

'Oh yes I was, but no one knew because I was in disguise.' There is amusement in his voice.

'How did you disguise yourself?'

'As a woman, naturally, that way no one would suspect me. Remember, I was a dresser by profession? I followed the cortege all the way to the crematorium and waited till her body was reduced to ashes; it did not take long.'

'And then?'

'The priest collected the handful of bone-dust and the navel, where life begins and ends, and which never burns away, and was moving to the river's edge when the *sanyasi* appeared on the scene.'

I almost fall off my chair in excitement, but the doctor raises his hand in caution and I subside, trying to hold myself in check. Ranjit raises his hand in a thumbs-up sign and I can sense his elation even at a distance.

The doctor continues, 'Then what did he do?'

'He took the earthen container with the ashes, opened the lid and scattered the contents on the waters of the river chanting mantras all the time. When the last speck was gone he dipped the container in the river, filled it with water and holding it with both hands, poured the water back into the river, repeating the phrase "I set you free" several times. Then he flung the pot as far as he was able into the river, turned on his heel and walked away without looking back once. By the time the mourners had realised what had happened, he had disappeared from the vicinity.'

'And then?'

'There was a police enquiry, but they never traced the criminal. I don't think they tried too hard either.'

'Why do you say that?'

'The people involved had too much power! They hushed up the case.'

'Have you any idea who these people are?'

'The same people who tried to kill me. They wanted the documents then and they are still prepared to take life to procure them, the bastards!'

I can sense that the doctor is slightly taken aback by this uncharacteristic violence, but he continues smoothly, 'Then why don't you tell us where they are? We will retrieve them for you and keep them in a safe place for your safety.'

Quick as a striking snake, there is the immediate rejoinder, 'Why should I trust you? How do I know that you are not one of them?'

After that Abdul goes into deep sleep, and it is evident that he is exhausted and will sleep through the night. We decide that we will meet the next day after he wakes up to devise the next step of our strategy.

~

On the way home in the car Ranjit says, 'Priti, we will have to find some way of convincing this man that his Ma wants him to tell us where the papers are! The taboo is so etched into his mind that no normal persuasion will work.'

'But how?' I counter worriedly. 'We have no way of knowing what will make him tick, literally, for we hardly know him, and it is quite evident that he does not trust us. In any case why should he? His association with us has hardly been congenial for him.'

'I realise the truth of what you say, Priti, but God has given us brains to surmount problems and I'm afraid you are not using them at the moment!'

Ranjit makes gentle fun of me as usual, but suddenly it makes me unaccountably angry. Perhaps the strain is getting to me finally? I burst into uncontrollable tears. Ranjit tries to soothe me by apologising profusely, but I just cannot stop. The pent-up disappointment of all these months is ultimately taking its toll and the sobs tear through me with a force over which I have no control. Finally, Ranjit brings the car to a halt, takes me in his arms and strokes my hair with his capable hands till I begin to get a grip on myself. Wordlessly he hands me his clean handkerchief and after I blow my nose violently a couple of times, I feel distinctly better. When I finally sit up and pay attention, he outlines a plan of such simple brilliance that I am left gasping.

We explain the plan to the doctor the following day. He too is very enthusiastic and thinks that the chance of success is high, and accordingly, we congregate in the same room two evenings later.

Abdul is in a less cooperative mood today and wonders aloud how the exercise is going to help any of us. However, he follows instructions as before, and soon drifts off into peaceful slumber in spite of his initial resistance. The opening salvo from the doctor is fiercer this time. It is evident that he is trying to disorient his patient so that he will have little opportunity to build up his defences.

'I think you were very disloyal to your Ma, Abdul. You should not have left her in the lurch and run away like a coward!'

'I left her in the lurch? How dare you suggest something so monstrous? I would have laid down my life for her! Surely you, who pretend to know so much, realise that!' replies Abdul furiously.

The doctor smiles broadly and lets fly again, 'If you were as loyal as you claim, how come you were not around to protect her when she was attacked?'

'Oh! How many times do I have to explain to you that Ma herself told me to leave with the documents? To her they were more important than her own life! I couldn't disobey her; it was unthinkable. You are too stupid to be able to understand my feelings about her.'

'But you failed her anyway, for you do not know where they are, and nobody can find them now when needed. I think she put her trust in the wrong person after all.'

Abdul's voice rises to a wail. 'I do know where they are but I cannot tell you, that's all. Will you please stop badgering me?'

The doctor holds up his hand to forestall a reaction from us that might interfere with the session and asks very deliberately, 'Would you tell us if Ma asked you to do so?'

'But how can she? No one can return from the dead.'

'Supposing we could call her back and *she* commanded you to tell us?'

'Only *one* person can make her return, but you cannot find him; he does not come unless he thinks it is necessary.'

'And that person is…?'

'The *sanyasi* of course! If you have not understood that you have grasped nothing.'

'Would you recognise the *sanyasi*'s voice if you heard it?'

The doctor is taking a huge risk and I am on tenterhooks for the success of our entire plan depends on the answer to this question.

Abdul sighs tremulously and says with hesitation, 'I don't think so. You see, he never spoke to me directly.'

Ranjit and I release our pent-up breath very slowly indeed.

'But would you recognise Ma if you saw her again?'

Abdul laughs contemptuously and asks, 'And, wouldn't you recognise your own mother if you happened to meet her now?'

The doctor's voice when he speaks again sounds very different. It has a sonorous, far-away quality as though travelling over a long distance. 'A-b-dul, I will now request the *sanyasi* to call Ma into this room. She will come and speak to you. Will you be able to bear that? Will you be afraid?'

'You cannot do such a thing! You are merely giving me false hopes to get what you want out of me. I know all your tricks!'

'Why would I trick you Abdul, what would I gain?'

'The papers of course, I know how valuable they are!' Abdul replies promptly.

We seem to have reached an impasse. The doctor looks at us as though for guidance. I look at Ranjit who gets up, moves to his side and whispers in his ear. Then the doctor moves away quietly and Ranjit takes his place. He imitates the doctor's sing-song, chanting tone in a much deeper voice.

'Gauri, please come into this roo-m…ro-o-m…r-o-o-m. Please, if you want your name na-me...n-a-me cleared, come, c-ome, now,…now,…now… .'

A shiver seems to go through Abdul and he peers around expectantly in spite of his scepticism. I press the play button on the player and another song by Tagore, oft-repeated in the diaries, floats in gently and sets the air vibrating in the room.

*O merciful Lord, stand before my eyes,*
*My heart craves your presence;*
*This earth is wide-eyed in its desire to behold you,*
*Flood it with sweetness,*
*In the vast, arid spaces of its domain*
*Arrive in a veil of verdure—O Lord.*

Abdul smiles for the first time and shakes his head appreciatively. He obviously wants the song to continue:

*Over all that distracts vision from you,*
*Across this entire world,*
*Filling and permeating my life,*
*Appear, where my thirsting soul awaits your presence eternally,*
*Alone and awake,*
*My Lord…*

The song continues, melodious and rhythmic; Ranjit scatters the white, sweet-smelling jasmine flowers he has been storing in a bag, for these are the flowers Gauri always wore in her hair. As the room fills with fragrance, Abdul tries to sit up but the doctor pushes him back to his reclining position. Then I get up and move slowly towards Abdul. Unaccountably, the thought that comes into my mind is: what would my grandmother say if she saw me now? For, clad in a traditional dancer's costume, with my plait entwined in *gajra*s, with heavy jewellery and bells around my ankles, I could easily be taken for a professional dancer. The judicious make-up applied by a theatre dresser makes my eyes appear enlarged, my nose more aquiline and my lips filled out. The greyed hair and discreet lines on my face make me look aged and dignified. I know that on stage I could easily pass muster, but I wonder if I could also get past Abdul?

Ranjit continues in his new persona.

'Abdul you are waking up…up…now… now…waking… waking…waking…you will slowly open your eye-s…e-y-e-s… e-y-e-s and see…see … see… .'

He moves away and I am now standing right in front of Abdul, rehearsing the lines we have put together so carefully. 'Will there be an opportunity to speak?' I wonder. Abdul opens his eyes, his gaze quite unfocussed.

Before he can get his bearings, I move in and say, 'Abdul look at me, look into my face and see if you can recognise me; you have not forgotten me surely? Abdul…Abdul, please say you have not put me out of your mind! You can't! It will break my heart if you do, for there is no one in this whole wide world who cares one bit for me or wants to see me! Abdul please, I beg of you on my bended knees, call out to your Ma once, only once. I promise you after this one venture, I will return to my shady abode far away, and not trouble you ever again!'

I am now kneeling before him in abject supplication, and suddenly I am pretending no longer; I am not pleading for Gauri, but as Gauri for my own deliverance. The unquiet wanderer who has sought so many avenues of communication and failed, has found a forum at last.

As though on cue, Abdul stretches out his hands, holds mine in a firm grasp and says, 'Ma, you must not kneel before your son; I have sinned enough without this last sin on my conscience. Please tell me what you want and it shall be done, as always.'

To my consternation, I find that tears are streaming down my face and that I have forgotten the moving speech I had prepared so carefully. So I simply whisper, 'Tell me where my papers are so that the ill fame that has dogged my footsteps in life and death may be obliterated once and for all, and I can go free.'

Abdul says, 'They have been trying for weeks to find out the whereabouts of this box, but I have not broken the trust you had in me. But now that you are here, tell me what can I do to help you?'

'You can tell Priti, she will know how to help me.'

'Do you trust her, completely?'

'Yes, completely.'

'Then call her into this room and I will tell her in your presence. You will then know that I have discharged my duty to the best of my conscience and she will absolve me of this responsibility, and I too, will have peace at last.'

His voice is emphatic in its command and it is clear that he will not agree to any other arrangement. Totally nonplussed, I look around for help but for once, Ranjit's resourcefulness seems to fail him and he has no solution to offer. The doctor too, looks crestfallen at the prospect of success slipping out of his grasp at the eleventh hour. Total silence reigns in the room for a few seconds, and then my own voice is heard clearly, but without my volition.

'Abdul, how absurd you are! Don't know that a disembodied soul cannot appear before mortal eyes in palpable form?'

The laughter in my voice is so genuine that Abdul smiles in spite of the tension under which he is labouring, and says lightly, 'Enlighten me then; tell me how you are standing before me?'

'I am using Priti's body, naturally; she is the only direct descendent I have who wants to clear my name. She has been trying for months and has brought us to this situation. She is doing this because my only son entrusted her with this mission. He wanted her to succeed where he had failed. It takes a woman's determination and courage, Abdul, to persist in the face of determined conspiracy to get at the truth. Don't you know as well as *I* do? Now in the name of God do your duty.'

And obediently, like a child responding to his mother, Abdul tells us where the papers are!

# 4

Three days later, a strange assortment of people find themselves on a train bound for the village of Manasabari. in the 24 Parganas, in which the temple is situated. There is Inspector Sharma with a couple of his men, Abdul and his grand-niece Sameen, Ranjit and I on the face of it, but we are aware that there are more people in the compartment whom we do not know, who are supposed to protect us in case of trouble. Their role is to be inconspicuous and they play their part to perfection, but it is comforting to be cognizant of their existence. In addition, I have the feeling that we are under surveillance from another quarter—that a group of people is travelling with us but whose members keep changing. So we cannot pinpoint a single person who is constantly present. Ranjit thinks I am imagining things, but to my surprise, Inspector Sharma takes me seriously and says it is entirely possible that a last minute coup is on the cards.

He says, 'It is obvious that the stakes are high or this business would not have gone on so long, and it would be unrealistic to expect that they will give up without a final struggle.'

I look triumphantly at Ranjit, but the uneasy feeling in the pit of my stomach refuses to go away.

The journey takes about an hour and when we disembark, it is almost eleven in the morning. To our surprise, we find that a cinema crew is waiting for us on the platform. It seems that a shoot will soon be in progress and that we are all expected to play a part! This is in response to the appeal we had put in the papers some months previously.

Today we are mainly doing local colour in a village. After a round of tea in the railway canteen, we set off on our mission. The shoot has naturally created a stir and it seems as though half the village is trailing behind us as we get under way. We stop at various scenic spots—by a large pond, one end of which is purple with flowering water hyacinth, a gnarled banyan tree with twisted buttress roots, a cottage with a courtyard full of children, a group of young women, brightly clad, carrying water urns on their hips. As we progress, the sun rises higher in the sky, but a cool breeze makes the walk pleasant and the various sights provide welcome distraction from our apprehensions. We laugh, converse, exchange pleasantries, drink more cups of sweet tea, and for a few moments, manage to put the serious intent of this trip out of our minds. But when I notice how careful Inspector Sharma is to keep Abdul at the centre of the group and how vigilant he and his men are, their hands never far from their holsters, my fears return in a rush and it seems, at least to me, that we are as far away from success as ever.

At one o'clock we stop for a break and packed lunches appear as do brightly coloured mats for us to sit on. Even though the picnic atmosphere continues, there is a tautness of expectation in Inspector Sharma's bodylines that belies his apparent joviality, and I begin to realise that we are nearing our destination. I look enquiringly at Ranjit, but he looks steadfastly away and refuses to respond.

By the time we resume our journey, the sun is well past the meridian, the novelty of the event is wearing off and the crowd begins to fall away in ones and twos. We move faster now, and

Abdul is definitely more animated as though old memories are beginning to stir. It becomes clear that we are following his lead and whenever he falters, Inspector Sharma takes his elbow, not only to reassure him but also to make his indecision less apparent. Abdul takes heart and continues on his way, but with each attempt his physical fatigue becomes more evident and I begin to fear that we might have to call off the quest after all. We walk another quarter of a mile and suddenly Abdul stops dead in his tracks; he rotates and moves his head in a gesture reminiscent of a dog sniffing the air, then takes a ninety-degree-turn and points confidently in a north-westerly direction, smiles delightedly and says, 'The *mogra* is in bloom; how Ma loved the fragrance!'

'So what does it indicate?' asks Inspector Sharma with a touch of impatience.

'That we have arrived at our destination, naturally! Can you see that old temple ahead of you? It used to be the haunt of an old seer who was very fond of Ma. When she left the box in my custody, she instructed me to take some of the more important documents to the old man. She said he would know a safe place to hide it. He did, and told me where to look for it if I ever needed to… .'

His voice trails off so fearfully that we turn to find him looking absolutely terrified. At that moment, a shot rings out and Abdul falls to the ground like an axed tree. Quick as lightning, Inspector Sharma turns and fires in one fluid movement bringing the man with the gun down, although he is more than fifteen yards away trying to shelter behind a tree. Blood spurts out in a dark, red fountain from the man's thigh, but I can only look at Abdul. My heart turns into a lump of lead in my bosom; having reached so close we have lost it all! Throwing caution to the winds I run to him, lean over him and implore him to speak to me.

'Abdul, please tell me that you are alive, speak to me, I beg of you; I can't lose you now, not after all your hard work and the trouble you have taken!'

Weeping hysterically, I cling to him in a paroxysm of agony and close my eyes. When I feel him stirring under my body, I will myself not to look, convinced that my imagination is playing tricks on my feeble mind.

It is Ranjit who pulls me to my feet saying, 'Give poor Abdul a break Priti, you are smothering him!'

When I finally have the courage to look, Abdul is sitting up and saying, 'Next to the temple, in the north-west, is an old disused well; the water dried out many years ago and it was abandoned; only the seer knew that there is a door at the bottom of this well that leads to the basement of the temple, and that there is no other entrance to the basement. If nothing untoward has happened, that is where the box containing the papers will be now, quite safe, I'm sure.'

I am still staring at him in amazement, when Ranjit leans close and whispers in my ear, 'Ever heard of bullet-proof jackets, Priti?'

The wounded man is taken into custody, placed on a ground sheet. Inspector Sharma examines his wound and concludes that the bone has not been touched. He dresses the wound with easy expertise. An attempt is then made to question him, but he is in great pain and cannot reply coherently. Inspector Sharma pumps him full of painkillers, and gradually investigations reveal that he is a hired, small-time assassin, commissioned by a man who had given him five thousand rupees in advance and promised him another ten on successfully executing the task. He had been told to shoot from a tree but that had not proved feasible. It is apparent that he is merely a cog in the wheel and has no knowledge that might prove of value to us. All this takes us away from the precious time at our disposal. However, the word of the shooting spreads fast. So by the time Inspector Sharma completes his interrogation and we near the temple, we are hardly surprised to find a delegation of men moving purposefully towards us from the village.

The edifice of the temple has an abandoned look. The tall, gnarled trees that surround it and the thick undergrowth clambering into it, impart a quality of impregnability, almost as though it were the castle of the legendary 'Sleeping Beauty'. The analogy seems particularly apt, and when Abdul warns us about snakes and scorpions, the picture is complete. Abdul advises that we wait till the morrow, but fortunately for me, Inspector Sharma is as eager as I am to get to the bottom of the matter, and instructs his men to clear the undergrowth around the well.

Before they can move however, a man of the delegation who claims to be the head of the village, the *sarpanch,* steps forward and says, 'I am Shanker, Sir. I advise you not to enter the temple without carrying out the required rituals, for if you do, I can assure you that you will neither find what you are looking for nor come out without mishap.'

He sounds so ominous that Inspector Sharma stops in his tracks and looks enquiringly at us.

I am about to speak when Ranjit breaks in decisively, 'I think Shanker is right, Sir. We should not precipitate or do anything to hurt the susceptibilities of the village folk. Why don't we wait till tomorrow?'

I am terribly irritated at Ranjit's proposal. If looks could kill Ranjit would have died on the spot, but as usual, Inspector Sharma defers to his 'good sense' and he gets his way. Arrangements are made though for a patrol to maintain a night-long vigil. A jeep is called for to drop us to the nearest circuit house. I am very uncomfortable and lean out of the vehicle as long as I can to keep the spot in sight, but finally it vanishes round a bend in the road and I am left desolate with the thought that this entire move is part of a plan to frustrate our attempt on the morrow.

The circuit house has no electricity; magnesium lamps emitting harsh glaring light that distort more than they clarify provide illumination. The architecture is of the time-honoured old British style, pretty much like a barrack, the living, sitting and dining rooms lying adjacent to a verandah that stretches along the entire building in the front. Bathrooms, kitchen and pantry that require running water are at the rear separated from the main rooms by a passage or corridor and verging on a kitchen garden of sorts.

As the only female members on the trip, Sameen and I share a room and we are both glad of each other's company. I find that she shares my apprehensions that some attempt will be made to get at the documents in spite of the police cordon, for she has been in their clutches and knows how ruthless they can be. She silently bares her arms and I am horrified to see deep gashes which have barely healed. 'The price of silence,' she says quietly. I realise, with a pang of guilt, that we have been so busy with our own plans that we have barely questioned her about her ordeal. She still refuses to speak about it, and only the naked terror in her eyes indicates the intensity of the suffering she has been through. Dinner in the dining room is a simple affair of mutton curry and rice, but surprisingly well cooked, and we fall for it suddenly realising that we are quite famished.

The man serving us, Ganesh, the caretaker, who doubles as cook and general dogsbody, is a ferret-faced fellow with sharp eyes. He has a helper who is obviously intimidated by him and runs to do his bidding with a degree of alacrity, which would be amusing if the situation were less forbidding. The constant eye contact indicates that messages are being relayed at speed between the two men but their purpose remains unclear, and my fears intensify till my throat feels dry and constricted. Fortunately, both Ranjit and the Inspector Sharma take note of this as well, and their eyes never leave the faces of these two men.

This obviously adds to their discomfiture and the helper appears nervous enough to bolt; it is only Ganesh's power over him that holds him to his post. He serves the food while Ganesh supervises, and all goes well till the sweets arrive after dinner along with the sherbet. Ganesh picks up the salver of sweets and brings them to us by turns and he directs his man to serve the drink carefully. The sherbet is in a jug and the man pours it into five glasses with great care.

When he picks up the tray to bring the glasses to us, Ganesh says with quiet emphasis, 'Be sure to give Mr Abdul the tallest glass. He looks very tired.'

Ranjit quickly intervenes and says, 'No, give me the tallest glass, I am very thirsty.'

Panic stricken, the man looks at Ganesh for directions and the glasses begin to rattle audibly on the tray. Ganesh swears viciously at him and crash! The tray with all five glasses falls to the floor from his nerveless hands. Ganesh, his face distorted with rage, fetches him a cuff on the side of his head that sends him sprawling to the floor and the prompt intervention of Inspector Sharma compels him to stop kicking his victim ruthlessly in the groin. While Ganesh and

Inspector Sharma struggle, the helper picks himself up and runs out of the room into the night. Ganesh is taken into custody, but I feel we have lost the better part of the bargain, for it would have been easier to make the other man talk.

While we have been otherwise engaged, a cat with her two kittens has lapped up much of the sherbet on the floor and is now sitting back licking her whiskers. She looks at me and meows gently. I bend down to scratch her head and she rubs her body against my leg, purring all the while. Sameen, meanwhile, has picked up one of the kittens, placed it on her lap and is playing with it. The kitten however is very lethargic and refuses to respond, and before long is fast asleep on her lap. Gradually, the mother cat too begins to lose energy, moves away and attempts to crawl onto the sofa which appears to be her regular place, but cannot quite make it. Claws embedded in the fabric, she seems to lack the strength to pull herself up. Before I can help her, she falls to the ground with a thud and begins to snore loudly. When I pick her up and put her on the sofa in the dining room, she does not stir. The third member of the family is discovered in a semi-comatose condition under an occasional table. The significance of this series of events is completely clear to all concerned, although the purpose is not.

Sameen and I lie in bed and make a determined attempt to sleep, but exhausted as I am, I cannot get the tension out my limbs or relax. I stare into the darkness trying to trace the flights of fireflies between the murmuring fronds of the coconut tree outside the window, listen to cricket chirping in the bushes and calm myself down, but my fears and apprehensions only mount steadily. Gradually, Sameen's breathing becomes more regular, and though I feel horribly envious and resentful, I am no closer to sleep than before. There is a glass of water on the table, but to reach it I have to get out of the bed. So I decide to check on the cat as well, and quietly open the door to step into the dark passage beyond. I don't know where the lanterns are, but have a hazy notion of the topography of the house. Realising that my torch is running a little low on power, I try to reverse the path I had traversed to my room from memory. As I come to the dining room where we had eaten the last memorable meal, I feel more confident and play the torch along the walls to locate the lantern last seen swinging on a hook. As I turn in a semi-circle I face the verandah that lies on the outer edge, where I can see the glowing ends of two cigarettes moving to the rhythm of what appears to be an animated conversation. I stop dead in my tracks, switch off my torch, and try to decide what my next move should be. I can raise an alarm, but this premature move could do more harm than good. I can try and reach Ranjit, but does he want to be reached? All evening he has been distant and secretive, and I have no way of knowing what his intentions are; he only behaves like this when he wants to keep me out of a project he considers unsuitable.

Suddenly, the warning bells go off with a jangle in my mind. It occurs to me that Ranjit and Inspector Sharma must have made a plan for the night in which they do not wish me to participate! So I return to my room, don clothing and footwear suitable for the rough terrain, put papers and torch in a stout purse and go back to the dining room. The pinpoints of light emitted by the glowing ends of cigarettes are still in view, so it is obvious they are chain-smoking; a sure sign that the tension is building to a crescendo. I sit down next to the cat, still snoring, and wait for the men to make the first move.

Almost ten minutes later, they throw away their last smokes and rise from their chairs; four men join them along with Abdul, and they start walking towards the jeep. I move quickly but noiselessly out of the room, fall in behind them and reach the vehicle without their noticing.

Inspector Sharma, it appears, will drive the vehicle himself, so he climbs into the driver's seat; Ranjit sits beside him, and the rest of the men prepare to get into the jeep with Abdul when I put my hand on his shoulder.

He quickly stifles the exclamation that rises to his lips and whispers in my ear, 'Want to come with us?'

When I nod wordlessly, he just holds my hand and pulls me in after him. The other constables look at each other, confer dubiously in whispers, but follow suit. The door is closed and the vehicle lurches into motion. The partition between the front and back seats is closed so I cannot hear the conversation in progress, but the solemn faces of the men travelling with me is indication enough of the dangers of the mission.

We traverse about two miles in silence. The men peer into the darkness around them to gauge the distance we still have to cover, and speak quietly to each other. Abdul puts his hand over mine and I find the gesture curiously reassuring, a reminder that we are the only people who care about Gauri at a personal level and that the fallout of the night's adventure will affect us more vitally than others, even Ranjit.

It is Abdul who first spots a procession winding its way towards the temple. They are visible because they are carrying flaming torches, what their purpose is or on whose side they may be, is purely a matter of conjecture. The jeep begins to slow down and I realise that Inspector Sharma is also trying to come to a decision about his next move. He takes a 180-degree turn and proceeds on his way, obviously planning to approach the temple from the rear. Abdul is clearly intimidated and moves closer to me; the men take out their revolvers to check on safety catches and magazines; the smell of fear is acrid in our noses and all our nerves are as taut as stretched wire. At the tail end of our journey, when the destination is in sight, what fresh complication awaits us? This frenzied question looms uppermost in our minds.

The vehicle slows down till we are practically crawling. A man steps into our path suddenly; I almost scream, but it appears that he is known to Inspector Sharma and has a message to convey. The man climbs onto the footboard and guides us into a narrow lane, almost a track, overhung with trees and bordered by bushes. The jeep has to mow down plants in its way to proceed and occasionally the man gets off to push aside larger obstacles. After travelling at a snail's pace for half an hour, we can finally see the temple, about a hundred yards away. The man dismounts and indicates that we should do the same. I look questioningly at Abdul, for concealment is no longer possible; in reply, he takes me by the hand and we disembark together. Ranjit's face on seeing me is a study in amazement, consternation and anger; the changing expressions chase each other across his visage like shadows and sunlight on a dappled field and the whole effect is rendered more dramatic in the light of dimmed torches.

He then steps forward, takes me fiercely by the shoulders, looks into my eyes and says, 'Will you never learn?'

When I shake my head, he looks helplessly at Inspector Sharma and asks, 'What shall we do with her?

To my surprise, Inspector Sharma smiles and says, 'Take her along with us, what else can we do? She loves cats, so maybe she has nine lives too! She has certainly survived so far. In any case, it is more dangerous to leave her behind at this stage when she can be taken hostage, than to take her with us. So come along young lady, and stay as close to me as possible.'

Ranjit is still hanging on to me for dear life, so I give his hand a reassuring squeeze, slip out of his grasp and sidle up to Inspector Sharma. The men, who are armed, form an outer ring and place Ranjit, Abdul and me in the centre. Inspector Sharma hands Ranjit a couple of grenades and instructs him to aim and throw as directed.

He slips a slim knife into Abdul's hand as per pre-planned strategy and says, 'Don't hesitate to use it if necessary.'

His grim tones brings home to us the danger we are in more effectively than the most flamboyant histrionics could have, and as we begin to inch forward, the thumping of my heart deafens my ears.

We keep within the shelter of the trees to avoid detection, but find that the ground around the temple has been cleared and that we have to traverse at least twenty yards without cover, to reach the edifice. There are, however, some large trees that provide vantage points, and Inspector Sharma tells two of his men to climb the trees that are about twenty-five feet apart, to provide covering fire. When they have taken up their positions, we walk quickly to two mango trees that have grown out of the same set of roots but away from each other, and which make an effective screen for us. We peer through the leaves and see that two torches have been stuck by the enemy forces in the ground near the door and one tied to a pillar to provide illumination. With the breeze, the flames are flaring high and burning low alternately, creating bizarre shadows and throwing into relief the human tableau on the steps of the temple. A lone man clad in saffron robes has his back to a closed door which obviously is the entry to the interior. There are four men standing on the steps desirous of access to whatever lies behind the door; that an altercation is in progress can be made out from their gestures, if not words. How long the man, however strong-willed, be able to hold out is anybody's guess.

As we watch, one man tries to move up to the seer, but retreats hastily in what appears to be abject terror, and the other men pull him back to a safer position, at the bottom of the steps. All of us are equally mystified, and finally, Inspector Sharma requests Ranjit to climb the tree for a better view and relay a message to us. He shins up the tree with surprising agility, leans out as far as he dares, and puts a pair of binoculars to his eyes. We peer up at him in acute anxiety for a minute or so, and then his sharp intake of breath is audible to us all, but intelligible to none. After what seems an interminable period, but is actually no more than a minute, Ranjit comes down and hisses one cryptic word at us, 'Cobras!'

It appears that the seer has a basket of snakes at his feet and is threatening to release them in case the men try to force an entry. He is actually holding one by the neck, and would have thrown it on the advancing man unless he had retreated so rapidly. This novel mode of self-defence causes Inspector Sharma to change his strategy, and after a whispered conclave, he and two of his men step into the open and call out to the enemy to surrender. In response, two of them whip out guns and warn us against advancing further, but it is clear that they do not have a plan of action ready, for they had not expected a two-pronged attack.

We seem to have reached an impasse; seconds lengthen into minutes, when suddenly the seer calls out to Inspector Sharma to approach him. He also bends down to replace the reptile he is holding in the basket at his feet, but before he can complete his task, a volley of gunfire rings out and he falls, blood fountaining from his chest. The basket is open, and the cobras, one after the other, climb out and slither towards the attackers. Without further ado the men turn to run, only to find armed men blocking their way. Like puppets all except one drop their guns and raise their hands above their heads. But before the man who tries to flee by trying to take a tangential route, has even taken five steps, something sings past my ears, and Abdul's knife, thrown with deadly accuracy, brings him to his knees.

While the police are putting handcuffs on the culprits, Abdul runs to the man he has injured and asks, 'Why Bihari, why? To the best of my knowledge, she never did you harm! Then why?'

The name is one I have heard before and now I walk up to them and try to get a look at his face, which he keeps steadfastly averted till Abdul takes him by the hair and compels him to look up. Bihari, our loyal gardener cum security guard, who has been away 'on holiday' for the last six months, looks tearfully but defiantly at me without a word.

Inspector Sharma and Ranjit have, in the meanwhile, rushed to the seer, and when I join them, they are trying desperately to staunch the blood flowing from his wound, but their efforts appear to me futile, for the man is too old to survive this murderous onslaught. I fall to my knees beside him and place my hand on his forehead. With agonising slowness he opens his eyes, looks up at me and a beatific smile radiates his heavily wrinkled, but still handsome visage.

It is evident that he wants to convey an urgent message, so I take my ear as close as possible to his lips, and in a voice as frail as the rustle of dry leaves, he whispers, 'I have kept my promise. She will know that Shourjo did not betray her trust; now I can go in peace!'

His eyelids droop, and soon Inspector Sharma and Ranjit declare him dead. I cannot for the life of me understand why a terrible desolation fills my heart or explain to myself the reason for the sense of loss that permeates my being. Why do I feel that someone very precious has passed on, and that the opportunity of communication lost irrevocably is an event I will rue all my life? After all, I had never seen him before, then why this emotion? Why this sense of closeness, of spiritual oneness? Almost without volition I lay my head down on his chest and will his heart to beat again, but though the body feels very alive, there is no answering echo. I feel as though I am battering my head against a door that will never open again!

Finally, Ranjit compels me to rise and wipes away with his handkerchief the blood from my face; my hair is clotted with it, but strangely I feel no revulsion and just bundle it out of the way. Ranjit, who knows how finicky I am normally, raises his eyebrows quizzically, but says nothing. Bihari and the other men are taken away and we sit down on the steps wearily to plan the ultimate stage of our long and arduous quest. All the while, like a thudding hammer at the back of my head rises the question: who is Shourjo, and where does he fit in this puzzle? Are the seer and Shourjo one and the same person?

Bihari's presence has confirmed my suspicions but jolted me more than I care to admit even to myself, for it has linked the entire sequence of events indubitably with our household, particularly my grandmother, as he is her trusted flunkey of many years' standing. As a matter of fact, his father had come over with our family from Bangladesh, remained with us since, and now his son Bihari, a small boy at the time, lives with his wife and children in our servants' quarters. My parents, taking their cue from my grandmother, have trusted him implicitly and never questioned the fact that he is away from home months at a time because he has always provided a 'trustworthy' substitute. Now I find myself wondering about the nature and purpose of these 'absences'.

Inspector Sharma takes the lead. 'First things first; we must recover the box, go through the contents, then decide on a course of action. Does everyone agree?'

I am just about to nod my head reluctantly, when Ranjit breaks in with uncharacteristic vehemence and says, 'I don't agree at all. This entire business was initiated by Priti for purely personal reasons. I got drawn in because of my concern for her, and we turned to you when we stumbled on to matters too big for us to handle. But it still remains her primary concern and it should be up to her to decide how much she wants to tell us. I don't think we should invade her privacy.'

To my surprise, Abdul nods in emphatic agreement and says, 'There are secrets in that box that were never meant to be revealed to the world. Why else would Ma go to such lengths to maintain security? Why did Priti's grandfather trust no one else but her? There is some information in that box that only concern the family, and I agree with Ranjit that she be allowed a preview.'

I can see that Inspector Sharma is displeased at this exclusion, so I speak up. 'One night is all I need. Thereafter I'll place the matter before you, with complete trust in your discretion. But if there's an official embargo on this procedure, I will do as you advise.'

Inspector Sharma turns to us, squares his shoulders and says, 'I had better acquaint you with a few facts and figures about the status of this case, so that you realise what odds we are up against. As you are aware, I was initially warned off this case totally; then there was a change of attitude on the part of my superior officer, and I was told "to utilise the information at your disposal, *not* to help you, but to get to the manuscript". Under no circumstance, was I to allow you access to them, once they were found. Now where does that leave me? I can either accede to your request and jeopardise my career, or whisk the box away from you now, so that you will never see it again. I wish to goodness that I had never got involved in the first place!'

His distress is so genuine, that my heart goes out to him in spite of the crushing disappointment, and I am about to say something conciliatory, when Ranjit breaks in impassionedly, 'Look, Sir, you can't do this to us now, not after we have come so far together! You have to find a way around this impasse so that, to translate an Indian proverb, "the snake is killed but the stick is not broken". For instance, I could stage a fight with you that would lay you out, and Priti and Abdul could take a peek in the meanwhile; how is that for a plan?'

Inspector Sharma smiles in spite of the dilemma he is in and says, 'It is a very bad plan, particularly with all my men present as witnesses. No, we will have to think of something better. There is one man with us whom I can trust absolutely, and we will leave him on guard here and return to the circuit house, ostensibly to rest and wait for full daylight before we tackle the well and the snakes. This will give you an opportunity to double back and get to the documents on your own within a reprieve period of about four hours, for it is three in the morning now, and we will be back by eight, at the latest. It is not much of an opportunity, and I rate your chance of success at about twenty per cent; but it is the best I can think of.'

He turns away brusquely; obviously piqued at his own lack of independence, and walks briskly towards the jeep leaving us trailing disconsolately behind him.

Back at the circuit house, the three of us lock ourselves in Ranjit's room and look at each other helplessly. We don't even know whether we can locate the well in the dark, leave alone find the entry to the crypt. The memory of the snakes slithering all over the steps is too fresh in our minds to discount, and even Abdul clearly quails at the prospect of taking them on by torchlight. Exhausted and without hope, I cannot hold back the tears that have been pricking my eyes and they drop on Ranjit's hand as he holds my hands in his own. When he looks up, his own face is lined with fatigue, but he says quietly looking steadily into my eyes, 'This won't do Priti, we just have to find a way. We cannot accept defeat tamely having come so far! So wipe your eyes, put on your thinking cap and let us review the affairs of the evening to see what ideas we can come up with.'

Bit by bit, we go over the events of the past few hours till we come to the point when we first saw the seer holding the hostile crowd at bay, and I say, 'Can you remember his exact position? What was his stance? What precisely was he trying to achieve?'

Both the men look uncomprehendingly at me for a moment, and then with partial understanding dawning in his eyes, Abdul says, 'He had his back to the door. He was trying to prevent those men from entering the temple.'

'And why would he do that? Why would he want to protect the interior of the temple?'

I ask again, surprised at my own insistence, for I do not have the answers to this question myself.

Abdul says, 'Perhaps he did not want them to defile the temple? After all, they were an evil bunch.'

'No, it was something else; he had a stronger reason, though I don't know what it might have been.'

While Abdul and I go over the events repeatedly trying to find a clue, Ranjit does not say a word. He sits with his eyes closed, and apparently does not pay much attention to the interchange.

But presently he jumps up, claps me on the shoulder and says excitedly, 'Bravo, Priti, you have found the answer which has been staring at us in the face all the time, but which we have been too stupid to notice! He was trying to prevent entry because there must be another entrance to the crypt somewhere within the temple, probably cleverly camouflaged, but which might be found if intelligently searched for. If the holy man was prepared to give up his life to protect a secret, it could have been nothing less vital than this. And if this is true, we have all of three hours to locate the entrance, penetrate the crypt, find the relevant documents, read them and then decide on a future course of action! Every moment wasted now is irretrievable. We have to leave this minute.'

We obviously cannot use the official vehicle, but the security guard at the circuit house possesses a motorcycle, which we decide to borrow without permission, and as it has a sidecar, it will take all three of us comfortably. We raid supplies for two powerful torches, a set of spare batteries, a crowbar, candles and matches; also, a couple of knives, a coil of rope, and a rope ladder. Ranjit carries the gun and ammunition Inspector Sharma had given him and failed to take back, perhaps a deliberate oversight? At the last minute, Abdul goes back for a water bottle, a pair of scissors and a stout stick.

Ranjit walks the vehicle to the gate of the circuit house so that no one gets to know of our absence and takes the driver's seat. I climb on to the pillion and Abdul into the sidecar. With a low hum, the powerful motor comes to life and gradually we slide away into darkness. As I look back, I can clearly see a man's figure silhouetted against a lone, lit window that belongs to Inspector Sharma's room.

Ranjit only has his memory to guide him and carefully follows the landmarks he had noted on his way back. The road is little more than a track and every few yards he comes up against bifurcations that are thoroughly confusing.

But Abdul is a great help and saves him from taking wrong turns. 'Keep to the east,' he says. 'Don't you remember that mango tree you climbed? That is your guide, for there is only one such tree, two sections growing out of a common stock, in this village.'

Fortunately, it is a clear night, and although the moon is a mere crescent, the starlight enables us to see and recognise some of the cottages and trees we have seen on our earlier visit, and before long, Abdul exclaims, 'There is your tree and to the left of that you can make out the outlines of the temple.'

We slow down till the vehicle is cruising at the minimum speed that allows it to remain upright, and as we come within twenty yards of the edifice, a man with a gun steps into our path and signals us to stop. Heart in mouth, I see Ranjit slow down to a mere crawl while his hand strays towards his own weapon, when Abdul rises in his seat and whispers in his ear. At this Ranjit relaxes, pulls level with the man and stops, and I see what Abdul has noticed earlier—the man is none other than the policeman Inspector Sharma had appointed to guard the building. He has been waiting for us impatiently and tells us in furious whispers to 'get on with it' as we have only three hours to complete our task; for even if Inspector Sharma tries to give us more time, our enemies and their supporters will certainly make an effort to put a spanner in the works as early as possible.

The task in hand seems so difficult that for once even Ranjit's indomitable enthusiasm seems to desert him and he has no immediate plan of action to offer. As we climb the steps, the memory of the gallant old man desperately trying to hold an entire crowd at bay returns with a rush and underlines the hopelessness of our enterprise. Where people better equipped than us, in greater numbers and with all the time in the world have failed, how can we hope to succeed?

The temple itself is quite large; there is a huge verandah, which can accommodate a thousand devotees for prayer; in the centre is a door, the one which the seer had had his back against, which opens onto this verandah and now stands ajar; and beyond the door is a large room which apparently houses the main deity, Goddess Kali. There are other rooms adjacent to this on either side, which are locked, obviously no longer in use. There is an air of general dereliction and the offering of a few perfunctory flowers at the deity's feet indicates individual rather than organised and regular worship.

We turn to Abdul for information and he begins, 'In the days of my youth, when I visited this village to meet the seer and handover the box Ma gave me, this was a famous place of worship. The local *zamindar* patronised several priests who performed all the temple rituals regularly. People came from far off places to seek favours of the "mother", and returned later with rich gifts when their prayers had been answered. Then catastrophe struck about twenty years ago.

'On the night of the main *puja,* a new moon night, the buffalo, perfect in every respect and earmarked months ahead for sacrifice, could not be found and the substitute was declared highly unsatisfactory by the head priest, the man who died here today, and he refused to continue the rituals. Angry words were exchanged and the priest left, vowing never to return. The assistant completed the *puja,* but every man left the scene with a sense of dark foreboding in his heart.

'Two days after this the *zamindar* fell from his horse and broke his neck; within a week, his only son succumbed to a snake bite; then his son-in-law in faraway Calcutta died of typhoid. By this time, the womenfolk were hysterical with fear, and spent their entire time at the temple, desperately trying to propitiate the deity and clinging to the last scion of the family, a boy of two.

'That night there was a terrible storm and in the morning the child was discovered, lying face down in a pool of rainwater, dead. The entire village found itself in the grip of dementia, and people refused to come out of their cottages or look at the faces of the remaining "cursed" family members. Later in the day, a little girl who had ventured out in spite of dire warnings, came running to her mother screaming, "Blood, blood, blood!". All the women of the family had killed themselves by driving daggers into their hearts, in a final act of propitiation. After this the great house and temple were abandoned, but the terror took years to subside. In recent times, a devotee would occasionally leave a few flowers more out of fear than devotion, but after what happened tonight, I doubt that they will return. Only the seer was seen once in a while in the vicinity, but nobody had ever dared to speak to him or approach him.'

So intently do we listen to Abdul's narration that we fail to notice the passage of time, and when Ranjit looks at his watch, he finds it difficult to stifle the oath that rises to his lips; but he still has no idea, looks helplessly at me and says, 'Where shall we begin?'

I, in turn, look at Abdul and am surprised to find him smiling gently and encouragingly at me. 'Think hard,' he says, 'because Ma wants *you* to discover the truth and no one else. Pray to her and she will show you the light.'

Obediently, I close my eyes and try to concentrate. Gradually an image forms on my mental screen—a page of a history book I had read in grade seven. Mahmud of Ghazni, who had raided India seventeen times, had repeatedly visited the Somnath Temple in Gujarat, but failed to locate the legendary jewellery that bedecked the idol in peace time, till he had decided to move the great idol itself. Beneath the idol he found a yawning aperture filled with gold and precious stones. These he had removed immediately, for being a Muslim, he had no superstitious fear of the Hindu idol.

I recount the story to them and ask, 'Should we not look in the vicinity of the idol, for the entrance to the secret crypt?'

For the first time in our association, Ranjit says I am 'brilliant', but I refrain from telling him that the idea has been 'conveyed' to me, but this is neither the apt time nor place; besides, we have no idea as to how we should put my 'idea' into practice, and when we call out to the policeman and ask whether he will help us, he turns distinctly green at the suggestion, folds his hands and begs to be excused. He explains that only a priest can dare to touch the idol, for he alone knows the right rituals. Ranjit and I look at each other in utter confusion; whether it is an inherent taboo or whether it is the effect of Abdul's narrative, neither of us wishes to undertake the task. All our emancipation, our much vaunted 'secularism' is of no avail when we come face to face with the fear of the unknown.

Time is ticking away with every heartbeat; the sky seems to brighten in the east. It could be my imagination, but the birds do seem to stir the trees; and we still stare at each other, in the grip of a terrible inertia, unable to think, plan or act, when suddenly Abdul speaks, 'Ma always said that donning the saffron is only the outer manifestation of *sanyas*; that release from desire and fear, as well as freedom from the shackles of the senses had to be achieved before the spiritual threshold could be approached. She also said that any act undertaken in the spirit of true altruism is necessarily free of personal motivation and could never be wrong in the eyes of the Almighty. Now, I guess her Almighty is the same as mine, and He would confer the status of *sanyas* on me in this instance, for I would undertake *any* hardship to carry out her behest without counting the cost. So, I will move the idol.'

Without further ado or the slightest hesitation, he descends the steps, walks to the little reservoir in the courtyard of the temple, washes his hands and feet, comes up the steps, pushes back the doors on their creaking hinges and approaches the deity. We watch with bated breath while the policeman looks steadfastly away. I think he expects Abdul to be struck down by lightning the minute he touches the idol, in the manner so dear to Indian chroniclers. Even I close my eyes and cling to Ranjit's arm when Abdul puts out his hands on the deity. After a minute or two, I venture to look and find Abdul exploring the figure with the gentlest of fingers.

The deity is the traditional one, the Mother-Goddess standing over Shiva with a look of consternation on her face at having stepped on him, mingling with the sweetest smile at his acquiescence. As the spare frame of the Goddess is too svelte to conceal a device of any sort, he bends to the base and runs his hand over the recumbent frame of her consort. Made of finely chiselled black marble, it seems again too smooth to house a device, and I close my eyes again out of sheer fatigue and frustration.

Eons later, six minutes by the watch, Ranjit whispers in my ears, 'Look!'

I open my eyes to find the idol occupying a position to the right of its former stance and a yawning aperture in the floor where it had formerly stood. Abdul in anticipation of having disturbed the sanctity of the shrine prays profusely with the beads in his hands, while tears stream down his face!

On closer inspection, we discover an ingenious piece of machinery below the ground—a moving dais connected to a series of pulleys, which permits the idol to move in a 180-degree arc when a lever between the feet of the image is twisted in an anti-clockwise direction. Since the entire piece of machinery is made of solid brass, no rust has set in and the contraption moves with amazing ease. To one side of the aperture is a brass ladder, snaking its way into the darkness below. We decide to follow Abdul for he wants to go first. I will go down after him while Ranjit will bring up the rear. The policeman agrees to stand guard though rather reluctantly, and promises to warn us in case of trouble. We carry torches, knives, a crowbar, candles and a box of matches; Ranjit takes the gun and Abdul his trusty stick. At the last minute, I decide to take along the water bottle even though the men look quizzically at me.

Going downward is easy as the treads are solid, the balustrade strong, and in no time, we find ourselves in a fair-sized room without windows, rather reminiscent of a large coffin, but obviously fitted out for habitation for there is a bed of sorts, some clothes hung out on a line, an earthen urn half full of water and a large trunk with a padlock on it. The air is fresh, and the room does not seem forbidding.

Abdul looks around carefully and moves purposefully forward to examine the trunk, for it is the only logical hiding place for his box. He tugs at the padlock, but to no avail; it stays firmly in place. Is it the last obstacle in our search?

We confer amongst ourselves on the whereabouts of the key—is it hidden somewhere in the room or did the seer carry it on his person for safety? We have no idea what was done with his body; presumably a cremation was arranged, but in that case, was the key found? If so, by whom? Would the person who found the key, make the crucial connection? If the key had fallen into the enemy's clutches, how soon will they put two and two together, and come in pursuit? If the key were in the room, where should we look for it?

After fifteen minutes of frantic deliberation, Abdul hesitates no longer and declares, 'I am going to break the lock,' and picking up the crowbar, he strikes at the junction of the hasp and staple repeatedly till they both give way, and the lock falls to the ground with a metallic thud. He lifts the lid. The jubilation in his voice is unmistakable when he says, 'There is my case!'

He reaches for the case, lifts it out slowly, places it on the ground, closes the lid of the trunk and hoists the case on to it to facilitate inspection. Then he turns to me and says: 'Go on and do the honours, for it is *your* right and yours alone!'

With hands that are shaking uncontrollably, I raise the lid of the case and stare at the precious papers within, afraid to touch them. Suppose they disappear like 'fools gold' when I touch them? It is Ranjit who finally picks up a sheaf and places it in my hands, and as soon as he does so, the room begins to darken, and we are just in time to see the trapdoor above sliding back into place, and to hear the 'click' of the bolt shooting home before total darkness engulfs us.

None of us will hopefully ever experience the total panic of that moment ever again in our lives as we cling to each other like children.

Only one thought occupies my mind and I tell myself, 'This then is the end of the road; here time will take its toll and we will pass into eternity gasping for breath, starved of oxygen, faculties failing one by one, like a flame that is extinguished inexorably, perhaps the end of our adventure, hope, justice, and the very end of life itself!'

I had read somewhere that the darkness in underground caves is nineteen times greater than the gloom of the night. The stygian darkness of mythology was to be our shroud and our tomb. We would die here, stifled, and I would never know the truth about Gauri!

When Abdul strikes the match to light up the candle, dispelling the darkness momentarily, I stare at the flame in stupefaction, then with growing comprehension as Abdul lights the candle, drops some melted wax on the floor and affixes the candle firmly to the ground.

The torches come to life; suddenly the gloom is banished, and gradually, my heartbeats return to normal and I can hear Ranjit, with great urgency in his voice, saying, 'Hurry up Priti, look for the crucial document before we are either rescued or captured! In either case, we cannot have them falling into alien hands. You have to do this alone; I can't help you because I cannot read Bengali and Abdul does not have your special knowledge! *You* and *only you* can find the answer to the riddle, so concentrate as you never have before!'

I pick up the precious sheaves of paper, glance through each one and reluctantly put it aside to pick up the next one, for each one is a veritable treasure trove of information in totality, a panoramic view of the years she had spent in the theatre in social and political terms; but they contain nothing that can be construed as personal history, till I reach the bottom and stumble on a sheaf with the words, 'THE ONLY SON', printed in bold letters on the cover. I flip the cover and a pen and ink drawing stands out. I wonder at the amazing accuracy of the image, perhaps another hidden dimension of Gauri's talents. The lions of the *Rajbari* in Bangladesh stare back at me with unblinking eyes, and through the gates, the path, covered in red cloth, winds its way towards the great house.

I turn to the next page and the script begins with the wedding of the second 'Kumar Bahadur', ostensibly Gauri's husband. I now turn the pages with feverish anxiety completely absorbed, and very soon the urgent need for secrecy on the part of my family becomes crystal clear to me. I am worldly enough to realise that everything in the end boils down to 'filthy lucre and property', but this revelation is beyond my wildest dreams, and really jolts me.

Ranjit and Abdul have been watching me with poignant anxiety, and they immediately recognise my predicament. Too sensitive to be curious, Ranjit merely asks, 'Satisfied?' When I nod in affirmation wordlessly, he says, 'Good, now see if you can hide them on your person.'

Since this is clearly impossible, I hand the papers to him; he places them inside his shirt, buttons up carefully and tightens his belt, and then nods to both of us reassuringly. The men then put the other papers back in the box, close it, put it back in the trunk and pull down the lid. And we settle down to a wait that appears to be interminable!

For a while, we make conversation feverishly, pretending that all is well, that it is only a matter of time before we are found and restored to civilisation, that the policeman knows where we are and will definitely inform Inspector Sharma, that rescue is the least of our worries. But as the minutes tick away into hours, our efforts become more frenetic but noticeably less successful. However, as we run out of any further topic discussion, our voices die down, and my fears which had been dispelled by the lighting of the candles return with redoubled force and threaten to overwhelm me.

Finally, Ranjit can no longer stand inaction; he rises from the floor, picks up the water bottle and asks us whether we want a drink; when we nod, he pours tiny portions into the cap and offers it to us by turns, before taking a few drops himself. Somehow this rationing of the life-giving liquid brings home the desperation of our predicament more strongly than words and I feel as though every nerve in my body is stretched to the maximum and will snap any moment, causing me to lose all control!

It is Abdul who suddenly sniffs the air, gets up, and takes a round of the room and says, 'We are twenty feet under the ground, in a room that appears hermetically sealed; yet the air is neither stale nor the room stuffy. Can someone unravel this mystery?'

Ranjit always comes to life whenever there is a problem to solve. He jumps up now, eyes shining, all his lethargy gone and pats Abdul on the back exclaiming, 'By all that is wonderful Abdul, you've done it again, and that makes a hat trick! There has to be a conduit somewhere for the exchange of air, and if we can find that we might also get a clue about the second exit out of this room. Right?'

Abdul's benign smile indicates his acquiescence, and without further ado we begin the search. Every inch of the wall is scanned, every crack in the floor explored, every niche is gone over with the greatest care, but not a clue emerges, nor is there an indication of an aperture of any sort that could remotely connect to a passage. After searching desperately for an hour we are compelled to concede defeat, and as we sit down on the floor and look miserably at each other, the tension builds steadily again. I am taken aback by a sudden, piercing scream that assails my ears like a red hot, sharp needle and continues without abatement till a stinging slap on the cheek brings me back to my senses, and I realise with a shock that the sound has been emanating from me! But I just cannot stop; the sound continues to flow, ricochets from the walls, and it is doubled, quadrupled, redoubled yet again till the world is nothing but sound, a raucous cacophony that will last through eternity, long after I have stopped breathing, feeling, loving! In blind need I turn to Ranjit, whose heart is beating as wildly as mine, and who draws on some invisible source of strength to find the courage to console me, holding me close and murmuring with total conviction that all would yet be well.

When I speak, the voice is not mine, nor is the language—both spring from a deep well of consciousness within my being of which I am quite unconscious.

*When in doubt, look within,*
*To be afraid is no great sin;*
*We are men, we are weak,*
*So guidance we must seek;*
*No problem is too great to solve,*
*But ourselves we must absolve,*
*Of guilt, fear, desires and sin*
*And pray hard to the God within.*

Abdul looks at me with a pale face, but I pay scant attention to him and say to Ranjit confidently, 'We have been working unscientifically, that is our problem; each one of us has the required knowledge, but none of us has looked inward. It is quite elementary, really! We must use a lighted candle to detect the draught and then play it by ear; after that, one step at a time.'

Three candles flare into life simultaneously, and the game of 'detect the draught' begins anew. We take a wall each and try to take the flames which burn without a tremor, over every inch of the surface as thoroughly and closely as possible. Ranjit, being the tallest, can reach higher than us, but stops short of the ceiling by a good two feet. Three walls are done, but the flames show no sign of movement, and with waning hope all three of us attack the fourth wall together and meet in the middle staring at each other in frustration, for the candles burn as steadily as ever. This time however, I feel no panic, and instruct the men calmly to find a way to reach the junction of the roof and the wall, for logically, that is where the conduit must be. When they look incomprehensibly at me, I explain loftily, 'Since the room is underground, how can the air enter through the soil? Obviously, the passage must be above the ground. It's simple reasoning, my friends!'

Even before I have completed my speech, Ranjit is bending over instructing Abdul to climb onto his back with the candle, and almost immediately, the flame begins to flutter, and as it nears the north-western corner, it almost goes out with the force of the draught. Abdul jumps down, his face alight, bows to me and says, 'What next, my mistress? Your wish is our command!'

Fortunately, the corner is next to the stairs down which we had descended, and it is possible for both the men to stand on them to explore the surface with their fingertips.

Minutes pass with agonising slowness and then Ranjit says in a voice taut with excitement, 'Pass me the knife, Priti, I sense a depression here.'

I reach out as far as I can to hand him the slim hunting knife that Inspector Sharma had given Abdul, and he bends down and takes it from my fingers, giving my hand a reassuring squeeze in the process. He inserts the tip of the knife into the dent, eases away the mortar which falls to the ground in little lumps, then feels around and discovers that he can push the blade horizontally along a fissure to the right, turn and move downward vertically, turn a corner move to the left, and then up again to delineate the parameters of a tile.

Abdul says in a voice barely audible, 'Give me the hammer.'

I hand him without a word and he uses it to drive the point of the blade deeper and retraces Ranjit's path around the tile and the tile falls to the ground and smashes to smithereens, leaving a gaping hole behind and letting in a rush of air! After that, it is a matter of minutes before other adjacent tiles are moved and an aperture created, large enough for us to squeeze through.

Abdul decides to go first and suggests that I follow him, while Ranjit comes last. We only take our torches, the water bottle, and the knife that has stood us in such good stead. None of us has forgotten the cobras slithering all over the place, but we manfully shut the image away from our minds. The path is clear and it is evident that we are not far below the surface, for the air is fresh indicating that there is a series of vents aerating the passage, but cunningly hidden so as to prevent detection. Abdul presses forward determinedly, pointing the torch to the ground to illumine his path, and we follow as close behind his heels as we can without stepping on his feet. As we climb a gentle gradient, Abdul stops suddenly and I actually bump into him. We find the way blocked. There is a solid fall of earth which we will not be able to dislodge in a hundred years! The torch drops from Abdul's nerveless hands and the light goes out, leaving us in total darkness, clinging again to each other like lost infants. Since our legs give way under us, we sit down on the ground, quietly hold hands and pray as we have never prayed before, concentrating our collective energies on one objective, to get out of this vault alive, so that we may tell the story that has waited so long to be told!

Ultimately, our energy drains out of us and the prayers die on our lips and hearts. One by one, we fall silent and stare fixedly into the darkness, quite without recognition, like zombies, like the damned in some gothic fable, condemned to confinement without reprieve or hope.

~

I don't know how long we sat there in a state of stupor, scarcely aware of our surroundings or feelings, scarcely aware that life was flowing normally elsewhere, scarcely conscious that we could not accept our present lot meekly and give up hope or give up the will to live. All our energy is at an end, and it is comforting to lie down, quietly go off to sleep and ultimately give up the ghost, so that we do not have to fight this losing battle any longer. Fatigue and disappointment finally catch up with us.

It is Abdul who takes the lead again and coaxes us back to life. His gentle but firm insistence compels us to rise, to wearily place one foot before the other and retrace our steps, to descend the ladder and return to the room we had recently abandoned in such hope! We ration out the water as carefully as possible and stare at the remainder in terror. There are easier ways of dying than dehydration leading to screaming madness! I remember a movie I had once seen in which a group of men cast adrift on the sea in a boat under the scorching sun, had slashed each other with knives to get at the blood that flowed in driblets with greedy lips!

Ranjit has been looking intently at me. He notices the growing desperation on my face and realises that I am close to breaking point. He jumps up and says, 'This will not do. Gauri would never have given up having come so far, or expected her great-granddaughter to do so. No, Priti, you have to get a hold on yourself and do some constructive thinking quickly, so that we can reveal the truth before more damage is done. The lie has lain undisturbed too long! The dust has practically obliterated the face of reality. You cannot allow this injustice to continue any longer. We need your power now, for you and you alone are the chosen instrument. Come, tell us what to do, as you did before.'

His words, confident and spoken with total conviction, echo and reverberate around the room, penetrate my consciousness millimetre by millimetre and gradually, I tried to regain control of my senses. Years later, I would recollect the gaping black hole and the temptation to jump in and float away to nothingness with blinding clarity, and would be grateful to Ranjit yet again, for having saved my sanity that day!

But now, obedient to his instructions, I sit down cross-legged on the floor, assume the lotus pose of meditation and try to concentrate on the visions of Gauri I have in my mind. Like a montage, various images flit by—the little girl on the edge of the pond looking at her own reflection in the water; the slightly older damsel, terrified by the blood oozing out between her legs; the ecstatic bride-to-be; the wiser young woman devastated by the sombre truth of the actual experience; the lonely figure fighting tooth and nail for honourable survival at the convent; then 'Gauri Sikdar', dazzling thousands with her brilliant performances throughout North India; and finally, the body of the beautiful old woman lying in a pool of her own blood shed by an alien hand, because she had made up her mind to reveal the truth that she had guarded with her life, and which she had wanted her son to know! Which of these would come to my aid? Had she known about this room, foreseen the situation in which we found ourselves, and left a clue for us to find? Obviously, I am not within the parameters of rational thought at this point, but I feel it in my bones that if I am to succeed, I must stretch out farther, to the level of consciousness that lies beyond human rationality.

I stretch out my hands and say to Ranjit, 'Give me the papers you are holding for me.'

He does so immediately. I flip the pages one by one, and almost at the end, a scrap of verse typical of Gauri, rivets my attention:

*To do right, you must do wrong,*
*That is the burden of my song,*

*For right is not right nor left, left,*
*Taking away is not always theft.*

*Pull to the right then turn the left,*
*Remember, you must be very deft;*
*Bear in mind whatever you see,*
*Is always not what is meant to be.*

*The prison is just another room,*
*Made by whom and for whom?*
*There is no prison for the bold,*
*Who can the human mind hold?*

*Time is of the essence, my friend,*
*Whether to mar, lose or to mend;*
*Gird your loins; get on with the job,*
*If you would not cry, moan and sob.*

I read it out aloud and can certainly not complain of lack of attention; both men listen with avid concentration and soon have the sense of the simple rhyme by heart. It is interesting to note how each of us responds to the riddle according to our cultural and personal codes.

Ranjit immediately observes, 'She is definitely referring to a mechanism that will enable us to get out of this room, provided we can find it.'

'I feel that this is a conundrum devised by Gauri to test our ingenuity; if we pass, we will be considered worthy of the solemn responsibility,' I comment.

Abdul speaks with quiet conviction, 'She knew something would come to this pass and prepared in advance. She was a great planner, always anticipating and preparing for contingencies.'

While we are theorising, Ranjit again lights up three candles. The largest of them illumines the room as brightly as possible. Ranjit examines the walls with minute attention. He comes up against the big hole we had made earlier, which seems to mock at us with its presence and ineffectiveness, and says, stifling an oath, 'The walls have nothing further to tell us, we must turn our attention to the roof.' And then with growing excitement, he continues, 'Of course, we should have thought of this earlier, there must be some way of manipulating the mechanism that moves the idol from inside as well as from outside. How stupid we have been!'

And I say with complete faith, 'Not so, Ranjit, it is time now. That is all—the last phase of the journey.'

Ranjit drags the bed to the centre of the room, puts the trunk on it and finds that he can reach the designated spot by climbing onto the box. With infinite care he feels around the contraption, keeping up a running commentary all the while, allaying our impatience.

'The pulleys are so cleverly interconnected that it is difficult to make out how they activate each other,' he observes, 'and I cannot afford to jam them by applying force in the wrong direction. There are several knobs of different dimensions, which is the first one? Do I go left to the right or the other way around?'

As he raises these questions, the bells go off simultaneously in our heads, and I repeat the verse, again and again, while Ranjit and Abdul try to find the connections and decipher the process, almost delirious with excitement at the prospect of escape.

Finally, we calm down and tell each other to keep quiet. Ranjit climbs down and we put our heads together in a serious attempt to make sense of the riddle. Ranjit tells us that there are three knobs and four handles, alternately placed, making a total of seven, pretty much like a bizarre musical keyboard. It is obviously a sequence, and unless we get all the moves right, the machinery will not be set in motion.

We go back to the poem and consider the words carefully again: 'To do right, you must do wrong…'. If we interpret 'wrong' as 'left' then the first handle should be turned to the left, but then at which end do we begin? Do we go from left to right, or vice versa?

I observe, 'In India, we write, play instruments, move men on the chess-board, from left to right, so, "wrong" must also indicate "right to left"?'

A chuckle from Abdul stops me in my tracks and he counters saying, 'Not all languages. What about Urdu? Does not the script go from right to left?'

Ranjit breaks in excitedly, 'You are right, by God! Don't forget that Urdu is more an Indian language than the ones that developed from Sanskrit, which after all came with the Aryans, whereas Urdu was born and grew in army camps, on river banks, a completely indigenous mixture. So, we go from left to right after all? "For right is not right, nor left, left; taking away is not always theft".'

'Sounds like absolute gibberish to me,' mutters Abdul. 'Really, Ma could be very annoying at times; if nothing is nothing, then what is?'

'Wait a minute!' says Ranjit. 'If neither left nor right are what they seem, then "taking away" must mean "front or back".'

But this time I have an idea and I break in, 'Tell me, are the knobs movable? If so, how do they move?'

Ranjit frowns in concentration, thinks a while and says, 'I presume they are attached to shafts with screws, and would turn on them.' His voice dies down.

Quick as a flash, Abdul asks, 'Do they turn from left to right, or the other way? And do they come away altogether, if you go the whole way? After all, "taking away is not always theft", do you remember?'

'So, what have we deciphered up to this point?' I ask warily, for honestly I am a little confused. 'That we begin from left to right, and unscrew the two knobs, one to the left and then one to the right of the spectrum? Is that right?'

'Quite right,' says Ranjit condescendingly. 'And now, tell us the next lines like a good little girl.'

I make a face at him but recite obediently.

*Pull to the right then turn the left,*
*Remember you must be very deft,*
*Bear in mind, whatever you see,*
*Is always not what is meant to be.*

'So,' says Ranjit, 'after I have unscrewed the knobs, I pull the handle to the right of the knob to the left, and turn the handle on the left—which way?'

'To the right of course,' Abdul speaks with complete certainty. 'But deftly and gently, feeling your way carefully all the time!'

Rather bewildered, I break in, 'That leaves us with the central and final knob, and that is the one that is of deceptive appearance, for "it is not what it appears to be"; how do we tackle this one?'

So we go back to the poem again, and put our heads together. Two factors emerge that appear to be of primary importance—one, human ingenuity is the key to the final solution, and two, the timing has to be very precise, or the whole project can be jeopardised.

Abdul says, 'I think that once you set the process in motion Ranjit, you cannot hesitate, or some mechanism will go drastically wrong. You must execute the whole series in one fluent motion and with complete assurance.'

Ranjit turns on him with a furious scowl and says, 'Why must you assume that I have to take the responsibility? Why can't you do it?' And then almost sotto voce, 'I too can feel scared, you don't seem to understand.'

Abdul and I look at each other, and then at Ranjit's pale and panic-stricken face with a sudden realisation of the tremendous strain he has been under, that he is close to breaking point, that he cannot, after all he has been through, face the responsibility of a wrong move that could trap us in this subterranean prison for ever. I also see how heavily I have leant on him throughout these months and how easy he has made it for me to take him for granted. This time I wrap my arms around him and then tell him as best as I can that whatever he ever did for me would always be right, that he need not have been here in the first place, that we were in the same boat for a reason beyond our ken, that we all had to die some day, and if this were our appointed time, then I would like nothing better than to die with him by my side.

Very slowly, the colour returns to his face; then he returns my hug, claps Abdul on the back and says in a husky voice, 'I am a fool! Let's get on with the job.'

We repeat the sequence we have worked out several times and Ranjit soon has it by heart. We all have a sinking feeling in the pit of our stomachs that we may have got the entire meaning wrong, in which case we are in for a massive disappointment none of us feels equipped to deal sensibly with in our present, fragile psychological condition.

As for the unknown quantity, the central knob, neither Abdul nor I would like to be in Ranjit's shoes, and both of us pray, as we never have before, as he climbs gingerly onto the box. Abdul and I stand in opposite corners so we can see his face clearly and he can see us in case of need, and with perspiration trickling down my neck and back like a hundred insects, I crane forward as he reaches for the two handles with both hands. They apparently move with ease, for his shoulder muscles relax visibly and he turns to me with a radiant smile for a fleeting moment, before returning to the job on hand.

I can make out from his movements that he is unscrewing the knobs and that they are moving in clockwise and anti-clockwise directions. As they come away in his hands he falls back with an oath, for two steel shafts come shooting out of the apertures so created, and would have struck him in the face had he been less vigilant. Ranjit, quite unfazed, drops the knob covers gently on the bed and reaches for the remaining handles. For a moment, he looks to us for confirmation and as we both gesticulate in perfect unison, he turns them confidently. Nothing happens for a minute. Then a whirring sound fills the air and the central shaft begins to gyrate, at first slowly, then faster and yet faster, with the knob still in place. As though divinely inspired, Ranjit stretches out and grasps the two steel shafts, pulling the right one forward and pushing the one to his left, back. The gyrations grow wilder. The last knob cover is loosened and falls off. A trident emerges from the final shaft and the three prongs fit neatly into three holes in the roof that we had not noticed before. The rotary motion stops, but the trident continues to rise, then moves smoothly to the right, and Ranjit finds himself staring straight into Inspector Sharma's startled face.

# Epilogue

Today there is a special *shradh* ceremony in our house. My grandmother, a shadow of her former self, has made all arrangements meticulously. My father will perform the actual rituals; my mother and I will assist him. Only the immediate family has been invited, but none of us has any intention of satisfying the curiosity writ large on their faces as to the reasons for this sudden revival. They all do a double take when they find that the venerable 'feet' have been relegated to far corners and the pride of the place is taken by the framed photograph of a beautiful woman clad in simple white. It is an old photo and the lines are not very clear, but there is something about the expression that inspires respect, even awe.

The police have refused to reopen the case because the entire 'episode took place a long time ago' and because 'the evidence unearthed is too vague to be admissible'. The trail is cold, the people who could have given first-hand accounts, are dead, and 'Abdul too psychologically fragile' to withstand the pressure of court procedures. Also, there are too many important people mentioned and too many questions about them in these documents. To disturb persons who occupy eminent positions in society today would seriously upset the political applecart, and no one wishes to take the responsibility, least of all, the police authorities. I am reminded of Metternich, the redoubtable chancellor of the Austrian Empire in the nineteenth century, who had said when he deserted Napoleon and re-joined the Allies who were fighting against him, 'political correctness is after all, largely a matter of date'. There is also the matter of the 'women's network', which hints at close family involvement, and frankly, even I have fought shy of that for, what right have I to play havoc with the lives of my own, living family members? That their own consciences, uneasy for years, were now exacting a heavy toll, I am fairly certain. So 'let the dead past bury its dead', and let the sweet flow of oblivion come with time—time that hurts, yet heals.

But in a strange way, I am content. I feel and Ranjit agrees too, that Gauri had not cared for public vindication She had only wanted her son and his family to know the truth and to judge her in its clear light. Life for her had been too hard and too real to make facile judgements about 'good' and 'bad', 'right' and 'wrong'. So she had wanted to hold up a mirror to what had been, and leave it at that. I assume the verdict has seemingly gone in her favour as far as the family is concerned, otherwise we would not have this ceremony in the house today, or I wonder, is it again merely a piece of 'political correctness'? For this time, my mother has stood firm and my father and grandmother have given in with apparent grace, but it could very well be that they have considered this course of action as the best policy calculated to win my trust.

Amazed and rather sickened at my own cynicism, I quietly go and sit down next to the family priest who looks at me with affectionate recognition and says, 'Not going to faint this time, are you?'

I cannot explain to him or even to myself that I have yet to come to terms at a personal level with the revelations that concern the family, and particularly my grandfather. How would he have reacted to this vital piece of information that has more to do with him than anyone else? Or had he suspected all along and desperately desired to be proved right or perhaps wrong? Had I after all, done him disservice by bringing the truth long buried, to light? But as the mantras recited in my father's deep yet musical voice flow over me in a lambent stream, I gradually experience such solace as I have not felt since my grandfather has passed away. I raise my eyes, find an echo in Ranjit's and then my mother's face, and I know everything that has been done is right. I can now conscionably give myself time to work out my own equation. As the poet says, *'Nothing is ever lost in this world of your creation, But we, of little understanding, fail to see.'*

At last the rituals are over; the priests have pronounced themselves satisfied with the proceedings and assured us that the soul of Gauri, the matriarch of this family, is at peace. My grandmother who has worked unceasingly to ensure perfection in every detail, is now seeing the last guests to the door, and my mother is presiding over the mopping up operations.

My father, obviously fatigued but content, puts his hand on my head gently, and when I look up, he smiles and simply says, 'Thank you.'

Then he reminds my mother to wake him early for work next day and goes away to his room. Ranjit also rises and says he must make a move.

At this my grandmother comes forward, takes him by the hand, looks straight into his eyes and says, 'Bless you for taking care of Priti, when we all failed to do our duty by her.' Then after a pause, she continues, 'Please tell your mother that I will be calling on her next week to complete a formality that has hung fire too long. Now that the past has sanctified the present, we can plan the future without fear… .'

As her voice trails off, I notice with sudden compunction how frail she has become in the last few days and the tremulous quality in her erstwhile strong voice falls on my ears and strikes me to the heart. I get up, put my arms around her and hold her close; she hugs me back almost fiercely, and as her heart beats steadily against mine, more blinkers fall away and I, for the first time, begin to see things from *her* point of view.

'Nature red in tooth and claw'—a mother or a wife, strikes, fights, and even kills if need be to protect her young, her mate and his family against encroachment, to prevent disaster from befalling them; and for this she does not even hesitate to condemn her own soul to perdition!

In the end, the force that had propelled my grandmother had been the same one that had driven Gauri. Gauri had realised this after the third encounter with her daughter-in-law and hence, she had authorised her own release. Her death had neither been suicide nor murder, but *ichha mrityu* or death by desire—the right to release the body from bondage when all temporal commitments have been met, a wish granted only to the spiritual elite, the true *sanyasi*; and the hand that had held the gun had been that of her deliverer, her mentor, her beloved! I think that night, both my grandmother and I saw the truth at last!

~

When I finally return to my room, it is well past midnight, for my grandmother and I have been so engrossed in our conversation that neither of us has noticed the clock ticking. I have seen her to her room before coming back to mine; I am concerned about her fragile state and do not want the burden to lie heavy on her any longer. To this end, I have enlightened her about the manner of Gauri's passing, and had the satisfaction of seeing her shoulders droop a little less, her eyes brighten for a fraction, and a modicum of her fighting spirit return.

She says to me before turning in, 'Don't think that because you have been getting your way lately, this state of affairs will continue indefinitely. When it comes to the wedding, you will do exactly as *I* say, and so will your parents and Ranjit! After all, I too have a debt to repay to Gauri and her son.' And she almost manages to keep the quiver out of her voice.

The jasmine is in bloom again and its intoxicatingly sweet fragrance has flooded my room. The moonlight too is pouring in, touching every article with silver including the darkness; Gauri's documents in the box are lying where I had left them—on the table—and although there is no breeze, its pages rustle as though impatient of confinement and eagerly awaiting release like the spirit that imbues them, that has waited so long for its tryst with its beloved, the tryst that is nirvana. I know what I have to do and it will be done tonight, but I must read the soul's cry in all its poignancy once more, before I place it beyond reach.

I begin reading the play, similar yet so different from the other pieces I have read:

*It is my wedding night. I am sitting on the bed; my heart beats wildly while I await my awesome husband. I would have happily given my life to please him. But I am so ignorant; how can I please a great man like him? When the womenfolk finally leave and we are alone, I get off the bed and stand with my eyes lowered till he draws near. I bend and touch his feet as instructed by my mother. He takes me by the shoulders and stares into my face for a long time, then holds me to his heart.*

*It is the same story every night. He blows out the lamps, undresses me with great care, takes off his own clothes and begins to caress me, but as he fails to get an erection and his frustration mounts, he goes for me like a wild animal, biting, scratching, squeezing, till I can hardly keep myself from crying out with pain. He ejaculates again and again, all over my cringing body, sometimes in my face, but never once inside me. This happens several times each night, after which he sleeps in utter exhaustion till mid-day. But I have to be up before dawn, bathe and get ready to assist Ranima with her early-morning rituals and worship. My best friend is the cold water in the pond which soothes my lacerated body like a mother. One day I will stay there and never come up to the surface again!*

~

*Several women are sitting in conclave with the lady of the house and commiserating with her on her daughter-in law's failure to produce a child.*

*Mrittika: It might have been better Ranima, if you had brought a plainer girl, but more fertile! You must not judge a fish by its scales; always check the smell.*

*Rohini: Well, you certainly spent a fortune on the marriage. A girl from a well-to-do home would have brought wealth in both kinds. I did suggest that you take a look at my brother's daughter, but you had to have a wingless fairy!*

*Kalyani: Your niece is too dark, Rohini; the Kumar would not have looked at her, but my friend's step-daughter is as fair as moonlight! However, Ranima paid no attention.*

*Mrittika: Yes, she is fair enough, but you must admit, her face is just like a frog's, particularly the eyes! (Peals of malicious laughter from others follow.)*

*Kalyani: Frog, lizard or fish, say what you like, she is live and fertile. Have you seen the fine baby boy she has borne recently? What is the use of a marble statue, bloodless and inanimate?*

*Rohini: And the Kumar is so handsome and virile! It must be very frustrating for him to be married to such a cold woman! Ranima, why don't you find him another wife? I think you have given her enough time.*

*Ranima: Do you think I have not considered it? It is my son who will not hear of it! I have spoken to him several times, but he is adamant.*

*Mrittika: Maybe she has cast a spell on him! Some women have occult powers. Tell me, have you ever seen her out in the garden in the evenings with her hair loose?*

*Ranima: Once or twice. Does that mean…?*

*Kalyani: Definitely. Don't waste any more time. Take her to the famous astrologer in the next village without delay and tell him everything. He will give her an amulet that will nullify her powers. Then the Kumar will agree to a second marriage like a fish takes to water, and Gauri…*

*Ranima: And Gauri?*

*Mrittika: Well, well, weren't you saying a little while ago that you require a special maid for the kitchen to help the cook? (More laughter follows.)*

~

*I do not think my husband is very well. He has been so irritable lately. I can do nothing to please him. Yesterday he almost knocked me over because the glass of water I had brought him was not cold enough, and tonight he kicked me away when I tried to press his feet! I went sprawling halfway across the room.*

*I picked myself up and went and stood on the balcony, for I am not allowed to go into the garden. The amaltas has flowered so profusely that the tree can hardly hold itself up! The flowers, bright gold in daytime are blanched to grey by the moonlight; the entire colour seems to have ebbed away just like my life now. I wish the cuckoo were less persistent; his plaintive call, piercingly sweet, drives me mad!*

*The book that no one reads,*
*The song that no one sings,*
*The house that no one enters,*
*The bell that no one rings,*

*The plant that will not grow,*
*The bush that will not flower,*
*The flower that no bee visits,*
*Beauty that fades in an hour,*

*A field where no child plays,*
*A tree where no bird nests,*
*A desert where no life grows,*
*An inn where no man rests,*

*A spring that has no flowering,*
*A summer that has no warmth,*
*An autumn that has no colours,*
*A winter that is cold and swarth,*

*A woman whom no one loves,*
*One who has no hearth or home,*
*Gauri is her name my only friend,*
*The wanderer who will always roam,*

*Roam and wander without end,*
*Till the glistening waters of a lake,*

*Beckon and lure with hope of death,*
*And her thirst, forever slake.*

I read on:

*The two brothers, Gauri's husband Anish and his elder brother Ashish are talking amongst themselves.*

*Ashish: You realise of course, that the group of* sadhus *living in the ruins on the edge of the forest are not what they appear to be.*

*Anish: When I heard that Shourjo, our cousin, has been seen with them, I began to wonder. Have you met him yet?*

*Ashish: I ran into him yesterday when I was out hunting. He is just as enthusiastic as before and just as determined! I must say I admire him a great deal.*

*Anish: But rather a hopeless cause, don't you think? I mean, enthusiasm is all very well, but where will it lead to ultimately?*

*Ashish: Perhaps nowhere, but does that matter? I think it's splendid of him to carry on, knowing that he has less than five per cent chance of success.*

*Anish: Is he not beating his head against a stone wall? What can he and his followers, a handful anyway, do to make a dent in the British armour? Surely, they are too strongly entrenched!*

*Ashish: He is not alone, you know, there are several groups operating on both sides of the River Padma, creating a climate of terror and instability that the administration is not able to counter. It is unnerving not to know where the next attack is coming from or what masks people are wearing. For instance, I am certain that his group had something to do with the robbery of the money on its way to the treasury last week, but there is nothing to prove the connection, for they cover their track very effectively.*

*Anish: That is what you think. You know the proverb: the bald man may pass under the* bel *tree once too often at the risk of his pate? Well, I am afraid it applies to our reckless cousin. He is far too arrogant and imagines that he bears a charmed, inviolate life. There are plenty of informers about. One of these days they will be betrayed. I wish Shourjo would pull out before they cart him off to prison.*

*Ashish: Perhaps you are right; I will invite him to the house one of these days, then we can both caution him.*

~

*I am not invited to meet Shourjo for I am not important enough, but he wants to meet Anish's wife, so I am told to serve him his food along with the other male members of the family. They are sitting in a row on woven mats on the floor with the glistening silver utensils before them, waiting to be served. I am terrified and my hands are trembling as I am afraid that I may spill the food! I never could have managed had Mala, Ashish's wife, not encouraged me. I am so grateful to her for her support.*

*Shourjo comes to the house once in a while to speak to Ashish. Anish does not care for him much, so he keeps out of his way. I see him the other day, crossing the courtyard and immediately bring the end of my sari down to cover my face partially and begin to move away towards the kitchen, at which he begins to laugh and says to my retreating back, 'You don't have to run away from me, I happen to be younger to Anish, and custom says that you may converse with your husband's juniors but must treat seniors with great respect, even reverence.'*

*Then he turns to my mother-in-law who has appeared on the scene and asks, 'Is not that true, my dear Aunt?'*

*The irony in his voice is unmistakable, and the lady rather flustered, says quickly, 'Of course, there is no question about that.'*

*Then to cover her embarrassment she immediately orders me to fetch tea and refreshments for him. The last thing I hear is his voice commending her on her choice of daughter-in-law: 'Pretty as well as hardworking, what a wonderful combination!'*

~

*There is a* baul *who visits our house intermittently. He stands in the courtyard and sings till someone comes out with rice and potatoes for him. My mother-in-law asks him one day why he does not come more regularly, for we all enjoy his songs, and he explains to her in all seriousness that he has been forbidden by his guru to do so because it is against their philosophy. I stand and watch his deeply etched face, his gnarled frame, his upright stance, and his animated eyes as he speaks.*

*'Man is steeped in illusion that makes him think that he has an individual identity when he is actually one with his maker, the reason for this is attachment to temporal things which evolves from our daily activities and the consciousness of the self. We must beg for food to develop humility and repay the debt to the donor by conveying the glories of God to his ears through the medium of song, but we must not visit the same house every day, for it is natural for man to form affinities. We must be like the bee that flits from flower to flower but tarries nowhere. That is why our activity is called* madhukari *and the bee is known as the* madhukar, *the collector of nectar!'*

*Then he takes his* ektara, *and sings:*

*I went and allowed my eyes to feast on him, to adore him,*
*I had not imagined that such glory could be contained in one body*

*Or be viewed by a pair of eyes;*
*I allowed my eyes to gaze on him till my heart was full,*
*I was lost in this beauty that lies beyond all physical attributes,*
*I responded to the passion in him, and my heart was set on fire.*
*I wonder if I will ever know such longing, such passion? Will my heart ever be ignited?*

*There is agitation in the village. The magistrate has mounted a raid on the ruined house that Shourjo's team inhabits and has discovered some incriminating material. They are not disclosing its nature nor has anyone been arrested, but the team members have gone their separate ways and so has Shourjo. We all miss his visits. It is as though the sun has suddenly been overshadowed.*

*Most nights I sleep on the balcony, for I have become the living image of his own incapacity and enrage him intolerably. But his pride will not let me out of his sight and my prayer to visit my parents has been turned down with the brusque command that I should try and forget my humble antecedents.*

*I love the balcony and its view of the garden and the river beyond. Here I sit and sing to myself the songs I have learnt from the* baul:

*'Tomorrow', said my beloved and left for the land of honey,*
*My dark one promised to be back tomorrow.*
*Time goes by but he does not return*
*Yet he said, 'tomorrow',*
*His time does not match with mine*
*When will that 'tomorrow' come?*

*Why does this song strike such a poignant chord in my heart, in my very soul?*

*Suddenly my attention is drawn to two figures moving stealthily under the balcony. One of them is definitely Ashish, but I wonder who the other is, wrapped in a blanket from head to foot moving as though in pain? Slowly they move out of sight and I get the impression that they have come into the house, but how? To the best of my knowledge, there is no entry into the building on the ground floor at this end. I peer over the parapet but all is quiet. Have I been dreaming?*

*Mala calls me into her room two days later, and tells me that she needs help urgently. She tells me that Shourjo has been injured in an encounter with the police but has managed to escape capture because one of Ashish's henchmen who happened to be in the vicinity, had pulled him onto his horse and ridden away at top speed. He had informed his master and Ashish had brought him home and hidden him in a cell that was usually reserved for incarceration of miscreants, and was usually kept locked, and to which Ashish only had the keys. The problem is to carry food, water and medicines to him without arousing suspicion, for if the servants get to know, he will be betrayed as the magistrate had announced a five-hundred-rupee reward for Shourjo, dead or alive!*

*My heart leaps as the meaning of the charade, seen two nights ago, becomes clear, but I turn impassively to her and ask,' What do you expect me to do? How can I help?'*

*'Well your brother-in-law was wondering whether you could carry supplies to him late in the night, when the house is asleep.'*

*'But then how can I get out of my room without my husband's permission? It is not possible.'*

*'Well we know that some nights you sleep on the balcony.'*

*'So with this knowledge you expect me to jeopardise my position further? Why?'*

*'We have noticed how generous you are and compassionate, how you care for the servants when they are unwell, so we thought…,' replies Mala, very embarrassed.*

*'That is only because I belong to the same class as the servants. I feel their pain as my own.'*

*'I know you have suffered a great deal through no fault of your own and we have been able to do nothing for you, but Ashish is very aware of the injustice that has been done. He also admires your courage and staying power tremendously and is confident that you will not turn down an appeal, particularly for such a cause.'*

*'What if Ranima finds out? How will I get to his room without anyone finding out?'*

*'We have heard that you were an adept at climbing trees in your childhood. Do you think you could climb down the balcony?'*

*'So a village girl has her uses after all! None of you fine ladies have ever climbed a tree in your lives, have you? Do you know that it will take me less than a minute to climb down, a few minutes to swim the river and escape from here forever? Do not think I have not considered this course of action but where and what would I escape to? No man can escape his karma, or so I have been told.'*

*'So will you help us?'*

*'I suppose so.'*

*That night, with my sari tied firmly round my waist and the supplies in a bag slung on my back, I negotiate the tricky walk along the outer ledge of the balcony, holding on to the railing for support till I reach the point directly above the hidden door—hidden by a thick creeper of jasmine that has been allowed to spread its tentacles into every available nook and cranny so that not only is the door concealed, but the pathetic and piercing cries that emanate from the regular inmates are deadened. This is my sole support and lifeline on the way down. The vine hard and woody with age takes my weight easily, and I am a few hands above the ground when I clutch a handful of leaves by error which come away in a bunch and cause me to slither down and fall awkwardly on my left foot, which turns causing excruciating pain. I lie stunned for a while, then pick myself up, hobble painfully to the door, insert the key in the hole and turn it cautiously.*

~

*Anish: Has Shourjo been traced yet? I hear that the magistrate has raised the reward amount to a thousand rupees! He must be a fish of deeper waters than we had imagined.*

*Ashish: Oh absolutely! But I have no idea where he might be.*

*Anish: I didn't ask you whether you did. Why are you so quick to react? Is it because you do know of his whereabouts? I wouldn't put it beyond you. You always admired him much more than I ever did. Just don't forget that you could bring great trouble to the entire family by your foolhardiness.*

*Ashish: How absurd you are! Would I jeopardise the good name of our family as loyal subjects of the Raj by such a silly undertaking? This is the reason why I sometimes think that you do not know me at all!*

*Anish: I know you a little too well, that is the problem. Well, you are aware that I am going up to Dhaka on some official work today, and will return in a day or two. Don't get into mischief while I am away! That is all.*

*Ashish: Really, if an outsider heard this conversation, he would imagine that I am the errant younger brother and you the wise elder!*

*Stop taking things so seriously, Anish. We have but one life after all and must live it as best as we can.*

*Anish: Yes, exactly. So, if you get to know something of Shourjo's whereabouts in my absence, do inform the magistrate immediately!*

*I have heard enough. I have no doubt in my mind that the 'official work' has to do with Shourjo, and I would not put it beyond him to return with a police force to comb the area. He has always disliked Shourjo, for he is everything that Anish is not—warm, courageous, idealistic. Also, Anish's great love of money is proverbial! For a thousand rupees, he would expend a lot of time and energy. There is no time to lose; a decision must be taken tonight, and by me. I cannot wait for Ashish to devise strategies!*

*When I meet Shourjo, I find that the wound is still raw but he can move more easily; still, when I suggest my plan to him, he looks doubtful, for he does not realise the danger he is in, even now.*

*He says, 'Will I be able to walk so much and then cross the river on my own? I very much doubt it. Besides, I don't think Anish would stoop so low! I think you are overreacting.'*

*So I explain to him exactly how low Anish can stoop and then relate the entire conversation I had overheard between him and Ashish that morning. Shourjo sits quietly for a few minutes, then makes up his mind.*

*'So be it! I will certainly do my best to stay alive. If I don't succeed, thank you for everything that you have done for me out of the goodness of your heart.'*

*His polite tone indicates that he has no inkling of my feelings, and I think to myself, 'Are men always so blind? Can't he see that not only my soul and heart, but my body is crying out for his touch?'*

*But keeping my face devoid of all emotion, I inform him that he is going nowhere alone; that I will support him till the water's edge, then row him across, and find him a place to stay where he will be safe; that we should start immediately or I will not be able to return before daybreak! He looks at me in wonderment for a while, then places his hand in mine and says that he has realised for the first time why a woman is called* Shakti *in our country.*

*I place him in the boat, make him comfortable, release the boat from its moorings and pick up both the oars. He quietly leans over and takes one of them from me and we hit the water at the same time as though we have been doing this for a long time. Some energy passes between us, and we are both aware of the exchange although neither of us can acknowledge it, leave alone act on its dictates. The river is ethereal in the moonlight and as we move along to the steady rhythm of the splashing oars, a snatch of a folk song comes to mind and I hum beneath my breath:*

*Oh my good boatman,*
*Who is the charmer to whose abode*
*You ply your boat?*
*Your boat that is the crescent moon*
*Sailing the blue sea of the sky?*

*Is her hair like a dark cloud?*
*Is her soft skin like moonshine?*
*Are her lips the colour of the coonch?*
*Are her eyes like the evening star?*

*Will you find a place for me in your boat?*
*Will you let me catch a glimpse of her face?*
*Will you fill my life with glory, just once?*
*Oh my good boatman.*

*He takes up the refrain in the second verse and soon picks up the words. He has a deep, melodious voice that blends perfectly with mine, and soon we have thrown caution to the winds and are singing with complete abandon, totally absorbed in the present, without thought of the past and certainly not of the future—a perfect moment encapsulated in time and space, an infinitesimal part of the complete human experience from the beginning of time that is preserved in time, but nonetheless unique!*

*It is as we are disembarking that Shourjo stumbles, clutches at me for support and I wrap my arms around him to steady him on his feet. After that things happen very fast and before either of us is aware of what is happening, he has taken me among the roots of a profusely blooming* kadamb *tree with its globular gold flowers and glossy, dark green leaves. The tree under which the immortal Radha-Krishna myth had been played out—the myth of incomplete and conventionally forbidden love which had been consummated only after death, when the human soul had found the Godhead:*

*The clouds parted, the sun broke through, and the moon came out to play,*
*We embraced and kissed like lovers, night clasped in the arms of day,*
*That which was never meant to be, came to be, we know not how or why,*
*A cosmic secret, out of time and space, came into play for us today.*

*The cuckoo crowed, the rook cooed, the rat was vicious, the tiger smiled,*
*The rose was bitter, thorns were fragrant, as I reached for the honey wild,*

*It skipped my grasp, came tumbling down, cascading on my upturned face,*
*My starving lips, my hungry eyes, my entire being was steeped in grace.*

*The years rolled but time stood still, happiness glowed but tears fell fast,*
*Time is neither mine nor yours, it uncoils and flees in the firmament vast;*
*It would never return, nor look back, or retrace its steps, but forward fly,*
*Be as that may, but today, both sun and time halted, and forgot to die!*

*Hand in hand, we arrive at Maryam Bibi's humble abode. There I explain who she is, what family actually means, and assure him that no one will think of looking in an untouchable's house for him, not even the British, for they pride themselves on their knowledge of local custom. At this point, he makes his one and only appeal: 'If you have a child, will you call him or her, Sadhan or Sadhana? Wherever I may be, I will get to know and rejoice, for this child will not be the fruit of lust, but the fulfilment of a prayer, the purest distillation of the creative impulse!'*

*On the way back I almost float on air! The sense of joy and exhilaration that fills my heart, the sense of physical well-being that permeates my body, are strangers to me, as though all the pent-up agony of yesteryears has been washed away in a torrent, a flood of joyous cleansing that has left no sediment of guilt behind, as though all that I had to offer, my beauty, my unrequited youth of eighteen years' standing, my longing, pain and yearning, my good and bad, have been mounted on one final pitch and toss of a gambler's throw, and I have come out as the winner! On the way back, the sky darkens, and when I take the oars it is raining in sheets. The water runs down my body like a caress cooling and soothing till the joy within and the exhilaration without mingle and become one…as always, I turn to Tagore to express my feelings:*

*The night that the doors of my room were blown down by*
*the storm*
*I did not see who entered my room,*
*In a moment all turned to darkness,*
*The lamp went out,*
*I stretched out my arms to the sky in search of whom?*
*For I did not realise that you had entered my room…*

*The current is strong; I am alone with both oars and despite my best efforts, the boat drifts in a westerly direction, away from our private landing-stage towards the village, and when I finally manage to pull the boat ashore, I find that I have arrived at the 'burning ground', the place where dead bodies are cremated. I cannot afford to leave the boat here for that would give the whole game away, so I decide to walk down the towpath, pulling the boat along after me. It is hard work and I have to pause again and again to catch my breath. My wet clothes dry out in no time and soon perspiration is running down my body in rivulets.*

*Finally, quite exhausted, I tie the boat to a tree and walk into the water to wash my sweaty face and throat, then plunge in further to wash more fully and get my clothes wet again to cool my body in preparation for the last lap of the journey. I swim for a bit under water, then strike out for the shore and when I lift my head out of the water and reach for a bush growing on the bank to haul myself up, I find myself staring straight into the eyes of a human skull that is sitting in the mud and grinning at me. Being a village girl, I am no stranger to death or the process of cremation, but this incident unnerves me completely and I leap out of the water and start running away from the river, intent only on escaping the leering, mocking face!*

*In my panic, I become unconscious of direction and time, and only when I stumble on a rock and measure my length on the ground do I stop and take stock of my surroundings. I appear to have come into the heart of the burning ground. There are some pyres that are still smouldering, some that have turned into a mere heap of embers, and some have gone out completely and dogs are beginning to pick at the remains of what were once human beings and are now chunks of singed meat fit only for canine consumption! I try to find a connection between the events of the evening, but fail totally to envisage a composite whole capable of encompassing the diversity. I am just about to return to my boat for my journey home when the flickering of a distant fire catches my attention, and almost involuntarily I move towards it till I am within twenty yards of a man clad in and seated on deerskin in the lotus pose, before a fire that is slowly going out. There are five skulls distributed evenly around him and he is addressing them in a low monotone, just as though they are living entities. Completely fascinated, for I have heard of tantric* sanyasis*, but never met one face to face. I inch forward to try and catch what he is saying. As he has his back to me, I feel comparatively free from the fear of detection.*

*It is a complete shock when I hear him say, 'I have been expecting you for some time, Gauri, for all that has happened is part of the plan! Come forward, stand before me and hear what I have to say, for you have no time to waste and must return before dawn.'*

*As I fall at his feet in total surrender, he places his hand on my head in benediction and begins to speak:*

*'The mountain mocks the sky with its grandeur*
*till the earthquake destroys its pride,*
*The falcon calls all space its own*
*till the eagle takes it by the throat,*
*The tree prinks its face in the brook-glass*
*till the lightning strikes it black,*
*The cobra rises and flaunts its poison*
*till the mongoose goes for its eyes,*
*The tiger is the king of the jungle*
*till the lion roars and makes it run,*
*Man swells in pride and he thinks he is God*
*till death lays him low, lower than the dust.*

*'There is great turmoil ahead! The earth shall be consumed by fire, lashed by the winds, washed away by water, struck by drought, parched by the sun, devastated by lightning—man will know suffering as never before and you too will not escape! The wheel turns inexorably and the poor monkey tied hand and foot to it imagines that he is in control, that he turns the wheel that turns him. How can we make choices that have been made for us without our will?*

*'In the span of a few hours today, you have known total fulfilment and come face to face with total annihilation, all without volition. Hold onto this truth with both hands! That is all you can do; and now, go, Go quickly! But remember, I will come to you in your hour of dire need for that too is part of the plan. Go in peace, Gauri!'*

*When I returned and climbed up the jasmine creeper to my balcony, dawn was just breaking and the people in the house were beginning to stir. Anish comes back the next day with a special mandate from the commissioner to search the countryside for Shourjo, but of course, he is not found. This not only embitters him further, but turns the family against him in a subtle way; even his mother, who has been his staunchest supporter is now revolted by this instance of treachery.She also finds out, I think from Mala, that the blame for failing to conceive could not be laid at my door and arranges for the* Putreshti Yajna, *and exactly eight months later my son is born! So delighted is the family that no one comments on the fact that for a slightly premature baby, he is exceptionally large and healthy, and one and all pronounced him as handsome as the 'moon'.*

*Anish goes for me with the knife exactly two years later in a fit of murderous rage when the family is away in Benaras and I am forced to flee, not only to save my life, but to prevent my son's father from being branded a murderer. After that he goes downhill very quickly, and the day he dies, I carry out my own funeral ceremony as advised by the* sanyasi, *for 'Gauri' is dead and nothing can, or so I think at that point, bring her back to life.*

*The night is very dark, for it is new moon. I sit on a deer skin and feed the fire with clarified butter and the flames rise higher and higher till they reach the sky. The night itself seems one with me, as though the world-mother is conspiring to bring about her own death to cleanse the world of evil. Her dark hair veils the earth; the moon, which is her third eye, is nowhere to be seen; she herself has put out the star-lamps one by one, so that none but I should bear witness. The* sanyasi *chants the mantras and I repeat them obediently:*

*'I, Gauri, hereby consign all desire, the fruits of all desire, and the desire for desire to the flames.*

*'I, Gauri, renounce all claims to happiness, peace, fulfilment, contentment and joy as the world knows it.*

*'I, Gauri, hereby abjure all longing for material gain, physical comfort, even pain, so that I may not long to be comforted.*

*'I, Gauri, do solemnly promise that I will not look back on my past life with any hope of renewing contact.*

*'I, Gauri, do realise that there is but one truth in life, and that truth is God, and promise to dedicate my life to the search.*

*'I, Gauri, do promise to preserve my body from defilement, whatever the temptation, for it is the temple of the living God.*

*'I, Gauri, will not falter on the path that has been marked out for me, till such time as He, in His infinite mercy, shall set me free from bondage.'*

*The ceremony, I realise later, is not the end but the beginning of the most arduous journey of my life. The shaving of my head and wearing of white clothes are merely symbolic of the novitiate, and it takes me some time to get used to it. The concept of* sanyas *is an intricate one, as I am only an ignorant village girl, with no experience of grasping the abstract. But with the rigorous training that the* sanyasi *puts me through, its meaning begins to emerge. For instance, on certain days, I am made to fast and on other days I am made to gorge till I feel bloated; some days I labour till I drop, on others I lie abed till the ennui gets to me; I am at times allowed to wear the most gorgeous sari possible, and at the next moment it is replaced by a piece of rag that barely covers my body. I read till the words lose meaning; I chant prayers till my throat is parched, I sit by the fire till I am almost scorched, I submerge myself in the cold river till I feel numb. In the beginning, there is just shock and stupefaction, but after six months of this rigorous and patterned routine, I begin to understand that he is trying to put me in control of my body, before he embarks on the mind and the spirit. But the day he makes me stand in the blinding sun for six hours without water and asks me to stare steadily at a fixed point fifty yards away, I rebel and declare that I am leaving.*

*Totally unmoved, he replies calmly, 'You won't be able to. As a matter of fact you will find yourself repeating the exercise at night of your own volition, for the conquest of the self is the most glorious experience available to man on earth!'*

*Certain that he is wrong, I pack my few belongings and wait for night to fall. I think I can escape when he begins his meditation and is lost to the world. I think that six hours will enable me to put many miles between us. But at the appointed hour my feet lead me to the river and I stand submerged up to my neck, staring at the Pole Star till it disappears from sight and dawn breaks. Precisely at that moment, for the first time in these many months, I feel a surge of power rising from the base of my spine to the cranium which leaves me dizzy and breathless! Afraid that I will faint and demean myself, I cling to the last shreds of self-control and manage to stay upright. Slowly the tide begins to subside; I feel the blood flowing through my veins and I find that I can move again! I turn around to find the* sanyasi *standing on the bank, with a smile of complete understanding on his face.*

*After this, there is no turning back. Though the rigours only increase; sometimes I find myself reading and studying twenty hours a day; sleep becomes a forgotten luxury; I analyse, debate, try to fathom tortuous texts like the Upanishads and the Bhagvad Gita and through it all an inexorable voice thunders in my ears: 'Who are you? Where do you locate yourself? What volition do you have? How much are your actions under your control? Are you dead or alive? Do you live through the body only? Is it possible to live without the body, and yet control the body like a living human being? Can the soul don the saffron while the body goes through the motions of life as the situation demands? Can the soul remain inviolate, while the body wades through mud?'*

*Finally, almost two years later, there is illumination—faint at first, then brighter and brighter, like the passage from dawn to the midday sun, and through it comes the realisation that lies beyond reason.*

*And one day, when autumn is setting in, and the leaves are blown hither and thither by the wind, the* sanyasi *says to me, 'It is time for you to leave the tree and surrender yourself to the wind to take you where it will. Your aim is to stay afloat and not fall to the ground; and if you do, despite your best efforts, to rise again untainted!'*

*And so, I set out on my long journey to the future, the I and the not I,—Gauri and the* sanyasi *Gauri—who coexist, hand in hand, towards an unknown destination.*

~

*Calcutta is a revelation in terms of sheer human misery—the extent and the depth are both staggering. I had not imagined such degradation possible or such depredation and exploitation. In the beginning, there is a sense of terrible helplessness, but it is soon replaced by smouldering anger and a sense of mission, and I increasingly feel that the training that I had received should not go in vain! I realise that I have no power at all, but then can I not speak out against all the sins around me? But how, I wonder. Why will anyone pay any attention to a poor refugee girl whose own antecedents are shady to say the least? In any case, 'staying afloat' is difficult enough for me, and it takes all my hard-learnt philosophy to do so.*

*I will believe as long as I live that meeting a man like Harish Sikdar, who gives me protection without a price and allows me my head as far as I want, is part of the* sanyasi*'s plan for me, for it is nothing short of a miracle! These are the best years of my life when I have the power to move the minds of men and to operate without fear!*

After this the page is blank.

Suddenly, the light goes out and I am brought up short by the complete darkness; but I do not put on the emergency light. I am glad to have an opportunity to go over what I have learnt of this amazing woman's experiences and character. I also wonder at what stage 'the play' had meandered into a personal narrative, a statement, and whether she had been aware of it. Had she meant to put it on stage and then shied away from putting her heart on display? Or was she confident that the 'truth' would come to light at the appointed time, for that too was part of the 'plan'?

I had all along found it difficult to believe that a woman of my grandmother's perspicacity should have failed to recognise the woman behind the mask, but now I feel that perhaps that too was planned so that I should have the privilege. Anything and everything seems part of a strategy plotted by this enigmatic character many years ago.

The light returns as suddenly as it had gone out dazzling me, but I go back to the last portion, for the night is drawing to an end. I turn the page and start reading again:

*And for many years I did not falter. But as time draws to an end, I increasingly feel that there is one duty I have not completed, one message I have not conveyed, one debt I have not repaid, one bond that even a* sanyasi *must recognise.*

*I have not told my son about his father; I have not told him that he was not conceived between the stale sheets of a jaded marriage bed, that his progenitor was not the impotent, half-crazy, murderous Kumar Bahadur, that there is no taint in his blood, that his mother did not leave him out of choice!*

*I must tell him that his was an immaculate birth, that he was the product of a union of pure joy where there was no thought of the past or future, only the living present, that his father was the kindest and most honest of men who gave his life chasing a dream.*

*I thought I had burnt every bridge behind me, but I was wrong. Before I die I want my son to hold me in his arms, to give me a chance to lay my head on his chest and release the flood of anguish that has been pent up for so long, that has not gone away despite my heartbreaking search for total self-abnegation, to grant and be granted absolution! It is his patrimony and my right, and we shall not be denied!*

I turn back to the present with a sigh and as I set fire to the document; leaf by leaf, the edges crumple, turn brown, then ignite in a blaze, and in this fire, I see Gauri's 'life entire'. I realise for the first time in my life, that Eliot was echoing the Gita in his timeless words: '*... in my end was my beginning...*', that the self only comes into its own when the self is completely annihilated.

Go in peace, Gauri!

# Glossary

| | |
|---|---|
| *Akash Ganga* | Milky Way |
| *alta* | liquid red dye applied around the feet of married women |
| *arakshaniya* | incapable of being protected |
| *baiji* | courtesan |
| *Baisakh* | first month of the Bengali year |
| bakul | large deciduous tree with sweet-smelling white flowers |
| *baul* | wandering village mendicants who sing with an *ektara* while begging alms |
| *bilaiti* | whisky |
| Brahmin | highest caste amongst Hindus |
| Brahmo Samaj | a reformist movement and an offshoot of Hinduism |
| *burkha* | gown with a heavy veil worn by Muslim women |
| *bustee* | slum |
| *chadar* | seamless piece of cloth worn on holy occasions |
| *Chaitra* | last month of the Bengali calendar |
| *chandan* | sandalwood paste |
| *chapatti* | unleavened bread |

| | |
|---|---|
| charak | folk festival unique to Bengal |
| *charpai* | bed made of jute rope and woven on a wooden frame |
| *chatai* | jute mat |
| *cheel* | hawk |
| *chhara* | rhyme |
| *chowki* | wooden planks on trestles |
| *churidar* | very tight-fitting trousers |
| dhaba | eatery |
| *dhak* | drum player |
| Didi | elder sister |
| *dupatta* | veil |
| *ektara* | one-stringed instrument |
| *gajra* | garland traditionally worn by classical dancers |
| *geet* | *light melodies* |
| ghat | bathing quay |
| *ghatak* | marriage broker |
| *ghazal* | *love songs in Urdu* |
| *Grameen* Movement | movement emphasising the empowerment of the village-folk |
| *hajak* | magnesium lanterns |
| hakim | native doctor |
| *haribol* | taking the name of God |
| *hom* | fire worship |
| Isa | Jesus |
| *jatra* | folk theatre |
| *Kaliyug* | an eon; last cycle of time as believed by Hindus |
| *kankurshinge* | catfish |

| | |
|---|---|
| *kantha* | embroidered quilt made out of many layers of cloth |
| *karela* | bitter gourd |
| *kingshook* | tall tree with red flowers |
| *kirtan* | devotional songs |
| *kosha* | spoon-shaped copper vessel used in *puja* |
| *kulo* | curved container made of bamboo |
| *kurta* | loose-fitting collarless long shirt |
| *kusha/durba* | type of grass |
| Lakshmi Puja | ritual worship of the Goddess of Prosperity |
| *laskar* | sailor |
| *linga* | phallic obelisk |
| Madana | Deity of Love |
| *madhukur* | the collector of nectar |
| *madhukuri* | the activity of bees collecting honey |
| mantra | Vedic hymn |
| Mashi | aunt |
| *maund* | measure of capacity or weight, around thirty-eight kilograms |
| *mela* | fair |
| *mofussil* | provincial |
| *mogra* | *bakul* |
| *muri* | puffed rice |
| *nagardola* | smaller version of the Ferris wheel |
| *nagra* | slipper with upturned tip |
| *namaz* | prayers |
| Nawab | Muslim title referring to the landowner |
| *nirvana* | spiritual oneness with the Godhead |
| one paisa | earlier equal to 1\64th of a rupee; now is 1\100th of a rupee |

| | |
|---|---|
| *paan* | betel leaf |
| *pajama* | loose trousers |
| *palki* | palanquin |
| *panchamrit* | a concoction of milk, honey, curd, clarified butter and Ganges water which is offered to the gods |
| Pandav–Kaurav | rival cousins in the epic Mahabharata |
| *payasam* | rice cooked in milk with sugar |
| *puja* | ceremonial offering |
| *raga* | arrangement of notes in the octave |
| *Rajbari* | a term often used by villagers in reference to the mansion of the local landlord |
| Rabindra Sangeet | songs composed by Rabindranath Tagore |
| Ramprasadi | devotional songs composed by Ramprasad, a poet and devotee of Goddess Kali |
| *reshmi* | silken |
| sadhu-baba | holy man |
| *salaam* | greetings for well-being |
| *samosa*s | savouries |
| *sanyas* | renunciation |
| *sanyasi* | Hindu mendicant |
| Saraswati Puja | worship of the Goddess of Learning |
| *sarpanch* | head of the five-man village administrative assembly |
| *shefali* | yellow jasmine |
| *shehnai* | flute-like pipes |
| *shola* | white sponge-wood carved to make decorations |
| *shraddha* | reverence |
| *sindoor* | vermillion applied on one's forehead |

| | |
|---|---|
| *singhadwar* | gateway flanked with motifs/statues of lions |
| *stree-shakti* | woman power |
| *tabla* | percussionist instrument used as an accompaniment with Indian classical music |
| *tanpura* | stringed musical instrument |
| tantric | a seer of an esoteric cult |
| *tola* | equals to 11.3 grams |
| *tulsi* | basil |
| *tulsi manch* | platform around the holy basil |
| *yajna* | offer oblations through fire |
| *yugantar* | change of epoch |
| *zamindar* | landlord |
| *zardozi* | embroidery with gold and silver thread |
| *zari* | gold or silver thread |